A Kind of Treason

A RINEHART SUSPENSE NOVEL

Books by Robert S. Elegant

A Kind of Treason

The Center of the World:
Communism and the Mind of China

The Dragon's Seed:
Peking and the Overseas Chinese

China's Red Masters:
Political Biography of the Chinese Communist Leaders

A Kind of Treason

By Robert S. Elegant

A RINEHART SUSPENSE NOVEL

Holt, Rinehart and Winston
New York   Chicago   San Francisco

Library of Congress Catalog Card Number: 66-13099

82255-0116
Printed in the United States of America

"It's only a small war, but it's the only war we've got."
"Don't despair. It'll get bigger."

—Conversation between two
unidentified correspondents
overheard in the bar of the
Hotel Caravelle, Saigon, December, 1963

A Kind of Treason

1

The narrow junk began to buck as soon as she left the shelter of the headland. Behind her lay the hectic Hong Kong inlet called Aberdeen, where sampans skittered between the slab sterns and sweeping bows of the great fishing junks. Before her lay the open bay, strewn with isolated islands against the long, low mass on the horizon that was the mainland of China.

Squinting into the morning sun, Harrison Gilroy eased the tiller and let the hemp lines run through their heavy wooden blocks. Pointing straight for dumbell-shaped Chengchow Island eight miles away, the junk sailed smoothly on her new course. White spray hissed along her teak sides, and dropped in pearl-like clusters from the ribbons at her prow where firecrackers had hung when she was launched. As the barren hills of Lama Island glided away on the left, the waves rose higher.

Sprawled on the scarlet cushions of the fantail, a glass of gin and lime juice cold against his palm, Mallory watched his host toy with the seven lines that shaped the muslin sail. Gilroy's body was as sleek and soft as if he were made of a cluster of pillows of different shapes, all stuffed near bursting with the finest down. But he manhandled the wooden rudder, half as big as a barn door, without apparent effort, and his sweeping blond mustache bristled against cheeks reddened by sun, wind, and gin. He wore only purple-and-pink swimming trunks and massive sunglasses.

Mallory was suspended between admiration and laughter by Gilroy's infinite ability to reconcile stark opposites, not only in his appearance but in his character. Two things the man loved —the mazes of secret intrigue and the ostentation of the opulent life. It was characteristic of his style that they should be sailing at six knots toward Chinese Communist waters in a junk almost as conspicuous by its scarlet-and-gold trim as by the enormous American flag that streamed from the mizzenmast.

The invitation had been heavily casual. "Gerry, let's take the new junk out and see what she'll do—just the two of us." But Mallory knew that sometime soon Gilroy would send the boat boy forward and shatter the holiday air with a string of words casually tossed into the wind's drumming. A week earlier it would have been hard to refuse any reasonable proposition. But now he could sit back with detachment and watch Gilroy perform.

The boat boy, his dark face alert as a Pekingese puppy's under his mushroom of a straw hat, refilled their glasses from an orange vacuum flask. Gilroy made a final delicate adjustment to the mainsail, tethered above them like the wing of a great brown moth, curved by the wind and segmented by bamboo battens.

"Ah Sum," he said in clumsy pidgin, "you go long frontside check foresail. I holler when you come back this side." Gilroy smiled an apology. "Gerry, didn't meant to hog the tiller. Why don't you take her now?"

Mallory knew he had been pinned down as neatly as if he were handcuffed to a chair under the knife blade of a spotlight. He would be struggling with a cranky new boat while her captain, his interrogator, lounged at ease in the cockpit.

"Gerry, tell me. Have things gone badly lately?" Gilroy was abrupt. "I haven't seen much of your stuff. And *Asia at Dawn* was almost five years ago. You can't live forever on a moderate best-seller—not the way you and I live."

Mallory bit down his irritation. The fat man was attempting to be subtle; the proposition must be particularly unpleasant. "Thanks for asking, Harry," he answered, his voice edged.

"But if anyone knows how I stand, it's you. Anyway, you could find out all you wanted in an hour."

"A simple liquor salesman like myself? I have no special sources as. . ."

". . .except the Special Branch, the Police Commissioner, the Director of the CIA, and, for all I know, Mao Tse-tung's secretary," interjected Mallory.

"You flatter me, boy. But have it your way. People are occasionally co-operative." Gilroy drained his glass and refilled it from the vacuum flask. "But," he resumed, "I'd like to know how you feel about your set-up, Gerry. I'm not asking idly."

"All right, Harry, I'll tell you what you already know. Things've been rotten the last couple of years. Alimony for Laura, schools for the two kids—they've eaten up every cent from the book plus more borrowed dough than I want to remember. I'm picking up a couple of hundred a week from the Syndicate, but it doesn't go far."

"I'm sorry to hear it," Gilroy broke in.

"And, since you've asked," continued Mallory, ignoring the interruption, "everything I've done lately is pure routine, carried by the name I'm fast losing. I've about run out of ideas—for another book or even a major piece. This hotshot correspondent is all dried up, just waiting till he blows away."

"That bad?"

"Well," Mallory admitted, "maybe not. If you don't know already, I've got a big one almost signed and sealed. It should pay well and, maybe, give me another book. But we'd better come about if we want to make Chengchow without a long beat."

The arched sails emptied of wind and swung ponderously across to fill on the starboard tack. A flying fish leaped in the tumbled water at the prow, glinting silver in the sun. As the junk settled on her new course, Mallory's deep voice was more enthusiastic.

"Somebody is having an attack of insight in that glossy madhouse of American liberalism, *Quest,* the fortnightly

11

everything magazine. It's time, they've decided, the great American public was told what's really happening in Vietnam and, *Deo gratias*, that I'm the man to tell them."

"What's your angle?" asked Gilroy, savoring his knowledge of insider's slang.

"No angle," snapped Mallory. "Neither *Quest* nor myself ever has an angle—except the truth. But the focus, as we say, is broad, penetrating, comprehensive, exhaustive, and detailed —all at once. Is that clear?"

"Well—no. It's not."

"All right, I'll try to make it clear. The last letter I had from McAllen—you know *Quest* always asks, never *tells* its contributors—he asked—and I'm quoting pretty closely—'We seem to be fighting a minor conventional war, or a major guerrilla action, in South Vietnam. Key to victory or defeat, sooner or later, will be the Vietnamese people. Yet we have seen no penetrating reporting on how do the Vietnamese themselves feel—peasants, workers, and, most important, the opinion-makers, the intellectuals? Do they really care who rules them? Can they provide the basis for eventual democratic government? Do they have the raw guts to stand up for what they believe—if they do believe? We hope you'll concentrate on the Vietnamese, but, naturally, would like to demonstrate American involvement by showing Americans in Vietnam. Finally, can we answer the big question: What does Vietnam mean to us Americans? How important is it to our interests? What are the moral questions involved in a war in Vietnam?' "

Mallory fished a Camel out of the limp packet in his shirt pocket. He took a deep drag, letting the smoke trail out slowly through his nostrils. Abruptly, he doubled over; he was coughing harshly, and his eyes were streaming. Gilroy made no move to take over, though the sails flapped in protest at the loosely swinging tiller.

"I'll learn that trick yet," Mallory wheezed. "I've been trying for twenty years."

Gilroy asked, "How do you plan to go about it?"

12

"What—learning to blow smoke out of my nose?"

"No. The Vietnam assignment."

"Oh, that—well, I guess I'll have to do something. They want to run twenty thousand words plus ten pages of color photos. I guess I'll just have to do something to fill all that space, won't I, Harry."

Gilroy did not reply. Two junks were trawling just off the tip of Chengchow and he was studying them through high-powered Japanese binoculars.

"All right," Mallory sighed, "if you must know. The normal routine, of course. But I'll also have to spend a lot of time among the intellectuals—such as they are—of Saigon and environs."

Gilroy let the binoculars dangle from the strap around his neck. He said slowly, "You do that, Gerry, spend a lot of time with the intellectuals, particularly those who're unhappy with the regime."

Mallory, trimming the sail in hopes of getting an additional half-knot out of the junk, glanced at his host. "For Chris' sake, Harry," he said. "Even McAllen doesn't tell me just how to cover a story. When did you take up teaching journalism, making assignments?"

"Just recently, Gerry, but I know what I'm talking about. I want you to spend a lot of time with the intellectuals, get to know those Americans who spend a lot of time with them. Then you can tell me about it."

"I can see how you have so many sources," snapped Mallory, "with your winning ways. But I won't play. I'm doing a job of reporting, and, I hope, getting a book out of it—not playing agent for a cloak, dagger, and microfilm *kongsi*."

"You're not making it easy for me, Gerry."

"I'm not trying to."

"All right, then," the fat man's voice sank, losing almost all timbre as he ticked off points on his fingers. "Your fat fee is ten thousand plus expenses. I'm prepared to add another ten thousand for a few bits of information that happen to interest me . . . that I don't want to ask anyone in Saigon to get. After you've agreed, I'll give you a little more detail."

Mallory ostentatiously studied the green and red wind pennants fluttering from the stays on either side of the junk. An additional ten thousand dollars would cover almost all his debts and still leave him six months free to work on the book. *Vietnam—Two Minutes to Midnight,* he decided firmly would make the best title after all. He turned back to face Gilroy, his decision made.

"No, Harry. This is different from working together during the war. Psychological static, you might call it, but still too much interference with my own work."

"All right, Gerry, if you want it straight and hard. You don't *have* to do anything for me. If you don't, though, you won't be going to Vietnam for *Quest.* Your friend McAllen doesn't know it, but we planted the idea for this story—and your name too. We can easily unplant it.

"Can you prove that?" asked Mallory.

"Could, but won't. I'm not accountable to you. But use your head, Gerry. Even if we hadn't set it up, I can think of a half-dozen ways we could foul it up. Even if we made it frontal, bad security, *Quest* wouldn't kick too hard."

"The hell they wouldn't. They love a cause like that," Mallory interrupted, rising and crooking his elbow around the tiller.

"Wrong again, boy. Nobody wants a hassle for your sake. No clear moral issue and no fun for *Quest.* If we decided to get really dirty—those Ho Chi-minh interviews in 1946; that stay in Peking after the Communists took over; that expulsion from Formosa; that flat statement that the Chicoms were, maybe, Communists, but so far off the main line and so Chinese that they'd be Chinese Social Democrats after a while —can you prove you didn't mean to deceive?"

Gilroy bit the tip off a cigar and spat into the sea. "But you're a free agent. You've got a choice," he said briskly. "Either go to Vietnam, do your piece and a little job of work for me, and collect twenty thousand plus expenses, plus, maybe, a book. Or don't go. Sit here and watch yourself trickle slowly down the drain. There's your choice, and this day, January 8th, nineteen hundred and sixty-four is your day of decision."

The fat man struck a wooden match on the deckboards and lit the cigar without taking his eyes off Mallory. The correspondent's head was turned to look past the whitecaps toward the small, green-pillared Confucian temple that capped the western tip of the brown island. Only the inch-long white scar on his left temple and the tip of his aquiline nose were visible. But a pulse throbbed unrhythmically beneath the scar and his wide-legged stance was rigid. His thin body was tense within the checked Madras cotton shirt, which hung open over tan swimming trunks, the waistband bulging over the beginning of a paunch.

Gilroy felt distaste stir. The incipient potbelly, somehow so vulnerable, diverted him briefly from his purpose. Mallory, just three years past forty, had begun to wear that badge of middle age only a year or so earlier. At the same time he had begun drinking neat Scotch by the half-tumblerful before dinner—and brandy by the same measure afterward. But only Mallory's hypersensitive conscience was threatened and Gilroy knew that nothing healed faster than a wounded conscience.

Mallory turned slowly. His wide, gray eyes glared an accusation under heavy black eyebrows, the right habitually cocked an eighth of an inch higher than the left in an expression perpetually quizzical. His broad mouth was twisted into a smile.

"Harry," he said, "I'm kidding myself I may still find a way out of your little maze. But I'm afraid you've got me pretty well trapped—as long as I don't have to emulate the master's tactics."

Wondering why some victories tasted so much like defeats, Gilroy laughed. "I'm sorry I had to get rough, Gerry. It's

15

almost ridiculous, the job's such a cinch. But the brass wanted you. And, damn it boy, I'm glad I could get you the break with *Quest*."

Gilroy reached into the ice chest under the cockpit seat. His broad, pink hand, befurred with yellow hair, emerged clutching a squat green bottle. Registering the brand of champagne, Dom Perignon, *blanc de blancs*, Mallory raised his estimate of his expenses by five hundred dollars.

"I'll give it to you fast," Gilroy continued. "I don't want to talk about it again. I promised Hazel some crab and shrimp. And I want to get to that little temple. One of the monks is selling off wood carvings from the back altar."

"It's your play," said Mallory dully.

"All right then. I want you to get in with the dissidents. I'm not interested in direct Vietcong connections; just the honest, sincere types who're never satisfied with the government—and won't be satisfied till Uncle Ho Chi-minh swallows them. And keep your eyes open for the Americans they see. But this isn't a smear job or a guilt-by-association deal."

"It sounds like a charming combination of the two," said Mallory. "But it's your ten thousand—I *am* sorry, twenty thousand—so go ahead."

"For your information, this is the background. The Vietnamese leak like sieves, so only about six men know the details of major operations—not just strikes, but even major campaigns and resettlement plans. Yet the Vietcong seem to know every major plan before it gets out of the planning stage. It didn't matter so much before, but now, with a co-ordinated long-range operation, it's killing us. Anyway, the Vietnamese insist it must be one of our people since we spread the poop much lower than they do. We can't admit it to the Viets, but they may be right."

"And how does my little mission fit in?"

"Laterally, very laterally. We don't want Saigon to know everything we're doing, so you'll pick up some minor pieces which might fit our puzzle. If it were anyone else, I wouldn't fill in the whole picture the way I'm doing. There's no danger —you'll really just be doing your own job."

"Aside from your subtle technique of seduction, it sounds very simple," said Mallory slowly. "I hope it stays that way."

"I said I was sorry," growled Gilroy, taking the tiller back.

He put the junk's head into the wind. With sails taut she beat into Chengchow harbor, circling the battered wooden shrimp boats and the steel-hulled ferry before tying up at the stone jetty.

2

The helicopters floated upward on fountains of red dust. Formed into tight vees, they churned toward the southwest, dangling cargo nets between their wheels like hawks flying homeward with their prey.

"Another big strike down south it looks like," said Lieutenant Gould, the trim young man from the Public Information Office who'd met Mallory at Tonsonnhut Airport. "When they resupply in the middle of the day somebody's having himself a fair-sized fight."

"How often," asked Mallory, "do you see this sort of resupply operation?"

"Oh, I'd say four, five times a week lately. Somebody's stirring things up. Uncle Ho seems to be getting a mite impatient."

Mallory pictured the companies of small brown men, some in jungle green, others in black, groping for each other with fingers of fire through the saw-edged swamp grass. Automatically, he began composing a lead for his article. Would you call the helicopters vultures? No, they were harpies dropping new weapons to insure complete destruction.

He pulled himself up short. Composing a loaded lead five minutes after touchdown was just foolish. He couldn't judge the whole show by Gilroy's raw tactics.

The blue-and-white Air France 707, which had carried him the nine hundred miles from the damp chill of Hong Kong dawn to the kiln heat of Saigon at noon in mid-January, stood about four hundred yards from the low terminal.

Closer positions were filled by towering Pinocchio-nosed turbo-props and droop-winged jets of the Military Air Transport Service. An ancient, potbellied Stratoliner of Air Laos, squatting among them, looked like the museum exhibit it should have been. A Super-Constellation of Flying Tigers Airlines was discharging a planeload of American women in crumpled dresses, each accompanied by one or two children. A long train of American soldiers straggled toward one of the MATS planes.

Every point of the compass on the expanse of flat land displayed its own bright yellow construction machinery. All the bulldozers, steam-shovels, and tractors were tearing frantically at the red earth. One piece of Vietnam, at any rate, was being transformed into the shape that Americans desired. On the other side of the field six propeller-driven T-28's with Vietnamese markings brooded over the turmoil, their silver sides shimmering astigmatically in the heat waves that spiraled upward through the pink dust.

"By the way, sir," said Lieutenant Gould, "Colonel McGuffey sends his regards. He had a conference or he'd have met you himself."

"Tell McGuff thanks and I'll call him," answered Mallory. "Big show you've got here. Is it always this busy?"

The pink flesh around Gould's brown eyes crinkled in surprise. He hesitated before answering, "Well, sir, I reckon it is. I've only been in Saigon three months, but every time I get out here—maybe, two, three times a week—it's just like this. Takes a lot of stuff to run an operation like this one. We're not just fooling around. We're right serious."

"You know," said Mallory, "the first time I landed in Saigon, about ten years ago, the terminal building was a quarter the size. The only activity was a Pan American DC-4 unloading maybe four or five passengers and an old single-engined Bobcat dropping down with a Frenchman in a leather helmet and goggles at the stick. All you'd see was a pair of Legionnaires or a couple of Senegalese sauntering around in berets and those tight, terribly short shorts the French wear. I liked it better. A more relaxed, maybe more civilized, way to fight a war."

The Lieutenant, who had been no more than thirteen when Mallory first came to Saigon, was obviously not interested in ancient history. But he was well-drilled. "No, sir, we're not fooling around the way I hear tell the French did. We're going to win this one and we're not counting the cost. What Vietnam wants, Vietnam gets, not only troops and matériel, but even moral-wise. The other day twenty-five teachers flew in for the dependents' school. When the Viets see that, they know we're not fooling; we're here to stay— men, women, and children. But not a good-looker in the whole lot," he concluded regretfully.

Mallory automatically followed the other passengers toward the terminal, but Gould took his arm.

"No, sir," he said. "We've set it up for you to go through the VIP lounge, faster and cooler, too. We know you've got lots to do."

They turned toward a small green concrete building with an arched roof, which stood fifty yards from the main terminal. A ring of Vietnamese policemen in white floated like whipped cream around the café au lait uniforms of Vietnamese and American Army officers.

"Just a moment, sir," said a tall Negro Military Policeman extending a massive arm. Mallory and Gould were halted before a wooden sentry box painted in red-and-white stripes. "If you'll just wait till the doctor is through," added the soft voice.

The interior of the sentry box was dark with shadow, but a pair of khaki-clad legs ending in heavy combat boots protruded from the narrow doorway, feet splayed in the dust. A rivulet of red ran between the legs, puddling where the strip of concrete pavement ended.

"Head wounds always bleed a lot," said a tall, white-haired American wearing Major's oak leaves and the cadu-

20

ceus. Facing a stocky colonel with a promontory of a nose, he wiped his hands on a towel and went on, "But he was dead two seconds after he pulled the trigger."

"Thanks, Doc," the Colonel said crisply. He looked around anxiously until his eye lighted on a Captain wedged in among the Vietnamese staring down at his feet as if trying to disappear.

"Horstmann," snapped the Colonel, "I'm putting you in charge. Take care of the body first, but remember we're going to have to write this up so make sure you've got witnesses all the way."

His decisiveness deserting him as visible doubt creased his florid brow, the Colonel turned to the Doctor. He asked anxiously, "Doc, you're sure medically that it was suicide? No chance of anything else."

"Colonel," the Doctor said slowly, "even a thirty-two makes a hell of a mess of a man's brain case. Medically I can't establish suicide or murder till I get him cleaned up on the autopsy table. Probably not even then. All I can say is that someone, the deceased or someone else, put a weapon into his mouth and pulled the trigger, spraying brains all over the General's nice sentry box."

He dropped the blood-stained towel into the dust and lit a cigarette.

"But you don't need a doctor to figure this thing out. We left them alone for about three minutes, then heard two shots. We got back and found poor Tham there," waving his hand toward a stretcher being loaded into an ambulance. "We found Tham flat on the ground and our other friend as you see him now. Only a magician could have shot them both and then disappeared. Relax, Colonel, it's bad, but not that bad."

The pouter-pigeon Colonel sagged for a moment, then pulled himself taut, his eye reconnoitering the crowd again. "Gould," he bellowed at Mallory's guide, "we're going to need your help. I want you to keep this as quiet. . . ."

21

"Colonel," interrupted the PIO Lieutenant, "who's in there?"

"Oh, you didn't know? It's Humboldt, young John Humboldt. He was going home. We thought we'd better get him out of here as quick as possible. Don't know what they'd planned back in the States, maybe a Good of the Service. . . ."

Gould interrupted again. "Colonel," he said quickly, "I'd sure like you to meet Mr. Mallory. He works for *Quest* magazine. Sort of come down here to look the war over and write a big piece about it. Mr. Mallory, Colonel Taylor is headquarters commandant."

The Colonel flushed, sagging and pulling himself erect in an instant. "Glad to meet you, sir," he intoned, pushing out his hand. "Glad to meet you. This business here—it's really nothing. I'm naturally disturbed because the poor guy was in a way my responsibility. He was just here too long. Needed treatment. Best say nothing about this—his family you know. Hope we can talk later." The Colonel turned away, throwing over his shoulder, "Gould, I'll call you at your office."

The crowd straggled away as the stretcher-bearers returned for the body in the sentry box.

In the khaki Chevrolet, driving between scraggly palms toward Saigon, Gould was withdrawn.

Finally he sighed. "Poor Johnny. I didn't know him too well, but he was a nice guy. Very tense though. Maybe that's why he went screwy. But, Mr. Mallory, before I forget, there's a cocktail party tonight at Mr. Hooghly's. He hopes you can come. And, Mr. Mallory, I've had a copy of *Asia at Dawn* since it came out. Would you mind putting your name in it for me."

Mallory signed the fly-leaf noting that the rubber-stamped "USIS Library, Saigon" was only partially obliterated.

3

"On the Hill," said the Senator, "some of us tend to get impatient, to think these people here ought to get on with it instead of whining to us for more help and more money."

He ran a bony hand through his white pompadour, depositing another drift of dandruff on his impeccably padded shoulders. "But after seeing for myself, I can understand what they're up against. I'm going to recommend we stay right with them, even if it means another eighteen months or two years of putting our dough and our boys on the line. We must keep faith with these people."

"Senator," trilled the tall blonde in the green net dress, a fined-down Brünhild clutching an enormous martini, "how encouraging it is to hear those words from a man of your stature. Trying to do a job for our country out here, we sometimes feel no one appreciates us, no one believes in the fight. What with the distorted press reports. . ."

The Senator's right hand deliberately took up another twelve-ounce drink the color of iodine. He shifted his cigar to the same hand and his left arm glided around the blonde's waist, sinuous as a snake in blue Dacron. "I can assure you, my dear lady, that some of us do," he said, his craggy face crinkling into lean ridges. "Just as I appreciate your finding me Jack Daniel and, well, Mekong water. . . ."

"If you tell him that Saigon isn't on the Mekong River, I'll break your arm," hissed a voice in Mallory's ear. "And restrain yourself. Don't tell him in two year's time we'll either be out on our asses or way over our asses in this mess."

Mallory turned to look into his host's blue eyes, bloodshot under the creased forehead crowned by a gray crewcut.

"Relax, Jim," he said, "I don't try to educate anyone any more, not unless I'm getting paid for it."

The Senator's hand rested comfortably on the upper curve of the blonde's left buttock. "My dear lady, now that I've seen everyone, I feel I really understand. The General, the Prime Minister, the Foreign Minister, even the Economics Minister, our own brilliant Ambassador and his generals— all gave me the frankest briefings. And that helicopter flight over the Delta—most informative. I go back feeling—if I may say so without immodesty—for the first time I have a true grasp of the situation here."

His hand wandered lower, but the blonde's expression did not change, even when she took a convulsive gulp from her martini.

". . . old goat, if he gooses Martha once more, I'll slug him," Hooghly breathed into Mallory's ear. "She'll give me hell afterward anyhow. The bastard spent more time talking than listening. That punk aide of his insisted the helicopters fly so high they could barely see the ground. . . . We'll talk more later. Right now I've got to go and keep the guests from each other's throats."

Awash in damp heat, the green walls of the broad room framed the vague and shifting figures of a dream. Scattered lamps thrust their dim rays through arabesques of smoke carved by the ceiling fans. The light cast a glow on copper or pink cheeks and struck crystals of light from upraised glasses. Split-bamboo jalousies hung across the broad arches that let onto the outside galleries.

"Sure, we've got Vietnamese guards outside," Hooghly had already explained to Mallory, "but there's no point in setting ourselves up like wooden ducks in an illuminated shooting gallery."

Mallory saw with a start that Hooghly had been replaced by another figure, just as tall but twice as bulky. Martha wriggled free and offered her hand.

"Senator, this is George Dietrich," she said. "He's our local press tycoon, runs *The Vietnam News;* George, do you know Gerry Mallory? He's here to do a piece for *Quest*."

The heavy man in white sharkskin took Martha's hand between his own. The massive head, its gray hair combed flat, leaned over his hostess' fingers.

"My dear Martha Hooghly, how good of you to ask me," he declaimed in a high-pitched voice that made Mallory think of pork crackling. "You know how long I have admired the Senator."

The Senator was arrested in mid-monologue by the weight of the publisher's presence. After wringing the Senator's hand, Dietrich observed to Mallory, "How do you do, sir. I have known you by reputation for a long time, but I do not believe we have met."

Years earlier Mallory had developed his only conscious social gambit. He shook hands in silence, since Dietrich's first words could presage either an attack or a gush of praise. Poised to repel boarders, he was relieved when Dietrich turned back to the Senator.

"I hope," he said, "that our charming hostess will excuse me if I venture to add one thought to the multitude already showered upon you. Senator, we almost destroyed our position here and gravely injured these good people of Vietnam by countenancing a betrayal only a short time ago. We can afford no more betrayals. The Oriental is a simple man. Above all, he prizes unshakable loyalty to friends and implacable hostility to foes. We must be true, if we are to prevail."

The Senator removed his cigar with an oratorical flourish. But Martha Hooghly took his arm and drew him away through the smoke and the bourbon fumes. "I'm sure, George," she pouted, "the Senator isn't interested in ancient history. Colonel Thai has just come in, and he's anxious to meet the Senator."

"That scrofulous bitch," Dietrich stated without emphasis. "She had to ask me, but I knew she wouldn't let me talk to that old Aeolus. Her husband, you know, is another of those bleeding-heart betrayers."

The man's conversational style was so stunning that revulsion yielded to fascination. Mallory asked with deliberate naïveté, "What do you mean by bleeding-heart betrayer, Mr. Dietrich?"

"Need you ask, Mr. Mallory?" The rejoinder was a high-pitched purr. "I should have thought that a man of your experience—but, perhaps like most of your colleagues, you don't know what actually happened here. I have references, sir, to the murder of President Ngo-dinh Diem. Your friend Mr. Hooghly played a particularly unsavory role in that treachery and disloyalty."

"Hooghly," objected Mallory, "took an oath of allegiance to the United States of America not to Ngo-dinh Diem. It may have been bad judgment, but certainly not disloyalty or treason."

The publisher's small blue eyes narrowed within their padded sockets, and his heavy cheeks flushed. But he mastered the threatened eruption and, sipping his whiskey and soda, said placidly, "Mr. Mallory, I should be delighted to discuss the matter with you at length. Pray forgive me if I impinged upon your loyalty to Mr. Hooghly. Loyalty is an admirable trait, but truth is more important—as is the nation's interest."

"It's not a matter of loyalty, Mr. Dietrich, but of fact." Mallory pressed his unexpected advanatge. "I never thought Jim Hooghly was infallible. But your argument contradicts almost everything I've seen and read."

"Coming from Gerald Mallory that contention demands serious discussion," answered Dietrich, his words portentous despite his light tenor voice. "I have always found your

26

recital of facts most impressive, though your conclusions are sometimes, if you will permit me, bizarre."

The correspondent replied lightly, "Mr. Dietrich, sometimes I find my conclusions bizarre myself. But then I often encounter bizarre situations."

"I'm sure I meant no affront, sir," Dietrich answered. "If you'll call me, perhaps we can lunch together soon. If I am a bit unorthodox in this secluded community, pray remember that I am in it but not of it. I, almost alone, represent American free enterprise. Besides, I have many Vietnamese friends, old friends, and that, too, is heretical in this community. But I must go now."

The Senator had disappeared on his way to a dinner party. Men in uniform—dress whites marking the Vietnamese, khaki the Americans—were drifting through the smoke-hazed double doors, convoying the pale cottons of American women and the bright silks of the Vietnamienne. Mallory joined the few remaining guests in an alcove formed by a pair of bamboo sofas cushioned in green-and-gold Thai silk. Holding himself firmly erect against the normal force of gravity, enhanced by four generous martinis, he accepted introductions.

A well-scrubbed, yellow-haired American officer: "Mr. Mallory—Captain Thayer." A Vietnamienne with a matte cream complexion and a delicately aquiline nose: "Miss Vguyenlee—Mr. Mallory." An intense Vietnamese, a lock of blue-black hair falling over his high forehead: "Mr. Mallory—Mr. Ngo-canh Vao." He nodded to Rosen of the New York *Times* and Levoncier, the Frenchman in his mid-thirties who was the local correspondent of the *Quest* empire.

"Have another drink," Hooghly offered, laying a heavy arm on Mallory's shoulders. "You've seen our two prize exhibits, Senator Everything-is-going-to-be-all-right-in-a-few-months and our local William Randolph Hearst, who thinks everything's been a betrayal since the day after Dewey took Manila."

27

Mallory slumped onto the couch beside the Vietnamese girl. "Welcome to our country," he entoned, waving his basinlike glass in a wide arc.

"I have long admired your work, Mr. Mallory," said Miss Vguyen-lee primly.

"Thank you, thank you. I couldn't have more charming disproof. . ." He gulped the crystalline drink, finding it bland as ice water. It was always the same on a new story: an airplane ride and then a cocktail party where you drank a lot, met a lot of people, most of them Americans, forgot most of the names, but made a few appointments—and discovered that you had committed yourself. You were trapped until the airplane took you away to another cocktail party in another country.

The Vietnamese girl leaned toward him, and he was suddenly aware of her. She was wearing a white silk tunic, the *ao-dai* which was the uniform garment of all Vietnamienne. The word literally meant "long gown," but the sweeping, ankle-length skirts, slit to the waist to reveal wide, diaphanous pantaloons, could only be a vestige of the time when Mongol tribes rode across the empty steppes.

"Welcome to our country," he repeated. "I simply couldn't have more charming disproof. . ."

"What do you mean by disproof and why 'welcome to your country'?" asked the Vietnamienne, a faint crease appearing between her dark eyebrows.

"I was beginning to think Saigon was a city populated entirely by Americans, with maybe a couple of spear-carriers disguised as Vietnamese to stand in corners at cocktail parties and evaporate whenever anyone talked to them. Delighted find it's not so . . . was beginning ask myself 'Where are the Vietnamese?'" He felt himself embarked on a talking jag, but didn't want to stop.

"Reminds me of Taggart Ali, man who worked for some paper with an unpronounceable name in Ankara. He came out to Tokyo early in '51 and never got to Korea but once.

Said he'd been over and found it not interesting, not as interesting anyway as locking himself in a room at the press club with five inventive Japanese girls. Then we took Seoul and Taggart had to fly over. So he went, spent an hour in the city, and filed his first dispatch. Entirety of it was 'Here I am in Seoul and everyone is asking where are the Turks?' Actually the Turks were doing a damned good job further south, but. . . ."

"Bullshit, Mallory, pure bullshit," a clear American female voice interrupted. His hostess' fixed blue eyes were regarding him without approval. "Just one of the troubles with you glamorous foreign correspondents is those quaint little stories—far-flung, all corners of the earth, naturally. Got one for every occasion, particularly meeting impressionable young girls." Martha Hooghly shrugged off her husband's restraining arm. "Take your hands off me," she snapped. "And give me that martini. Mallory, if you sons of bitches spent less time telling tales and more time working, less time lifting skirts and more finding out what's going on in front of your noses, less attacking people trying to do an honest job and more. . ."

The young Vietnamese tossed his hair back from his forehead and rose, taking the girl's hand in his own. "If our masters are fighting among themselves, I think it is time we left, Tuyelle."

Martha Hooghly waved an abstracted good-by and turned back to Mallory. But her husband forestalled her.

"Not tonight again, honey, please. Gerry's just doing a job. You didn't talk this way when I was doing the same job. . ." Hooghly tilted his martini glass back, finding to his sorrow that it was empty. Sighing, he went on, "And it wasn't nice for Tuyelle. She came like a trouper, even though Johnny. . . ."

Martha Hooghly turned on her husband, her voice sinking low. "As for you, you rumpled propagandist, you sweat-stained diplomat, don't worry about the girl. She had to come. It's her job. Hell of a job *you* did as a correspondent, in and out of every bed between Hong Kong and Singapore. And *who's* doing a job here? It's not in the marriage contract and not in your commission from the President, but I'm going to have a permanent scar on my ass. Being the Public Affairs Officer's lady—since when does it include bony-fingered hick Senators? That man's got a grip like a sex-starved octopus."

Rosen lifted his slight body from the couch, saying, "To paraphrase our young friend Vao, this is obviously turning into a private fight."

Descending the broad, whitewashed steps between Rosen and Levoncier, Mallory noticed that he was still carrying his glass. He drained it and set it precisely atop the stone gatepost. A small Vietnamese sentry watched, his muddy eyes unmoving beneath his steel helmet.

4

"New rules, Gerry, since your last visit," said Rosen brightly. "No more *pous-pous* at night and no taxicabs ever. Pierre's heap, hire cars, if you know the driver, and not too much walking."

"You birds are getting regimented living with the military. But your rules might snatch a few lives from Saigon drivers."

"Who walks anyway? After eighteen years here I have never met anyone who did not recover from such mania in the first two weeks," said Levoncier in his Maurice Chevalier accent. He squeezed his squat body through the gap in the wire grill surrounding the Chinese restaurant grandiloquently called the Arcenciel. "If they make this entrance any more narrow, they will keep out not only grenades, but also the customers."

The three walked slowly through the heavy tropical night that veiled Saigon's sister city, the largely Chinese commercial metropolis called Cholon. After Szechwan duck, fried twice for crispness, and a half-dozen other dishes, Mallory's head was reasonably clear, despite the platoons of beer which had flanked the dinner. The red-and-green neon signs revealed themselves as well-defined if incomprehensible Chinese characters. They were no longer the pinwheels of molten light they had been before dinner. Behind the steel grills which cut them off from the clattering throngs on the sidewalks, endless streets of shops received streams of customers, though it was nearly midnight.

Everything had settled down nicely. Since Levoncier was

eager to be helpful and Sid Rosen was essentially an earnest type, Mallory had learned a good deal: names, places, dates, and general assessments, the essential background he needed before he could even begin planning his story. Time enough to worry about an original approach when he knew where the bedrock lay.

For the first time since his arrival, Mallory allowed himself to think about his other assignment, the mission for Gilroy. Since he'd taken no money, he *could* just forget it. But he would be inviting the enmity of Gilroy's employers— damn it, the Central Intelligence Agency; euphemism could go too far. As Levoncier fumbled with the cranky lock of his ancient car, Mallory decided to worry about the problem tomorrow. Things had a way of turning up.

The boxy old Citroën smelled of oil over damp rot, and clumps of filthy wadding protruded from the torn upholstery. The car quivered as Levoncier cut across the channel of light that was the main street and began to thread a maze of dark alleys.

"Where are we going now?" demanded Mallory.

"Madame Jahn's," Rosen answered.

"For Chris' sake, Sid, I've got to start working tomorrow. It's too late."

"Never is it too late for Madame Jahn's," Lavoncier observed cheerily. "Anyway, you must first soak up the atmosphere before you can write. Sidney and I, we give you this evening as a present for your return."

"Damn you, Pierre," Rosen said mildly, "I told you not to tell him. What would Mr. Sulzberger and the auditors say?"

"The only solution, *mon cher* Sidney, is to pay for it yourself, if you feel so."

"I may at that," Rosen brooded.

The Citroën halted shakily at the head of a lane too small for its splayed fenders. With the ignition off, the engine chattered wearily for nearly a minute before halting with an explosive gasp.

32

"The *essence*, it improves daily," Levoncier murmured.

"And the car, Pierre, the car marches better with every decade that goes by," said Mallory, following them down the lane and into a cavernous doorway.

The iron-barred wooden door creaked open to throw a slat of light across them. After a pause a chain rattled loose and the door swung wide in the hands of a Vietnamienne who could not have been older than sixteen. She looked no more than twelve in her short green tunic over black silk trousers.

"*Bon soir, Messieurs*," she lisped in pidgin French. "Madam Jahn will be pleased."

"Maybe so pleased tonight she won't tell us about her *plus grande* establishment in Hanoi, so much better than this hovel," said Rosen.

The dark corridor ended in a small room lit by a single wall lamp swathed in red silk. It was crammed with four long low wooden tables covered with grass mats and flanked by small stools with brass tops. On each of the burnished stools rested a small spirit lamp, an ash tray, an empty glass, and a box of matches displaying a clipper ship under full sail. A gaudy calendar was suspended from the light fixture. It bore a colored photograph of a Chinese girl in a blue bikini and a message advertising Sunlight Soap in English, Chinese, and Vietnamese. Against the opposite wall a cracked mirror stood on a teak cupboard.

A black curtain in the far corner was twitched aside to admit a stout woman in her fifties. She wore a dark brown tunic unbuttoned at the neck. When she smiled, her eyes closed to slits and her parted lips revealed teeth stained the purple-black of the betel-nut addict.

"*Bon soir, Messieurs*," she said, her French fluent though marred by the Vietnamese sing-song. "M'sieu Rosen, M'sieu Levoncier, my old friend of better days in Hanoi, and M'sieu —I remember the face, but not the name."

Levoncier sketched a mock bow as he shook the woman's

hand. "Madame Jahn, may I have the honor of presenting once again the famous American writer, M. Mallory?"

"*Enchanté*, M'sieu Mallory. Welcome once again to my hovel. But, M'sieu Levoncier, is everyone you know nowadays a famous American writer?"

"Certainly, Madame Jahn, every one of them. But some are more famous than others, and M. Mallory is of the most famous. He writes not only for the journals but books as well, books that tens of thousands of people pay hundreds of piastres each to buy and read."

"How I wish I could apply the same principle," Madame Jahn sighed. "It is the wholesaler, not we poor retail merchants, who makes the grand profits. But it is, alas, impossible. A *fin à l'eau* while the pipes are being prepared?"

The three men slipped off their shoes to lie on the hard wooden divans, and the doorkeeper sidled into the room carrying a bottle of Bisquit and a carafe of water.

"Welcome to my house, Messieurs, and especially welcome to you, M'sieu Mallory," Madame Jahn said formally, raising her glass. "I hope I shall see you here often."

"If you can bear it," whispered Levoncier behind his hand. "The prices are reasonable, when one thinks that here one can enjoy all his vices. It is so compact, so efficient, so—almost —American. But it is very hard on the constitution."

The doorkeeper was joined by an older girl. Her short red tunic over flapping white trousers curved in at a waist that was slender despite the peasant solidity of her hips and the heavy breasts firm against the silk. Her broad face, enlivened by no spark of animation, was the face of ten thousand peasant girls. From the teak cupboard the girls took four pipes made of lacquered bamboo tubes with porcelain bowls the size of half-oranges set into them. The openings in the bowls were no larger than cherrystones.

"Watch the experts, Gerry," Rosen advised.

"No, Gerry, watch *Madame l'expert* if you have forgotten. I do not practice enough, for which thank God."

Squatting before the small blue light of the spirit lamps in the posture of acolytes, the girls dipped into a silver jar with metal rods like slender knitting needles. They plunged the points into the flames, returning again and again to the jar until gummy black wads were transformed into sleek gray balls. A musky, sweet odor filled the small room, and the girls pressed the pea-sized globules into two pipe bowls, withdrawing the needles with deft twists.

Madame Jahn reclined on the divan with her head propped on her hand. She held her pipe inverted over the open flame, drawing in the smoke in a constant stream for more than half a minute while the fingers of her free hand tapped rhythmically. Levoncier took longer, his inhalations less regular.

Mallory watched hazily, sipping his cognac and water, as the girls prepared pipes for Rosen and himself. The drug offered a suggestion of sweetness and an aftertaste of burning autumnal leaves. He drew the smoke deep into his lungs before letting it trickle slowly out between his lips.

"Just relax and let it work," Levoncier advised. "We have plenty of time and I would exhort you to do as I do—not more than seven pipes."

Mallory lit a cigarette, savoring the detachment which was the drug's first gift. Rosen and Levoncier looked far away, though their voices rang with unusual clarity.

"You know, I always feel decadent when I have a few pipes with our charming, clean-cut hostess here," said Rosen, smoothing his sleek black hair.

"Sid, that's not the most profound observation of the day," Mallory said.

"Not in that sense, Gerry. There's something so gracious and archaic about opium today. In the States, in Hong Kong or Macao, heroin's the stuff. It pays a thousand times better and it's a thousand times tougher. With opium I feel like an empire-builder of the 1880's rewarding himself with moderation for his labors."

"I, too, agree, Sidney," Levoncier mused, "though I have never even tried heroin. The raptures—they are not dignified. But opium, it is not bad. I have seen more men ruined by alcohol, many more."

"Alcohol," objected Mallory, "is for us Westerners; socially, even economically, we are attuned to alcohol. You *would* have seen more men ruined by liquor, Pierre."

"Still, Gerry, I have seen many colonial Frenchmen who became men of twenty or thirty pipes a day. But opium is somehow more gentle than liquor. Even if it ends in self-destruction—and many times it does not—it takes longer and it is much less violent."

The heavy-set Frenchman paused, his smooth face with its small, precise features cast in an incongruous frown of concentration.

"Take young Humboldt, of whom everyone was talking tonight at the party. . . ."

"Everyone talking?" asked Mallory. "I meant to ask you about him. I saw the body when I came in, but I didn't hear a word about him at the party."

"Of course not, Gerry," Rosen said. "You were a distinguished new arrival rubbing shoulders with the nobs. Martha runs a very well-disciplined party—before she gets loaded. But the working folk, with whom Pierre and I mingled, knowing our places, they talked of little else."

"Young Humboldt," Levoncier went on doggedly, "adopted the wrong way of destroying himself. Liquor—and he talked and talked and talked; it made him feel worse instead of better, and he made everyone else feel worse too. If he had taken to opium, as I told him, he would have relaxed, been at a distance and not caring so much."

"What was driving him?"

"Oh, to say that is hard." Levoncier tossed off a large Gallic shrug which rippled gently from the tips of his fingers to toes encased in checked green socks. "He did not like the way the war was going. Who does? He did not like American tactics. Who does? He did not like your allies. Who does? He did not like most of his fellow officers. So, again, who does? He also did not like the climate very much. I do, but who else does? So he started drinking, then shot himself. Who may not do the same in time?"

"Pierre is being French, superficial, and unfair to both Humboldt and himself," Rosen said, his tone assertive and precise.

"All right, *mon cher* Sidney, you tell us then."

"Yeah, Sid. If young American officers are blowing out their brains, it's damned interesting."

"It's not, Gerry. It's hardly typical. But take a very bright boy from the Middle West and send him to Harvard. Remember, he's not only got a first-class brain but also a passionate, idealistic nature."

"All right. What happens next to this paragon?"

"No paragon, as will emerge. Send him to Korea in 1952 with a brand-new ROTC commission and give him command of a company at Old Baldy and Porkchop a year later. After the armistice, he volunteers to extend his tour because he's fascinated by a civilization totally different from his own. Besides, he's always wanted to write. God preserve me from young men who want to write."

"Amen, Sidney, amen," breathed Levoncier. "That is why I am working for an American magazine. Not only because the Americans have the money but because I cannot write in English. So I am ideal for them."

The attendants were preparing another round of pipes. Mallory let his fingers trail across the thighs of the girl in the red tunic. She glanced at him obliquely, her eyes dull. Levoncier was stroking the shoulders of the young doorkeeper as if she were a favorite cat. Rosen was immersed in his tale.

"With one thing and another, John Humboldt doesn't get out of the Army until 1955. He decides to take a Master's at Yale in Oriental civilization—whatever that is. By now it's

37

1958, and he decides it's time he went out into the world. But first he acquires a wife, an intense little brunette whose father is a professor of law at New Haven and, incidentally, heir to a soap fortune. She thinks Johnny's brilliant and loves him for it; after all, she was brought up to value the intellect. But she also thinks he's going places—though even she doesn't know where."

Rosen broke off to accept the proffered pipe, his spare form expanding as his lungs filled. Levoncier, his second pipe expended, was toying with the doorkeeper's long black hair. When Mallory handed back his own pipe, the girl in red sat on the edge of his divan and placed her hand firmly on his thigh. Her face, contemplating the wall calendar, remained without expression.

"Another toast to Madame Jahn and her unique hospitality." Mallory raised his glass. "Pierre, why not be efficient and combine the two means of self-destruction always?"

"Did I mention that Humboldt wanted to write?" asked Rosen. "Yeah, I guess I did. So, like many a fool before him, he listens to advice—he gets a job on a small paper, some sheet in Upper Overshoes, Maine. After a couple of years, he's still covering church socials and high-school graduations, while his wife is getting sourer and sourer. Every attempt to move to a bigger paper—or the heaven of a foreign assignment—is stymied. When the Army wants him back, he's ready; figures he'll get out to the Orient again and take his discharge here, then pick up some kind of job. Lady Macbeth back home agrees, though after a while he's wondering if she'll ever join him. Poor goof is still in love with her. Something to do with sex I'd say as a guess."

"*Mon cher,* you make it so romantic—and so tawdry. Do all Americans know so much about each other?"

"No, Pierre, but I was interested in this boy. And I had a lot of drinks with him once," answered Rosen, wiping the side of his index finger along the curved bridge of his nose. "I thought I could get him on with us, if he'd forget about wanting to write. Be patient, the tawdry story's almost finished. Anyway, it's better to have a couple of facts instead of just your Charlie Chaplin shrug and a big load of well-rounded, rhetorical Gallic horse manure."

"Pray continue, Sidney. We are enthralled by your solid all-American facts."

"The Army, as usual, disobliges. Humboldt sits in Washington until about ten months ago, when they finally send him out here. But he gets a damned interesting job—almost ideal for him. Sort of utility liaison man with the Vietnamese Army, the Embassy, and our own headquarters, with a special brief for intelligence and deep assault work that takes him into the paddies and the jungles."

"Fascinating job, Sid," Mallory broke in. "With your promised patronage he should have been happy as a leech in a herd of buffalo. Or wasn't he getting laid?"

"*Au contraire,* Gerry, as we say in Saigon, Vietnam. About six months ago he meets a girl who's everything his neurotic wife isn't. She's interested in him, not in his pretensions, and she wants him to be happy, not jet-propelled.

"But, in a way, that's the beginning of his real troubles. He's guilty as hell about his wife and, worse, he begins to see the Vietnamese as people, not just a fascinating study. He's ever more depressed by Saigon. Let's see if I can remember some of the things he said—purple as hell, I told him. Yeah! Vietnam is a playground for Americans and a few Vietnamese, but it's purgatory for ninety-five per cent of the people. Saigon is a flawed diamond on a dung heap, a twisted petal floating in a honey bucket. It's Pompeii and the volcanologists have predicted the eruption, but hardly anybody believes them; and those that do, they can't get away."

"So he talks too frequently about this bad situation, and the Army it gets—how do you say it—gorged up, and decides to send him home," said Levoncier. "So that is the end of the story. Another cognac, anyone?"

"Pierre's right, Sid," Mallory interposed. "You've told me everything except why he went wild and shot himself. It wasn't quite the end of the world, particularly if *you* were still in his corner."

"But that I have already explained, concisely and Gallicly. He does not like the war, the tactics, the allies, his colleagues, and, above all, he does not like the climate. But also he does not like to go home. So, poof."

"I don't think it's got much to do with your story, Gerry, but if you really want to know ask his girl. She'd know, if anyone would."

"Who's she?"

"You met her at Hooghly's—Tuyelle. She came to the party because she had to. She works in the Information Ministry. Ask Tuyelle."

"I may at that."

Levoncier rose, letting his hand slide down the green silk of the young doorkeeper's sleeve until he grasped her hand. "You permit, Messieurs. Come, *ma petite*," he said, leading her out of the room.

"That Pierre has strange tastes," Rosen sighed. "They call her Little Sister. Madame Jahn keeps her for old Chinese tycoons, a few Vietnamese past their prime, for emergencies when everyone else is taken—and for Pierre."

Madame Jahn had vanished, and the girl in red was preparing two more pipes. A Vietnamienne of about twenty-five swirled into the room in a low-cut sequin evening gown. She kissed Rosen enthusiastically, but evaded his clutching hands to stand humming to herself while she studied her gamin features in the mirror.

"Since Jeanne-Marie is being elusive, let me tell you about my latest project, Gerry. It will make a fortune. Pierre and I are writing a *Cookbook for Corespondents*, no, not correspondents, corespondents. . . ." Rosen's dry voice trailed off.

The Vietnamienne had casually stepped out of her evening gown, revealing a white-net brassière and a skimpy half-

40

slip. She lay down on the divan Levoncier had vacated, the half-slip rucked up around her honey-colored thighs, and put out her hand for the pipe prepared for Rosen.

". . . the cookbook," resumed Rosen, "will take the prospective corespondent through all the stages. He starts by eating lightly, if discriminatingly, so that he can appear to his lady wan with desire but yet a man of taste. Then, as seduction grows nearer, the quantity and quality of the food and wine rise to crescendo. There is a middle period, a plateau, of mutual enjoyment. Now, we come to the crucial phase—the withdrawal phase. He must live on fried hamburgers and onions, washed down with cheap beer, belching bountifully to discourage the lady. Finally, we prescribe a list of iron rations—an escape kit if he must flee. It will make a. . . ."

"Who's your friend?" asked Mallory, nodding at the Vietnamienne, who had unclasped her brassière and was slipping it halfway off and then on again. She caressed her breasts with her fingertips, delighting in her own touch.

"Oh, Jeanne-Marie. She sings at a cabaret near here, the Van Dam. Sometimes drops in for a pipe or two—and what she can find. Tonight she's found me. Unless you'd like me to put in a word for you? She is, frankly, experimental—and a little nuts."

"No, Sid. Thanks a lot. She frightens me. I'm content with my silent friend here."

The girl in the red tunic followed Mallory out of the room. She opened a door down the corridor and motioned him into a dim room about half the size of the first. The blue-white light of a street lamp came through a small window high in the wall and fell on a blackwood divan covered with a red silk quilt.

Still silent, she unbuttoned his shirt and drew it down over his arms, running the back of her hand gently across his chest. Standing close, she hooked her thumbs in the elastic at the waist of her pantaloons and slid them down her legs. She stepped out of the froth of white, gathering it up and folding it carefully to put it on the bedside table. Turning her back, she undid her red tunic and shrugged out of her brassière. She folded those garments, too, and laid them on top of her pantaloons.

As she moved toward Mallory on bare feet, her face expressionless, he caught his breath. Her waist was as slender as he had thought, and her coffee-colored hips were amply curved, but her generous thighs tapered into slender calves.

Mallory placed his hands on her hips, letting his fingers slide gently over the cool skin until he grasped her buttocks. He stepped forward toward a brief oblivion.

5

Motes of dust danced in the shaft of sun that transfixed the muffled room, intruding through the imperfectly drawn crimson drapes above the antique, gray air-conditioner. The band of light crept slowly toward the head of the figure sprawled on the double bed. When the jagged golden halo touched the high cheekbones and the long-lobed ears with a brief glory, Mallory woke abruptly.

Groaning, he closed his eyes and sank back on the pillow. As Rosen had warned him, the scarlet drapes and the crimson-brocade walls made him feel as if he were "waking in the whale's stomach." Groping for the telephone, he ordered. *"Café complet avec jus d'orange."* Slowly he put his feet on the floor and knotted his orange plaid sarong at the waist.

When he emerged from the bathroom, Mallory shook a cigarette out of the crumpled pack of Camels and drew the curtains back. He recoiled under the impact of the glare that revealed worn spots in the crimson rug and scars on the blond furniture. Stepping onto the narrow balcony, he shivered as the heat cloaked his chilled skin. The scent of Saigon drifted up to him—woodsmoke and musk, garlic and sweat, fish and flowers.

On his left began the tree-shaded Rue Catinat, which had hopefully been rechristened *Tu Do*—Freedom—almost a decade earlier. Jewelry shops, curio merchants, and raucous bars tempted the pale giants of the American Military Assistance Group, who were Saigon's latest army of occupation.

Ngo-dinh Diem had contemptuously referred to his critics as "Radio Catinat." The swelling of discontent in the cafés of Catinat was, once again, the only articulate public opinion in the shattered state of Vietnam. The power of decision lay elsewhere—in Washington and Moscow, in Hanoi and Peking. Yet the ultimate verdict of Radio Catinat would determine not only the fate of Vietnam and, certainly, Thailand and Cambodia as well, not only the results of elections in Maine and California but the destiny of children growing up in Rio de Janiero and Sicily and the shape of new nations under the African sun. If, Mallory reminded himself impatiently, almost querulously, if Vietnam were really as important as it appeared to him.

Rue Catinat ended at the broad quay along the narrow Saigon River. The denizens of the quay, ragged in the golden sunlight, sought their livings indifferent to the anguished attention the great capitals were giving to their affairs. Grimy boys of eleven or twelve offered cigarettes and chewing gum from trays slung around their necks. Teenage girls in dark tunics squatted behind displays of a few bony fish laid on newspapers covering the pavement. Others offered baskets of spiky red and green fruits or pairs of protesting chickens hanging head down from poles. Slender women in shiny black Chinese tunics and trousers narrower than those of the Vietnamienne peddled graying chunks of raw flesh suspended from filthy strings.

Mallory shifted his eyes. Far to the left, past the foot of Catinat, an American freighter lay at the quay and a shabby ferry launch carried a load of squealing pigs and resigned peasants to the river's far bank three minutes away. Directly in line with the ferry, but easily two miles from the river, he saw a ship sailing majestically upon the paddy fields. Her steep gray sides rising from a clump of trees, the small carrier maneuvered serenely on solid land with not a finger of water visible around her. Her flight deck was jagged with helicopters and the folded wings of propeller-driven medium bombers. He watched, fascinated, as the towering hull executed a sharp turn in the midst of the green rice, though he had seen after the first delighted shock that the carrier was following the serpentine course of the Saigon River from Cap St. Jacques and the open sea.

Twin trickles of sweat running down his bare sides broke his reverie, and Mallory realized that the glare was making his eyes ache. He stepped back into the room and saw that his breakfast waited beside the typewriter on the spindly blond-wood table. Selecting five different colored pills from the vials in his leather case, he washed them down with orange juice. After pouring equal amounts of coffee and hot milk into his cup and buttering a croissant, he opened the heavy square envelope which rested on a folded copy of *The Vietnam News* beside the plates. The message was short: "I should be very pleased if you would lunch with me today. Unless I hear otherwise, I shall expect you at L'Amiral at 1 PM." It was signed George Dietrich.

Reflecting that Dietrich, the man who believed in victory but did not believe in the means employed, was as good a place to start as any other, Mallory leafed through the newspaper. GOVERNMENT PROMISES COMPLETE PROTECTION TO PEASANTS, ran one headline. He skimmed others: AMERICAN OFFICIAL SEES TIDE TURNING; PARIS, PEKING AND MOSCOW CALL FOR CONFERENCE ON LAOS—PATHET LAO TAKE NEW TOWN; PROVINCIAL GOVERNOR GUARANTEES SAFETY OF HIGHWAY IN RAINY SEASON: RANGERS DESTROY THREE VIETCONG CAMPS—OUR CASUALTIES LIGHT. He carefully folded the paper and laid it aside, wondering why he bothered to keep it. Its columns, he reflected, offered a view of the reality of the war through a periscope made of distorting mirrors.

Mallory carried his cup to the bedside table. He opened his notebook and lifted the handset of the telephone. A deafening alternation of buzzing and whistling reverberated through the crimson room. He shook a cigarette out of his pack with one hand, his right eyebrow cocked high in an unconscious parody of astonishment.

"Can you get me 28145?" he asked after a full minute, when the tumult had subsided.

"Yes, sir," a male voice replied.

After a series of clicks he heard a thin, far-away ringing. It continued for two minutes, ending just when he was about to hang up. A forty-five-second silence was followed by a flow of explosive Vietnamese.

"Is that the American Embassy?" he asked.

Another spasm of Vietnamese.

"C'est l'Ambassade Américaine?"

"Non, Monsieur. C'est le residence du Doctor Quay!"

"Oh, pardonnez-moi."

He put the handset back in its cradle and lit a cigarette before picking the telephone up again. The dull silence of an empty room greeted him. He jiggled the plate up and down, switching hands from time to time. The hollow silence was unbroken. Crushing out his cigarette, he tried again, finally eliciting a reply after five minutes.

"I was just feeling a sensation of terrible isolation," he said softly.

"Sir?" the voice inquired.

"Nothing important. Would you try 28145 again please?"

"Oh," said the voice, startled. "Not 28154? You want another number?"

"No, the same number—28145."

"But that is not the number you asked for earlier."

"Don't worry about it, just try 28145."

"Yes, sir. Number 28149."

"No," Mallory said very slowly, feeling his face flush and the sweat dripping down his neck, "Two eight one four *five*."

"Yes, sir. Number two eight one four *five*." The voice was tolerant of his eccentricity.

A silence, followed by clicks and another silence, broken

after two minutes by the voice he was beginning to hate.

"I have listened myself this time, and the number is busy."

Mallory gripped the handset hard to keep himself from throwing it across the room. "Then try 28146."

"Yes, sir. Number 28146."

"Wonderful, right the first time." Mallory felt he should rush out and light a candle in thanksgiving, but he was tied down to the vicious black instrument.

"I am sorry, sir, but the number does not answer," reported the voice. It added in earnest explanation, "Nobody is there."

"Look, there must be someone there. Please try again."

After another two minutes a female voice responded from the bottom of a mine shaft: "American Embassy, good morning."

"I'd like to speak to Mr. Nelson in the Political Section."

"Just a moment, sir," she said; then, after a full minute, "I am ringing your extension."

Breaking into the first ring, a hearty American voice boomed, "Attaché's office, Sergeant Swenson."

"Look, Sergeant," Mallory weakly said, "I'm calling from outside, trying to reach Mr. Nelson in the Political Section. Can you get the operator back for me, please?"

"I'll try, sir." Was there doubt in the hearty voice?

Sergeant Swenson's morning began to collapse upon the wreckage of Mallory's. Mallory heard the connection broken and renewed time and time again as Swenson pleaded: "Operator! Operator!" Then silence, marred only by the rattle of a typewriter.

"I'm trying, sir, but these girls are a mite slow."

"Thanks, Sergeant. If I hang up I'll never get through again."

"No trouble, sir. I know how it is."

Finally that distant voice, "Operator. Can I help you?"

"This caller wants Mr. Nelson—Nelson—in the Political Section."

"Trying Mr. Nelson."

A series of clicks preceded total silence. After two minutes Mallory jiggled the plate gently. A dial tone rewarded him. He hung up and walked deliberately to the bathroom. He returned, mopping his face with a towel.

"Once more into the breach," he murmured, picking up the handset. "Number 28146, please."

"The same number, sir?"

"Yes, the same number please, 28146."

The faraway female voice came on immediately. "Good morning, American Embassy."

"I'd like to speak to Mr. Nelson in the Political Section," Mallory said, slowly and distinctly. "Mr. Nelson in the Political Section. Nelson, have you got that?"

"Yes sir, of course." The voice was hurt, a breath of sorrow from a distant land.

On the second ring a female voice dripping with magnolias and Spanish moss said, "Mr. Brown's office."

Mallory felt a rush of pressure behind his forehead. But he kept his voice even. "I'm terribly sorry, but I'm trying to reach Mr. Nelson and I'm calling from outside. I wonder if you could ask the operator. . . ."

"Mr. Nelson is also on this extension, sir."

Suddenly birds sang and he asked lightheartedly, "May I speak to Mr. Nelson?"

"I'm sorry, sir." The magnolias were blooming so thick he could smell them. "But Mr. Nelson is out of Saigon. I don't expect him back till tomorrow."

"Look," he said desperately, "will you ask him to call me, Mallory at the Majestic, as soon as he gets in."

Two hours later the ash tray was overflowing, Mallory was drenched in sweat, and his appointment book was almost bare. Out of fifteen numbers, five had actually answered. He had garnered one firm date and one promise to call back. He stretched and started for the balcony to escape the clammy air-conditioning. A tattoo of resounding knocks was played on the door.

"Coming, damn it," he shouted.

"Open! Open immediately! Urgent press," cried a voice in the corridor. "Extra, extra."

"Come in, Pierre," Mallory said in a lower tone.

The open door framed Levoncier's innocent face. His eyes rolled in an exaggerated circuit of the room before he flung the door open and bounced in, waving a blue telegram form. His chest was crisscrossed by straps supporting three cameras and he carried a camera bag.

"I just wanted to be certain you were alone. *Mon Dieu,* it was not easy separating you from the temptation last night. I bring you a *communiqué* from our masters."

Mallory read the cable: QUEST SAIGON/LEVONCIER PLEASE PASS MALLORY COLON CONFIRMING TWENTYFIRST FEBRUARY FIRM DEADLINE FOR TWENTY TO TWENTYFIVE THOUSAND WORDS STOP ALL SET ROLL COMMA GIVING YOUR TAKEOUT SPECIAL PRESENTATION AND PROMOTION STOP PLEASE COORDINATE PHOTOS WITH LEVONCIER WHOM CABLING SEPARATELY PARA AS WE SEE IT FROM DISTANCE STORY LOOKS MORE AND MORE LIKE SEARCHING EXAMINATION MORAL WELL AS POLITICAL QUESTIONS DASH DILEMMA OF TWO NATIONS STOP HOPE YOU AGREE STOP WILL KEEP YOU POSTED LATEST WASHINGTON THINKING FOR YOUR INFORMATION COMMA BUT HOPE YOU WILL CONCENTRATE UNDERLYING ISSUES COMMA LEAVING US INFILL WASHINGTON APPRAISAL IN BRIEF SIDEBAR BEST REGARDS MCALLEN

Mallory let the flimsy sheet flutter to the table. "Christ," he said, "everybody goes mad in cables—words, and more words, ninety per cent of them unnecessary. What did they say about pictures?"

"Nothing of a startling nature. I am to go where you go and shoot tens of thousands of pictures—black-and-white, white-and-black, Kodachrome, Ektachrome, infra-red, ultra-violet, and ultra-violent. So you must put up with me for the next three weeks continuously."

"Just as long as you don't block my note-taking hand. Did you say three weeks? My God, that means just four weeks for reporting and writing. Hell, it could take two weeks just telephoning."

Levoncier had raised a Nikon to his eye and was snapping the shutter rapidly, advancing the film with flicks of his thumb.

"What are you doing?"

"I did not tell you, but they also want many, many pictures of you working, talking to people, being heroic in helicopters and foxholes. You are to be big in this story, my friend—but I took none last night."

"Yeah, very big in a dirty sarong brooding over a stack of dirty dishes. I'm going to shower. You and your cameras can stay out here."

"Oh, Gerry. They have already held an inquiry, and the body of Humboldt is to be shipped away today. As I said, they decided he shot himself because he didn't like the way things were going. 'A highly disturbed state of mind,' was the main point."

"Dammed quick, wasn't it?"

"Not necessarily. You know how it is in this climate. Nothing lasts very long—governments, countries, reputations, even bodies."

"If you're through playing Hamlet as a tropical remittance man, you can do something for me. This girl of Humboldt's—Tuyelle? You know her, don't you? Could you ask her to have dinner with us tonight? I'd like to talk to her about Humboldt, see if I can't find out more about him. I've got a feeling he might make a few good paragraphs, though Rosen and you don't. But I can't tackle the phone again."

Levoncier came to stiff attention. *"Avec plaisir, mon general,"* he said.

"And order another pot of coffee, *mon caporal,"* said Mallory, retreating into the bathroom.

Fifteen minutes later, Mallory found Levoncier sipping a cup of coffee and reading the newspaper with little exclamations of pleasure and surprise.

"This is an interesting country, this Vietnam they are writing about. I should like to go there someday," he said. "Mademoiselle Tuyelle accepts—after much urging, for she does not like to go out. But I have told her it could be of service to what people think of Johnny Humboldt and, perhaps, Vietnam. You are certain you are interested only in him, not in her?"

"Of course," Mallory snapped. "I hardly looked at the girl."

"So be it, Robespierre. Now we must get you many, many cards of identity. You have thousands of little pictures of yourself?"

"Thousands, naturally. But, before we go, I want a cup of coffee and you can tell me about George Dietrich. I'm having lunch with him today. He's paying."

"I wonder what he wants?" Levoncier breathed. "But perhaps that is not fair, for he is a man of fearsome opinions. Maybe he wants only to convince you."

"Of what?"

"Oh, that Vietnam must be most strenuously defended because George Dietrich has so much property here. But I am being unfair, as Sidney would say. I must try to give you a better idea."

Levoncier leaned back in the easy chair and placed his fingertips together magisterially. "Pierre's private biographical information service," he entoned, "will now provide excerpts from Dossier D-108. George Dietrich came here in 1952 as a merchant. He was not popular with my countrymen because they knew that he was a close friend of Ngo-dinh Diem. The little man was then in exile, living on the American Catholic Church. Dietrich, incidentally, had met Diem through a brother who was a priest of the Maryknoll Order, which gave Diem shelter.

"Dietrich was also not popular because he *would* use phrases like 'stinking colonialism' when he became too hot in argument. He was almost thrown out of the country three of four times, but he stayed and built up a little importing business. When Diem came to power, Dietrich's interests expanded—he founded *The Vietnam News* as a sideline. The paper makes money, though nothing compared to what Dietrich makes on his export-import business and his contracts with the American military. When Diem was killed, Dietrich was in trouble, but he seemed to find a sponsor in the new government—even I do not know who— and he hung on. These, *mon general,* are the facts."

"And the gossip, the rumor?"

"That is harder yet. Rumor had it that Dietrich survived in the bad old French days because he was a cohort of our noble Commander in Chief, General Raoul Salan, in the opium trade. Salan preferred a non-Frenchman for certain purposes. I do not know. In Hanoi, he used to patronize Madame Jahn's grand establishment, as did everyone. He does not go to her poor hovel here, as few do."

Mallory, shrugging into a white-linen safari jacket, gestured impatiently as Levoncier's voice trailed off. "And what do you really think?" he asked.

"That is the hardest. I am a reporter, not a pundit. But I should say that *le gros Georges* is, in parts that are equal, a man who likes money, and a man of conviction. Now he puts his passions all into the cause of the Vietnamese. He hates the Communists and he loved Diem. Unfortunately I cannot share his faith." Levoncier gulped his coffee and rose. Waving toward the door, he said, "But I shall continue the briefing as we go."

The room lay silent for almost an hour after the pair had left, the air-conditioner laboring away ever more noisily as the heat outside increased.

The black door to the corridor opened slowly to admit a young Vietnamese in a white jacket and trousers. Noting that the bathroom door was ajar, he drew it carefully shut and pulled on the handle of the door leading to the balcony to make sure that it, too, was closed. Moving without haste, he stacked the used dishes on a tray.

He read Mallory's cable with frowning attention. Slipping a notebook out of his jacket, he laboriously copied the message. He shuffled through the debris in the wastepaper basket, but found nothing of interest. Balancing the tray on one palm, he moved toward the door. His feet shuffled across the crimson carpet, and his gaze was cast down.

6

The narrow spiral staircase trembled on the vertical iron bars that were its only support. Despite the coarse-meshed fishermen's nets stretched between the rods, Mallory was as tense as a novice trapeze performer until he stepped from the last flimsy tread into the air-conditioned room where anchors and rigging blocks hung on the walls.

George Dietrich seemed even heavier and more imposing in the small room, crowded by just four tables, than he had appeared the night before. A giant in white sharkskin, he rose with one well-manicured hand resting on a polished brass ship's lantern. He drew Mallory into the room as much by the smoldering vitality of his presence as by his ostentatiously firm handclasp.

"My dear chap, so glad you could come," Dietrich piped. "I've taken the liberty of ordering drinks."

Two crystalline martinis in outsize champagne glasses were endangered by the sweep of his broad hand. A perfect crescent of lemon peel floated in each, like a boat with decks awash.

"I've finally taught them to make a proper martini here— at the cost of much effort and no small expenditure. These are precisely twenty parts of fine gin to one of vermouth."

The cocktail drenched the back of Mallory's mouth with a spray of ice. He wondered why Dietrich was as effusive as a nervous Chicago hostess eager to impress a spurious Italian count. Perhaps it was just his normal manner; perhaps he truly enjoyed practicing the art of hospitality; perhaps he was merely anxious to put his deeply felt convictions in the most persuasive atmosphere. Perhaps, Mallory told himself, it was time to check the reporter's instinct to question every word and every deed. Dietrich was probably lonely; he probably disliked eating along.

"I've taken a postgraduate course in reading this," said Dietrich, flipping the purple scrawl of the bill of fare against his thumb, "and it's been worth the tuition. If you'll allow me to suggest a *paté du chef*, followed by *ris de veau granmere en cocotte*, and, last, *fraises du bois* from Dalat. With them, I think, a *rosé*, Tavel."

"Sounds fine," said Mallory. "And another martini as a tribute to your training."

He, too, would be uttering rolling Edwardian phrases if he did not curb his instinct toward mimicry. He lit a cigarette, taking sensuous delight in the hissing air-conditioning and the restorative martini. What, he wondered, would Dietrich do if he said out of the corner of his mouth, "All right, buster, shoot. It's your nickel."

Instead, he said, "Nice place Marcel's got here. It's been so long I'd forgotten."

"Yes, if you know what to order, even if it is run by a Frenchman. The tragedy of this country is somehow epitomized—the best non-Chinese restaurants in Saigon are all French-owned. The Vietnamese make excellent chefs, but they will simply not attend to the instructions of another Vietnamese."

Mallory's pleasure at the direct approach was mixed with irritation at being taken so definitely under control. He recognized the manner of a man utterly determined to impose his views on a visiting correspondent and, presumably, through him on the American public. It was a familiar phenomenon, indeed it was the *sine qua non* of the reporter's trade—people who wanted to talk. For his own unknown reasons, altruistic or self-seeking, Dietrich, who was hardly first but by no means last in this middle-size Asian city, had chosen Gerald Mallory to transmit his convictions. Mallory settled down to listen, for that was his trade.

The big man sipped his martini delicately. "When Ngodinh Diem still lived, before he was murdered with the complicity of the Department of State, it was different. The Vietnamese were growing toward independence."

"Why did the people turn against him?" Mallory asked.

"The people did *not* turn against their president. But, to answer properly, I must go deep into the Vietnamese struggle for freedom."

"Go ahead, it's your nickel!" Mallory could not banish the temptation, but he added hastily, "I've been looking forward to hearing you talk on a subject you know so well."

Was there a hint of resentment in the small blue eyes? Did the thick fingers, powerful beneath their cushion of fat, tense angrily for an instant? But Dietrich resumed in his normal tones, as ever, slightly unctuous with the shadow of the hard bone beneath the surface.

"The peoples of Indo-China have lived under alien domination so long that they are now incapable of ruling themselves or of finding their own salvation. The one man who could have led them to maturity is dead. Americans must now assume direct leadership. The Boy Scout generals in the seats of power must be directed or the struggle is lost. The cancer of communism is consuming this country like a forest fire driven by raging winds. We must assume the power, as well as the responsibility."

Another martini blossomed before Mallory and he took it gratefully. The fat man might have much to say, but he had a thirst-provoking manner of discourse.

"How can we assume real power and how exercise it?" Mallory asked, his deliberately goading frivolity wholly abandoned as he concerntrated on the thesis. Dietrich had ideas, that rare commodity, and he was therefore well worth attention, even if all his ideas were later rejected.

The publisher tasted the chilled *rosé* appreciatively and

cut a fastidious slice out of his *paté* before replying. If he was a man obsessed, as appeared likely, he was a mono-maniac with remarkable self-control.

"Mr. Mallory, someone must assume control. If we Americans do not, the Chinese will. A wonderful small nation will disappear, and the American position in the Pacific will be untenable. If necessary, we must move our men into every ministry and every platoon."

"What channels are open to us?" Mallory was now wholly the professional interrogator. His private fears were forgotten. The nervous darting of his right hand to his ear lobe and its perplexed passage over his crewcut were stilled.

"Mr. Mallory, there are even more opportunities to exercise power than there are problems here. Intelligence networks, communications, military discipline, civilian confidence, mobility of troops, economic betterment—all cry out for direction. President Diem was moving when he was destroyed. Many of the Americans who acceded to his destruction with so much joy were undoubtedly agents of the Communists."

"I'll pass on that," Mallory said, side-stepping a direct confrontation. "You know you're considered Diem's chief champion around here?"

"And proud of that distinction. . . ."

"Everything I saw on my last visit before the coup made me feel Diem was through. He was weak, isolated, and the country was going to pot. . . ."

"No, Mr. Mallory, he was biding his time." The high tenor was still silky, but the heavy cheeks were suddenly florid, and the small blue eyes glinted dangerously. "The old power structure had to collapse before he could apply his own solutions."

"He was close, wasn't he? Things were going to hell in a couple of handbaskets. What role did Diem's brother, Ngo-dinh Nhu play?" pressed Mallory.

"Even the greatest man must have someone he can trust

57

implicitly," Dietrich retorted. "That is the only role Nhu played. Diem made his own decisions."

"I'm *not* going to let *that* pass," Mallory said. "How do you explain. . . ."

They argued amicably through the meal. The tender sweet-breads with just a suggestion of tarragon, the tiny strawberries, the second bottle of wine, the bitter coffee accompanied by pungent *marc de Champagne,* the brandy which is the essence of the vine, frugally pressed from the skins, pits, and twigs that remain after the initial pressing—all came and vanished amid torrents of words, ideas, and hopes. Dietrich was surprisingly pleasant in his contention, always in control of himself.

Desending the spiral staircase was more precarious than the ascent had been. The wooden slats creaked when Dietrich set his feet upon them. They ceremonially shook hands with Marcel, the tall Frenchman who stood behind the long bar on the ground floor, and waited for a small Vietnamese boy in a white sailor suit to open the glass doors.

The stickly heat of midafternoon enveloped them. It was equally impervious to the hint of rain in the air and to the fitful wind that chased eddies of dust over the broken pavements and toyed with scraps of paper in the doorways of shuttered shops. By the time they had walked the short block to Rue Catinat, Mallory was once more drenched in sweat. He could feel the alcohol bubbling through his bloodstream to percolate under his skull.

He thanked Dietrich for the lunch, and the big man, his suit still crisp and his blue foulard tie still precisely knotted, replied, "I am glad that you enjoyed the meal as much as I did. I hope it was also of some value to you."

"I've got some ideas from you to mix with my own preconceptions." Mallory decided the publisher deserved a certain measure of frankness. "But I badly need hard facts—actual incidents and talks with the Vietnamese. Still, if the situation is so close to hopeless, I don't see how we can help by diving head first into the muck."

Dietrich might have merited frankness, but he did not receive it well. For an instant his control faded. The heavy hands clenched and the broad, fleshy forehead tightened into a scowl. "I am not, sir, seeking to convince you or educate you!" The high voice had a momentary edge like a yellow diamond; then the tone changed apruptly. "Forgive me! I feel too strongly about this tortured country. Of course, Gerald Mallory has a duty to be skeptical, but I shall arrange for you to meet some Vietnamese whose words and experiences will naturally carry more weight than my own. *Adieu.*"

Mallory watched the bulky, erect figure walk rapidly past the marble-and-glass façade of the Air France office in the Caravelle Hotel. He turned the other way. Along the three blocks before the Majestic only one shop was open, a narrow bar, crowded with American soldiers. Mallory heard a swelling patter like the tread of a pursuing throng. He broke into a trot and an instant after he stepped into the Majestic the skies opened. The rain fell so thick he could not see across the street.

Riding up in the cage-like elevator which was guided by a miniscule Vietnamese boy in a crimson uniform, Mallory knew that the story was beginning to assume definite form. It was good to be back at work again. Talking with Tuyelle —the family name eluded him—should assist its growth. She might also provide him with contacts to discharge his nebulous obligation to Gilroy.

7

A hint of a frown marred the high narrow forehead. The suggestion of a crease appeared on the soft buttercup-cream skin between the dark eyebrows that swooped outward like the wings of a moth.

"Ngo-dinh Diem was many things to all of us," Tuyelle said slowly. "The one man who stood against both the French and the Communists. A fanatic ascetic out of the early history of the Church, who feared women as the very principle of corruption."

"Are you a Catholic, Miss Vguyen-lee?" Mallory asked.

She accepted the question as he had offered it—a simple matter of identification in the confused Asian context. So might she ask whether he preferred to write for newspapers or magazines.

"No, I am if anything, a Buddhist, but all of us had French and Catholic educations, those of us who were educated." She paused, then added hastily, "Please Miss Tuyelle or just Tuyelle, if you prefer. There are too many Miss Vguyen-lees. But I shall call you Mr. Mallory."

"I'd be happier if you'd call me Gerry in turn."

"No, I think not." The softly pointed chin moved decisively from side to side above the high yellow collar. "I was telling you about Diem. He destroyed monsters like the gangster who kept a pen of crocodiles and a caged leopard on his private island off Cholon. That man's enemies went to the crocodiles alive and their bones to the leopard. The French supported that man with money and arms, and he

60

bought—actually bought—control of the Saigon police force. The French legacy was corruption and decadence. Diem cleared these stables of the filth of centuries." She hesitated. "I am talking too much about things that do not interest you."

"They do indeed," Mallory said.

"Finally, Diem became what his opponents had always charged—the complete fanatic. He listened only to his own voices—and the hatred of his brother Nhu. He was completely cut off from the people. He did not fight the Communists effectively, but maneuvered only to keep any general from becoming strong enough to challenge him. Our weakness was an invitation to a new Communist attack. Diem made eunuchs, like himself, of the men around him, and he pretended that women did not exist."

At the sidewalk café of the Majestic, they were surrounded by American officers and their Vietnamese girl friends. Mallory had a cognac in front of him; she had a crème de menthe. A hundred yards down the quay the jeep carrier *Mindanao* was tied up, her cranes swinging helicopters and stub-winged planes onto flatbed trucks in the glare of spotlights.

They had met at a restaurant called the Hong Kong, its red-painted booths just like those in any unpretentious Chinese restaurant in California, but the Cantonese food was infinitely better. Even Mallory, who did not particularly like Cantonese food, could not fault the fresh crab with black-bean sauce.

Levoncier had muttered, "Ah, the duenna!" as they entered the restaurant, for Tuyelle was seated beside Ngo-canh Vao, the young Vietnamese with whom she had left the Hooghlys' party. Thin, intense, his long, frail fingers nervously flicking back the lock that fell over his forehead, Vao had said almost nothing except to admit grudgingly that he worked for the daily *Than Dan* and wrote occasional articles for *The Vietnam News*. But his presence had effectively inhibited any but the most general conversation.

Halfway through the cold dessert of lotus seeds in almond milk, the waiter had whispered to Levoncier. The Frenchman explained, when he returned from the phone, "The PIO's office. I told them where we'd be to save them the trouble of getting the wrong information from Vietnamese intelligence. I must go the the airport. A big fight in the Camau, and they are bringing in the wounded and dead, a few Americans, many Vietnamese."

"I'll go with you," Vao said. "We can drop Tuyelle off on the way."

"No," she had said decisively. "I shall go and sit in the café of the Majestic with Mr. Mallory. You can pick me up when you are through. No one will see us. No one looks at the faces of the girls with Americans there."

To Mallory's surprise, Vao had agreed without further protest, only admonishing sternly, when the black Citroën pulled up in front of the hotel, "Now you wait here for me. It won't be long."

But time had spun itself out. Its passage was almost imperceptible through the cloying tropical darkness, except when flashes of heat lightning lit up the far shore of the river and the palm trees stood out, carved violet shadows against the yellow glow.

Intent on the activity around the carrier, Mallory missed a few sentences. "I'm sorry, I was wool gathering," he said.

"Wool gathering? Oh, thinking elsewhere." It was the first fault he had noticed in her English. "I was just saying that Diem was killed, and the new men came, and everything suddenly seemed much worse—or perhaps we discovered how bad things had already become."

"And where do you go from here?"

"I do not know. If my family did not come from the north, if I did not know the Communists, I could say, like many of my friends, 'The Communists will rule and all will be well!' Nonetheless, the Viet Minh *will* come!"

"Must they win? Is there no hope?"

"Hope?" The slender hands sketched a circle in the air before the scarlet nails came to rest, gently touching the sides of the bright green glass. "Hope? There is always hope. But there is each day less and less."

She took a pack of Marlboros out of her beaded purse. Mallory was glad of the pretext to stare at her intent face through the flame of his silver lighter. The black hair lying on her shoulders framed the long, pale face dramatized by dark eyebrows and a broad scarlet mouth. Her nose was slender and slightly arched, and her nostrils flared delicately. He eyes were wide, with green in their brown depths. Somewhere, there was a touch of northern blood, Mongol or even Turki, out of the great melting pot of Central Asia. Except for the wide eyes, it was the same narrow, fair, acquiline face which showed itself in old prints of the Japanese aristocracy.

Mallory felt that she was being honest, but her reserve was formidable. Even the movenemts of her hands and body seemed slightly contrived, as if she were exercising tremendous restraint.

"I was," he probed, "talking to George Dietrich. He thinks the war can still be won—if the Americans assume more dircet responsibility."

"Mr. Mallory, George is a gentle bear, but he talks nonsense. If you Americans are tenacious, the people will merely suffer longer." She paused to sip the crème de menthe, wincing when a loud American voice called across the table, "Hey, Jack, come and meet Zelda. She's a real number, equipped way beyond specifications."

"But," Tuyelle went on, "let us consider American self-interest. One hears little else here. Mr. Mallory, if an artist recognizes the impossible, he is finished. How different for a general. If he persists in commiting his forces when even a general should know there is no hope of victory, he compels disaster." She tilted her glass to her lips.

The same American voice bellowed, "Yeah, a ball-bearing action—and what a universal joint."

Tuyelle ground her cigarette out. Her cheeks were flushed and her eyes sparkled. "Get out, Mr. Mallory," she said. "Tell your people to get out and leave us to tear each other to pieces as we have done for centuries. There is no hope, really, not even hope. Get out before you destroy yourselves or become as corrupt as we are."

She stopped abruptly, placing her hands palms down on the table before her. "I'm sorry," she said quietly. "I think I'd like a brandy now, please."

Mallory gestured for the waiter without taking his eyes from her face. The amalgam of tortured emotion and cold political analysis that made up this woman was new to his experience. The politics of her troubled homeland, Byzantine in their intricacy and in their cruelty, were an incongrous preoccupation for so much loveliness. But how, he asked himself, could she, or any literate Vietnamese woman, help being dominated by the contending forces. True, she was a unique individual, but she had been shaped by Vietnam and battle. American women only heard the bray of distant trumpets over the waters; the Vietnamienne had always known guns behind her and the dead falling beside her.

"How long," he asked, "have you felt this way?"

"For months, I suppose. But I had not thought clearly till yesterday, till Johnny. . . ."

Mallory ordered two more cognacs, glad of the interruption. His stomach knotted and the muscles of his neck tightened involuntarily. His body was protesting against the intrusive questions he must ask. Someday his sense of decency would prevail and he would be finished professionally.

"You know," he said, making his voice neutral, "that I want to talk to you about Captain Humboldt? I can assure you that it is not simply curiosity. Perhaps what happened is important to all of us, Vietnamese and Americans as well."

"Yes." Her voice, initially so low that he could barely hear, rose slightly but remained flat in timbre. "I knew you wanted to talk about Johnny. That's why I said I'd come. Now I'm not sure."

"Just tell me that you wish to," he said, the gambit ready from a hundred similar conversations. "I'll write nothing that'll embarrass either you or him."

She studied her ringless fingers, flicking a bit of ash from a pointed nail while the waiter placed the cognacs on the table.

"Mr. Mallory," she said, sweeping her hand through the air to indicate her glowing yellow *ao-dai* and bright golden slippers, "you see that I am not in mourning, and here I sit talking with you amid these *poules*. I have no right to mourn, not in men's eyes or in God's eyes—not even in my own. Only that woman in America may mourn the man she never knew."

". . . not even in your own eyes?" prodded Mallory.

"Not more than a friend may mourn, Mr. Mallory; I was not in love with Johnny and I don't know if he was in love with me." Her voice dropped into inaudibility and she sat silent, pleating her skirt between thumb and forefinger. With sudden decision, she lit another cigarette and resumed in normal tones. "Mr. Mallory, I have explained to no one else. I do not know why—really not—but I shall tell how it was. Johnny and I were lovers, of course."

Her voice hastened onward precipitously. "That is, I was his mistress, as the French would say with precision. But how could I love a boy, a boy who was thirty-four years old. He needed me and, I suppose, I responded. I hated it when he was leaving. And then—it is terrible—but I felt a strange sense of relief when I heard . . . It seemed, somehow, good that he had finally made up his mind about something, even if it was the end. . . ."

"Aren't you being too hard?" he asked as gently as he

65

could. She was beginning to talk, but it was not the emotional entanglement that really interested him. His own response to her, the compassion that urged him to drop his questions and simply take her hand in his in comfort—that compulsion he must resist.

"Yes," she replied, her voice normal. "I suppose I am. He needed me and he was open, and I could talk with him as with no one else. His enthusiasm—he loved the country— first as a puzzle then as one loves people who are suffering, but, toward the end perhaps, as one simply loves people."

She drained her brandy and Mallory signaled the waiter.

"Somehow," she added irrelevantly, "it is not easy to talk to Vietnamese. I could not tell anyone what I am telling you, but still. . . ."

"Did his feelings toward this country change?" Mallory interjected.

"No," she said, "except to become stronger. Then he began to talk not only to me and to my friends but to other American officers. And they said he was drinking too much, and told him he must be more circum—circumspect. That meant not seeing me any more. We met in secret and nothing happened for a few weeks. Then, in a day, he was to go home. The rest you know."

Composed once more, she sipped her drink. Mallory was urgently aware of her as woman, not Vietnamienne or symbol, aware of the silken grace of her body and the slender, eager hands. He raked his palm over the stubble of his crewcut and shaped a prosaic question.

"One thing I don't quite get. What specifically did he do to get sent home?"

"I do not know. I saw him only for an instant after they told him he must go. They said he talked too much; he was a source of disturbance. And they threatened him if he spoke out when he got home."

Mallory decided to give up. Humboldt would make no

66

more than a paragraph unless he could wheedle more information out of the Army. Still, it was worth a last try.

"If something else occurs to you, I'm very much interested. I'd like to feel—you would too, I think—that Captain Humboldt's death was not an incident, not entirely meaningless."

Her voice was doubtful. "I'll think, but I have told you all I know. . . . You know, Mr. Mallory, we Vietnamese and you Americans are allies. I am grateful because I know the Communists. But most Vietnamese do not like the Americans. It was different with the French; toward the end we hated them, but they had stamped something French on us all."

Mallory nodded abstractedly, his eyes fixed on the *Mindanao*. He did not want to hear the pain that touched him behind the words his mind filed for later quotation.

Hearing a dull explosion downriver a few minutes earlier, he had dismissed it as the sound of a distant gun. But the unloading of the carrier had suddenly stopped and a platoon of MP's was cordoning off the quay where the ship was anchored.

"Let's take a walk, Tuyelle," he said.

Tottering on spike heels over the cobblestones, she took his arm. The shadows, sharp and black wherever the floodlighting died, made it difficult to judge, but the flight deck seemed canted.

"All right, buddy, keep moving," a heavy-set MP sergeant said. "*Vite, vite, comprez?*"

"Press," Mallory said, showing his identification card. "What's happened?"

"There's been an accident, sir."

"What kind of accident," Mallory persisted. "I'd like to talk to the captain."

"Just an accident. I'm sorry, my orders are no one goes aboard and everybody keeps moving."

"But," Mallory began.

"Sorry, sir, you'll have to keep moving. Any suspicious characters will be stopped and searched."

The sergeant stared appreciatively at Tuyelle. She was trying to keep the skirts of her long gown from whipping around her waist, fighting the wind that also nipped at the broad folds of her thin, white silk pantaloons. Her slim grace was silhouetted by the floodlights behind her.

"Not," he said with a grin, "that the lady could be hiding anything."

8

The dawn was dove-gray over the estuary of the Saigon River, streaked with iridescence about to burst into glowing pinks and violets. The *Mindanao* sagged wearily against her moorings, her broad, inclined flight deck a tangle of broken airplanes and helicopters. Her guard boats found no better targets for their automatic rifles than an occassional water-logged tree drifting slowly toward the sea or a brace of drowned chickens, their brown feathers matted with oil. The enemies, who had sunk her at her moorings, were far away, asleep in hidden hovels in Cholon. The crew of the *Mindanao* slept too, except for a small damage-control party clanging away in a confined space low in the hull.

As the cooks began to awaken in their canted bunks aboard the carrier, the telephone shrilled petulantly in the red room in the Majestic Hotel. Mallory turned on his stomach, pulling the pillow over this head. The ringing became peremptory, and he reached out with an uncertain hand for the instrument.

"Mon dieu," Levoncier's voice exploded in his ear, "it is like a cave of *Morphée* down there. First the central will not answer and then you."

"Yes, Pierre. What is it?"

"Rise and shine, *mon cher,* I shall be there in ten minutes. We must be at Tonsonnhut in an hour."

"Where?" asked Mallory from his half-sleep.

"The airport, Tonsonnhut. Start getting dressed. I shall explain all when I arrive."

Mallory winced as the curtains creaked open and the light pierced his eyes. It was just 4:35; three hours sleep would have to carry him through whatever the day held.

As Mallory was buttoning his jungle green safari jacket, Levoncier hurtled into the room. He, too, was dressed in jungle green, his trousers tucked into high-laced canvas-and-rubber boots. He carried another pair of boots which flapped against an empty musette bag.

Flinging the boots on the bed, Levoncier glanced approvingly at Mallory and said, "I am glad to see you knew what to wear. You know, Gerry, you are quite intelligent for a semi-pundit. Perhaps that is why you are only a semi-pundit."

"Quit the clowning," Mallory said glumly. "Am I supposed to wear those things?"

"They are about your size and well broken in. Do you have thick socks?"

"Yeah. Where are we going?"

"On a little flight, followed by a picnic. I will tell you more in the car. But first you must pack enough for overnight, in case we do not get back."

Mallory began filling the musette bag automatically—socks, underwear, towel, toilet articles, whiskey, cigarettes, and his pill case. Checking his pockets for notebook, sunglasses and lighter, he demanded, "What about my appointments?"

"The PIO will cancel them for you. I assure you, this is worth-while."

Mallory allowed Levoncier to bundle him into the Citroën. The streets of Saigon were just beginning to stir. A stream of cyclists peddled along and occasionally a jeep roared by filled with soldiers in green or policemen in white. Thin dogs trotted on their morning rounds, and the bells of the cathedral tolled a paean to the new day. As Levoncier swung the protesting Citroën wide to pass a pair of light tanks, Mallory wakened from his lethargy long enough to demand, "All right, *mon caporal,* where are we going?"

"That I do not know exactly. Somewhere in the Mekong Delta on what I would call a reconnaissance in force. Your countrymen call it a 'pounce strike.' We shall learn more en route. They only called me a half-hour ago. It will be interesting."

"I hope so," Mallory answered listlessly. "What about the carrier—anything new?"

"That is why I say you are a semi-pundit, going to sleep while those of us who are sharp as mustard waited for the hot news. There is nothing much new, except that the Navy admits someone placed a small bomb gently against the ship and then paddled happily away."

"Is that all?"

"They said all must have been in readiness for some time. But I say the organization, the direction, the espionage—it was superb. And the captain congratulated himself for allowing the ship to settle. At sea, he said, they would have repaired the hole without the necessity for sinking to the bottom. But this way the work of reparation can be done faster."

"How many planes did we lose?"

"That is classified—high secret—since it is well known from the way they make their bills that the waiter-spies at the Majestic cannot count. Otherwise, of course, they would just lean out the window and count the wreckage on the deck."

At the fork which marked the end of the city, Levoncier put his foot down hard and the Citroën rolled along at seventy-five, shuddering and creaking. Skidding to a halt on the asphalt parking lot, he led the way to a small restaurant beside the arrival hall. Two American officers in fatigues and jungle boots sat at a table beside the row of flower boxes which separated the restaurant from the field.

Gould, the young Lieutenant who had greeted Mallory on

71

his arrival, jumped to his feet. "Good morning, Mr. Mallory," he said. "How are you, Pierre? I'm coming along to help if I can. Major Harkness, this is Mr. Mallory and Mr. Levoncier of *Quest*."

Mallory studied the quiet Major while they finished their bitter café au lait. He was no taller than five feet seven. The taut skin over his high cheekbones and his small, delicate nose were the color and the texture of an old saddle, which had been scarred by much use and lovingly rubbed smooth again. His eyes, startlingly large in the drawn face, were liquid drops of iodine spattered with hazel flecks. His compact body was at rest except for his right hand, which squeezed a pair of red wooden handles mounted on a spring.

"Where are we going?" Mallory asked, breaking the silence.

"You gentleman are very welcome on this exercise," Harkness answered, "as long as you understand we'll do things my way."

"You're in charge," Mallory said.

"Good. I can't tell you where we're going just yet, except that it's down south. We're taking along some Viet Rangers—even their commanding officer didn't know about this operation till we routed him out a couple of hours ago. I'll brief you in the chopper."

A jeep carried them to the far side of the field, making a broad circuit around the busy runways. Harkness hoisted himself onto the ridged metal floor of the waiting helicopter, disdaining the boarding ladder. When the other three had followed, the rotors whirled faster, their tips flexing upward. The clumsy craft rose, spraying red dust.

Over the head of the Vietnamese Sergeant who had seated himself in the open doorway, his legs dangling outside and an automatic rifle cradled in his arms, Mallory saw another heavy-bodied passenger helicopter rise and take station alongside. Two smaller helicopters darted up from another part of the field. They fell sedately into formation behind the larger craft, but, like sportive dragonflies, soon tired of the pace and darted ahead, occasionally returning to swing in circles around the passenger helicopters.

"HUEYS," Harkness said, jerking his thumb toward the pair. "Our escort. They carry rockets and heavy machine guns. But I'm pretty sure we won't need them today."

A grizzled, husky Vietnamese officer, taller than Harkness, was seated beside Mallory. He wore two small, golden rosettes on a strip of cloth pinned to his chest and carried an automatic carbine.

"This is Lieutenant Tuey," Harkness shouted above the engine. "Mr. Mallory, Mr. Levoncier."

"A Tonkinese from the north," Levoncier said, his lips close to Mallory's ear. "Undoubtedly a professional soldier. Promotion is still slow as fate for those who have not the proper political connections."

"Lieutenant Tuey has an augmented section of Rangers with him," Harkness shouted again. "Twelve in this chopper. Seventeen in the other. It's a tight fit, but they're small men—luckily."

They were indeed small men. Mallory glanced at the dark faces under the steel helmets, some impassive, others working with nervousness. All carried hand grenades and knives in addition to their firearms. The soldier opposite gripped his ammunition belt with slender fingers; his tensed wrists were so thin Mallory wondered how he could possibly fire his heavy rifle.

"Tuey," said Harkness, straining to make himself heard through the noise, "let's tell the pilot to go up to about five thousand and then get the door closed. After briefing, we can come down out of long eye range."

With the door closed, Harkness could make himself heard by raising his voice only slightly. Disdaining to wipe the globules of sweat from his face, he pulled a transparent folder from his canvas map case.

73

Mallory leaned over the large-scale map of southern Vietnam, watching the Major's forefinger stab down on a red cross drawn in grease pencil north of a hamlet called Chaŏ Doc. It lay almost on the Cambodian border in the salient where the Mekong River splits into two broad streams to flow eventually into the South China Sea through more than a dozen channels.

"This is Hieptre, a village of about four hundred men, women, and children," Harkness said. "There is nothing special about Hieptre, except that it lies almost on top of one of the many supply routes the Vietcong use to bring men and equipment from their bases in 'neutral' Cambodia."

Mallory saw the faint dotted line passing from Cambodia into Vietnam near Hieptre.

"We had two choices with Hieptre—incidentally, please don't use the name in anything you may write about today's excursion. Gould?"

The Lieutenant nodded. "I'll remind Mr. Mallory, sir."

"Fine. We could've moved the entire population. The Vietcong would've been cut off from local intelligence and some food. But policy is to avoid dislocation if possible. Besides, the village is not that much use to the Vietcong. It's too close to home base."

Mallory interposed a question. "Have there been many relocations elsewhere recently?"

Harkness stared hard at Mallory, then swung his gaze to Gould.

"Mr. Mallory understands," the Lieutenant began.

"Look, Major," said Mallory, embarking on his standard lecture for officers nervous with the press, "I'd like to make one thing clear, now that I'm awake. I won't quote you on anything that would embarrass you. I'm interested in facts and seasoned opinion, not quotes. But you people aren't going to get the support you need unless the public gets really interested in Vietnam."

"I can vouch for Mr. Mallory's discretion, sir," a conciliatory Gould offered.

"All right," Harkness answered, his brown lips drawing back in a brief, tight smile. "I'll help all I can, but no quoting me. And, Mr. Mallory, don't forget the Special Forces."

Mallory relaxed. He could not make out the driving force in the man. Whatever it was—vanity, pride, dedication, or intelligence—it promised reasonable co-operation. Too often he had been frustrated by the withering fear of bureaucrats in uniform.

"Right, Major." He grinned. "I won't, but what about relocations?"

"I can tell you now that there've been a number of relocations in sensitive areas recently. But they haven't worked too well. The Vietnamese feel they alienate more than they help. But I can't go on with this now. We've got to come down soon and I want to finish filling you in."

"Maybe later?" Mallory asked.

"Sure," said Harkness with the same thin-lipped smile. "The second alternative we adopted. We've moved into Hieptre, given them a hand with their problems—fertilizer, medical aid, some seeds. We've fortified Hieptre. You'll see how. We put in half a company of Home Guards with an Army sergeant and a couple of soldiers to run a radio. The object is first to neutralize the village and later—well, we'll see."

"And why are we going down today with these gentlemen?" Levoncier asked.

"I was coming to that. We call it a pounce-strike. The main object is to show the flag, remind the village those Home Guards are backed by the full force of the Vietnamese government."

"And the United States of America," Lieutenant Tuey inserted in painfully slow English.

75

"Yes, that too," agreed Harkness, flipping the folder over to a large-scale map. "We'll come in low through this ravine and land in this field in front of the village." The finger traced a course. "We want the Vietcong to know we've been there, but we don't want to set ourselves up for an ambush. Then, we'll look around for a while, resupply, and relieve the radio detail. You gentlemen can talk to anyone you want to. That's about it. Any questions?"

"Yes," Mallory said. "What are our chances of running into the Vietcong? The area, I gather, is pretty thoroughly infested."

"I think I'll ask Lieutenant Tuey to answer your question. After all, it's his show. How about it, Tuey?"

"It is," began Tuey, in his stumbling English, "a place of heavy *infestation,* but we. . . ." He broke off and began talking to Levoncier in rapid French.

"He says that the chances are not great," reported Levoncier. "We might run into some Vietcongs by accident. But they cannot prepare an ambush because they cannot know we are coming. Although the flight was decided perhaps twenty-four hours ago, Saigon has not told Hieptre. We want to surprise our own people too."

"Do you speak French, Major?" Mallory asked.

"No, but we communicate. It just takes a little longer."

Tuey punched the pilot's shoulder, and the helicopter began to descend. The Sergeant took up his post at the open door.

"We won't get down to tree-top level till we're almost there," Harkness explained, as the craft levelled off at about five hundred feet.

Harkness dropped into a corner seat and closed his eyes. Mallory stood behind the Sergeant, watching the ground through the door. The racing shadows of the four helicopters cast a momentary darkness across the silver sheen of the flat, water-logged fields. The few roads were empty of traffic, except for infrequent military convoys. Twice, flights of bombers overtook the helicopters.

Tired of standing, Mallory wedged himself between Tuey and Harkness and closed his eyes. He awoke to feel a hand on his shoulder and to see Harkness leaning over him, mouthing, "We're down at tree-top level and getting ready to go in. When I jump, follow me—and keep moving."

The trees stretching high above them on either side cast an overwhelming green light into the dim cabin, and the roar of the rotors reverberated from the undulating wall of foliage. The helicopter slowed down as it emerged into sunlight.

When it hovered to a stop, the Vietnamese soldiers began jumping out. Mallory, in the middle of the queue, flexed his knees and stepped forward. The ground came up to hit him. He lay with his nostrils full of dust for ten seconds before chasing after the soldiers. Levoncier was already far ahead, racing past the short Vietnamese. Three times he stopped to shoot a string of pictures. Glancing over his shoulder, Mallory saw the helicopters clawing back into the sky.

The sun was just beginning to bake the fields, and no wind stirred the tall grass. The earth was still, except for the running soldiers and a pair of water buffalos rolling in a mud wallow. Directly ahead, on a little knoll, lay Hieptre, hardly maintaining the dignity of even a village, except for its brand-new bamboo palisade. At intervals along that wall Mallory saw the heads and shoulders of sentries. Concertinas of barbed-wire protected the pallisade, cascading across an improvised glacis. The flat-packed earth was studded with six-inch spikes of sharpened bamboo, except for a narrow path which wound to open wooden gates. Down the path a proud brown hen clucked, commanding six toddling chicks.

Easily outdistancing the soldiers, Mallory entered the open

gates a few seconds after the leaders. Harkness, Tuey, and Gould were staring across the small open square.

At the far end stood a large hut with two banners draped across its front. One was in Vietnamese, the other read AMERICAN IMPERIALISTS GO HOME! A naked man sagged from a stake, his intestines spilling green and yellow and red around his legs. A pair of hens pecked at the ground, ignoring a dirty gray dog sniffing the pool of blood.

The officers stood unmoving while the rest of the unit spilled through the gates. Lieutenant Tuey recovered first, snapping out twanging commands. A pair of soldiers detached themselves from the group and disappeared between the close-packed huts of bamboo and thatch. The rest of the unit retreated behind the hut nearest the palisade, but Levoncier lingered for a moment, frantically shooting pictures.

"Get back here with us, you fool," Harkness shouted.

As Levoncier tumbled into shelter, the Major said tautly, "Tuey's men are checking the village. If they come back, we'll know it's clean. If not, they'll manage to fire a shot before they die. But they won't find anything."

A pair of soldiers was struggling to close the heavy wooden gates. One was the nervous private with the thin wrists who had sat opposite Mallory on the helicopter. Slowly, agonizingly, the gate swung under the men's weight.

Lying full length behind the corner of the hut, Mallory raised himself on his elbows to watch the tableau in the sunlight. A sharp explosion pressed him to the ground. The gate sagged against its post, and the thin soldier stood in a cloudlet of gray smoke, staring in astonishment at the stumps of his arms. The bright blood gushed rhythmically from the raw flesh and began to well from rents in the jungle green tunic. The soldier stood frozen for about twenty seconds before falling face down. One of his fellows began working on the shattered form. Glancing at his watch, Mallory saw that it was not quite five minutes since he had jumped from the helicopter. Thirty seconds, he estimated, had passed since the booby-trap's explosion.

The scouts returned, shaking their heads.

"All right," Harkness said, "we've done everything wrong up to now. Let's start doing things right. Check the station radio and man the stockade."

The soldiers scattered and Harkness looked up at the sky. It was empty, except for a bank of gray clouds and the molten-gold disk of the sun.

"Damn them," Harkness swore. "Sneaking off to refuel. And the HUEYS have to stick with the big fellows."

Tuey appeared, trotting across the square, hardly sparing a glance for the figure at the stake. He spread his hands palms up.

"Radio smashed; if fire flares, maybe helios can see. Also make pack radio work. Hope can hear," he said, smiling for the first time that day.

"Gould, alternate with Tuey's man on the radio. See if you can raise the HUEYS," Harkness ordered. Then to Mallory. "Come with me, I'll show you something."

They climbed the spindly bamboo ladder to one of the sentry platforms. Mallory saw with annoyance that Levoncier was focusing on him with a telescopic lens. Edging past the soldier who crouched below the level of the fence, Harkness pointed at a silent, black-clad figure standing erect and gazing out across the fields. The Home Guard was lashed to the bamboo palings with grass rope.

"Take a look at his face, but don't move him—and don't let your head show," Harkness said.

The sentry's eye sockets were empty red pits, and a bamboo stake protruded from his heart.

"Killed 'em below, then brought 'em up here," said Harkness. "Gutty bastards figured they had plenty of time."

Harkness pulled out a knife and made slicing gestures, pointing to the corpse. The sentry said, "Okay!"

As Mallory and Harkness reached the bottom of the

ladder, the corpse dropped past them, crumpling as it hit the ground. An instant later a shot sounded outside the stockade. At the same moment a flare sailed up from the courtyard to burst red over the village.

Harkness, crouching with his eye at a crack between the palings, grinned happily. "I thought some fool would get eager," he said. "Tuey, let's mark it."

As the other Home Guards' corpses dropped to the ground, an irregular volley sounded outside the stockade. A few puffs of smoke blossomed in the long grass at the edge of the ravine.

Tuey, beside Harkness, said briefly, "Okay, mark." He moved off, speaking for an instant to each of his sentries.

An automatic rifle began to swear above Mallory's head, and cartridge cases streamed to the wet ground. A sentry was firing through the bamboo. After a five-second burst, he dropped to the ground and another automatic weapon down the line took up the chant. The bursts played back and forth, irregular in length and skipping without pattern from one post to another.

"Well, Mr. Mallory, you can relax now. If we can get the helicopters back fairly soon, there's no sweat." Harkness smiled.

"Relax? I thought this was the time to begin worrying."

"Hell, no. If we drew no fire, I'd worry about what they were planning. But this is just putting the cherry on top of the sundae."

As they worked their way back to the square, Harkness added, "Of course, they might want to suck in more troops. But I'd guess no. It's too close to the border."

Gould and a Vietnamese sergeant were crouched over a field radio, alternately speaking into the microphone.

"Any luck?" Harkness asked.

"No, sir. They must be out of range. We've fired five flares. Only another five left."

Harkness strolled off to check the wall, jauntier under fire than under questioning. Mallory, slumped against the rough thatch side of a hut, saw that Levoncier had acquired a carbine somewhere. He was alternately firing bursts toward the Vietcong and photographing the soldiers.

Another flare burst above the village.

Mallory considered Harkness's reassurance. The Major might be right about the Vietcong's intentions, but his record that day was not impressive. If he were wrong, if the Vietcong were tempted by their weakness—Mallory shuddered.

The terrible essence of this war was its loneliness. Little groups of men were islands in a sea of potential enemies, sustained only by their technical devices—helicopters, radios, and bombers. Temporarily stripped of these advantages, its ammunition limited, Tuey's tiny force was naked before the enemy. Mallory marveled at the Home Guards who garrisoned such isolated villages. It was not remarkable that many defected and others were overrun, but it was a miracle that any remained true.

Mallory shuddered again, the tremor rising deep within his chest and spreading involuntarily to his arms and legs. He was, he suddenly realized, totally exhausted, and he closed his eyes, slumping back against the hut. But he could not lie still, for the bile was rising in his throat. He spat heavily, hoping to clear the taste of old copper pennies from his mouth. But the bile rose irresistibly and he leaned over, retching. The vomit tore at his throat until he slumped back exhausted.

Too much crab and liquor, he told himself wryly. But he knew that it was exhaustion and naked fear that had forced the spasm. If Harkness were wrong and the Vietcong did attack in force, how long could they hold out? And how much unfinished business would he leave? Very little, he decided. *Quest* would give him a fine obituary and find someone else to do the piece. A divorced wife might grieve for him, as might a pair of children he had hardly ever seen. The next thought came unbidden—it would have been nice to have known Tuyelle better.

Another flare burst, its red glare almost lost against the sun.

Harkness, strolling back across the square from his circuit of the wall, said to Tuey, "Let's hold the rest of the flares. We may need them."

As Tuey gave the order, Mallory heard a throaty whine high overhead. An explosion tore him from his lethargy, ripping the banners from the hut and toppling the corpse at the stake.

"Mortars," said Harkness, smiling without mirth. "That changes things."

"No success, sir," Gould reported.

"Goddamn those pilots," Harkness swore. "I'd like to have them down here. It's beginning to look bad."

A second mortar shell fell on the other side of the village, kicking up dust and long splinters of wood and bamboo. Two more followed, neatly quartering the enclosure. A high cry, almost a squeal, ended abruptly in a gurgle.

Tuey dashed through the narrow passageway between the huts. In less than a minute he was back, grinning broadly. "*Un cochon*—the good chance—if no can evacuate this night, we have pork." His face fell. "But one *soldat*—splinter in arm."

A short, squat soldier came slowly down the passageway, supporting his right arm with his left hand. Tuey bound up the wound with a field dressing, talking earnestly while he worked. The Sergeant handed his microphone to the wounded soldier and trotted off to take his post.

"I'm getting something, but it's too indistinct to read," Gould said.

The mortar shells continued to fall at irregular intervals, smashing the close-packed huts.

"Just one tube, I think," Harkness said. "But even one can slaughter us. We're too tight here. I think it's about time."

Tuey nodded and moved off. Mallory suddenly became aware that the unit's rate of fire had dropped off appreciably. The soldiers were firing individual shots at long intervals. In the relative silence he heard a burst of automatic fire from the field. The soldier on the platform above their heads straightened up and pitched off his perch, falling face up almost at their feet. A shining red-and-black baldric was stretched from his left shoulder to his right hip, blood welling out of a series of holes as precisely spaced as machine stitches.

Mallory saw that Levoncier had caught the soldier in his lens as he fell. He opened his mouth to offer an ironic compliment, but Harkness interrupted. "Follow me."

They clambered up the bamboo ladder to the stained platform. Harkness checked the automatic rifle and handed Mallory his carbine.

"Can you work this? Fine. We're trying to suck them out by dropping our fire. Keep your eyes open."

A mortar shell dropped almost at their backs, but Mallory, concentrating on the field outside, hardly noticed. Two black figures rose in the green grass. Mallory felt his carbine, set on full-automatic, buck against his shoulder. He heard Harkness' automatic rifle barking its deeper note. The pair disappeared, one falling backward, the other, erect for an instant longer, before crumpling to the grass.

"They've got some damn fool recruits too," Harkness said with satisfaction. "One down."

Mallory felt the carbine's barrel hot in his palm and reflected that he had been abruptly transformed from a noncombatant. In the silence he heard a chicken cluck and the labored breathing of the wounded soldier at the radio.

A metallic voice boomed out over the village, so portentous, even in high-pitched Vietnamese, that the men involuntarily glanced toward the sky.

"It's not the angels speaking," Harkness chuckled. "They've got an electric megaphone. That *is* a new wrinkle."

Levoncier and Tuey were suddenly beside them on the platform, waiting patiently till the voice finished with a resounding, "Imperialists go home," in an accent almost unintelligible.

Tuey spoke rapidly in French to Levoncier, who explained to Harkness. "They call upon us to surrender, saying it is the only way we can spare our lives. They promise fifteen minutes to consider with no shooting. They promise those who wish to may join them. The others will be allowed to go free. They promise to injure no one."

"Like the Home Guards," said Tuey. "But we save ammunition."

Mallory sprawled flat on his stomach, watching Tuey pacing up and down in the square. A soldier appeared from a passage on the other side of the gate and joined Tuey. The Lieutenant shook his head decisively and pointed back to the passageway.

His head hanging dispiritedly, the soldier walked slowly past the gate. When he was five feet from the opening, he dropped his rifle and began running. Tuey fired a burst from his carbine, but the soldier's momentum carried him through the gate. He twisted down the path, suddenly falling headlong to impale himself on two bamboo spikes.

"I've got them," shouted Gould. "I've got contact, Major. They're coming back."

9

The long angular helicopter hung between the trees and the sky, a bird cage of metal and glass suspended from the invisible net of the spinning rotors. A red chrysanthemum blossomed alongside the cabin and a black projectile shot forward. Moving ever faster on the filament of black smoke it spun behind itself, the rocket burst in the tall grass. A jagged wedge of black smoke eddied upward from the red flame, growing broader as the helicopter fired again and again. The wet grass was smoldering sullenly when the helicopter climbed away in a broad spiral.

An identical craft dropped into its place. As the first rocket detached itself, an automatic rifle yammered high-pitched from the edge of the jungle. A jagged spiderweb appeared on the helicopter's windshield and an answering stream of fire spewed out of the aircraft searching the grass with lazy grace. The remaining rockets still unfired in their pods, the helicopter broke away, fleeing just above the tree-tops away from the border. A shiny slick of black oil stained its side.

"Christ," said Gould, crouched above the radio on the sentry platform, "they got the co-pilot."

Beside him, Levoncier was focusing a camera with a lens a foot and a half long.

"It's a rough party," said Harkness, working his hand-exerciser. "Keep talking them in."

"What next?" asked Mallory.

Harkness mimed surprise at the question. "It's all over now. They'll pick us up and send in another unit to try to nail our friends out there. With three, maybe four dead, and five wounded, this section's not a fighting unit any more."

When the fourth and last helicopter had dropped into the invisible groove in the sky, fired its rockets, and spiraled away, Harkness spoke again. "They'll be back with choppers for us. Want to take a walk?"

They strolled through the muddy lanes of the miniature village, from time to time edging in close to the woven palm sides of the huts to skirt a filthy pool or a pile of manure. Mallory felt exhaustion sinking its tiny, barbed hooks into the muscles of his legs and shoulders, despite the wine and the *paté* sandwiches Levoncier had produced. All of Harkness' jauntiness seemed to have deserted him. He walked splay-footed like a heavy old man.

The sour odor of half-fermented rice mingled with the acrid ammonia of urine. Aside from the scrawny brown chickens, darting about crazily on their long legs, and a yellow dog, ulcerated skin stretched tight over its protruding shoulder blades, the weary soldiers were the only movement, the only life.

They turned a corner. Beside a shattered hut, a sway-backed sow lay on the edge of a pool of blood. One pink stoat tugged at a swollen nipple on the dirty-gray abdomen with choked squeals. Abandoning the body, the stoat tentatively lapped at the blood, then plunged its crimson muzzle deep into the puddle.

The sparsely thatched roof of the hut lay at a crazy angle, almost touching the ground on one side. A hole in the thatch the size of a silver dollar showed where the mortar shell had entered. On a rough-hewn table, bearing a crudely colored picture of the Buddha, a bright-green Thermos jug still stood upright. Its sides were punctured and tea had run out to stain the red-and-white runner beneath it. In the corner white grains spilled from a torn rice sack.

"They're nasty things, Mr. Mallory," said Harkness, nodding at the shattered hut. "Small and light, easily carried. A nasty little toy of a mortar. It's a Chinese design, but now the VC make their own right here. Anything sophisticated—recoiless guns, machine guns, even rifles—still comes down from the north. All carried on men's backs. Of course they still capture a lot." Harkness looked glumly at his toes. He lit a cigarette with a shiny Zippo lighter and leaned against an intact corner post.

"You know," he continued, "I've been doing a lot of reading out here. They talk about sadness after sex. But I never felt that sadness. After a fire fight though. Everything stops —and you feel like cutting your throat. It's bad if you win, and ten times worse if you've made a horse's ass out of yourself. Like this time."

Mallory wordlessly offered Levoncier's silver flask of cognac.

"Thanks," said Harkness, wiping his mouth with the back of his hand. "It's too hot for cognac, but what the hell! You know there are only two reasons you're alive right now."

Mallory was profoundly immersed in the disquiet of his own discovery that he had overdrawn his reserves of courage. In Hieptre, without the comforting presence of flanking units and formidable machines, he had, for the first time, felt fear as an overwhelming physical reaction. His mouth was parched and sour and his forearms trembled. But he mustered up enough interest to ask, "What were the two miracles, Major."

"Call me Jack," Harkness said.

"The name's Gerry," Mallory said automatically.

"First, our friends out there didn't have four or five mortars. Even with those little babies, with that many, they could have whipsawed us to pieces. The second was the real miracle. It shouldn't have happened, but some Home Guard down the line saw our flares. Miracle number one. Then he managed to get through on the radio to call up the choppers. Miracle number two."

"But the choppers would have come back to pick us up," Mallory objected.

"Yeah, to pick up the pieces. How long do you think Tuey could have held his men? Damn those Viet chopper pilots to hell. Sneaking off to refuel."

"Look, Jack, it wasn't your fault."

"Maybe not, Gerry. But I wasn't brilliant. I wasn't even competent. But these birds—it's like using a knife that splinters in your hand."

Mallory muttered a vaguely affirmative noise.

"There's so little to work with. You can't fight guerrillas without intelligence, a real fine net like the Limeys had in Malaya. But it's the other way around here. We know nothing —and they know more and more. Those bastards knew we were coming."

Harkness transferred his red-handled toy to his left hand and pushed his right hand out, palm up. He nodded his thanks when Mallory handed him the flask, and went on.

"What hurts most, they don't even care about letting us know they've got a pipeline into headquarters. This strike was ordered about noon yesterday. We planned it, not the Viets. And they had to know by nightfall yesterday to set up this party. Twelve hours and a couple of dozen—maybe fifty, sixty—lives gone out like matches."

Through his weariness, Mallory felt a surge of pleasure. He had a fine piece of his story; he'd learned more about the nature of this war in half a day than he could normally have discovered in weeks. But there was something else.

Of course. Humboldt. He had almost forgotten about the young Captain. Humboldt, who had died two days ago, could not have provided the information that allowed the Vietcong to ambush an operation planned only twenty-four hours ago. Since it was beyond likelihood that there were two agents in the American headquarters, Humboldt could not be involved. Mallory would have to check on this boy some more. The young idealist could still provide a central figure for his story. He threw back his shoulders and felt the fishhooks let go. The old instincts still worked. He was still functioning as a reporter.

"The whole thing's upside down," Harkness complained. "We were trained as Special Forces, deep penentration to organize counter-guerrilla units and lead them. Instead, we're trapped in defensive battle around hamlets."

"But you're buttoning down the edges of the jungle, aren't you?"

"Yeah, I suppose so. But it doesn't do any good to button down the edges when the center's lousy with Vietcong."

"But," Mallory objected, "they can't conquer the country this way—by nibbling—not as long as we're pouring in support. It's a stalemate at worst."

"That's right, Gerry, a stalemate. But how long? Tuey was lucky he had to shoot only one man, and we were lucky it was Tuey with us and not some commissioned playboy. It's a miracle that the men still fight. But soldiers aren't martyrs. They fight because they want to live, not because they want to die."

"As long as they've got officers like Tuey," Mallory suggested.

"All right, take Tuey. He should be a colonel, but he's only a first lieutenant. He comes from the north, like most of their best officers. And the southerners don't trust them. And he's got no connections. He's only a Goddamned good fighting man. If he didn't know the Communists and hate them, even Tuey'd be over the hill."

"What will happen to the people of the village?" Mallory asked.

"I can guess. The Communists made an example of the headman and the Home Guards. The Army sergeant and his two men also disappeared. Chances are they'll be treated well, at least until the peasants are let off the hook, allowed to return to Hieptre. Then the soldiers will either go over or be killed. 'Lenient treatment,' they call it, for the army. Killing the Home Guards first thing drives the wedge between the peasants and the military."

"What's the percentage for the Vietcong?" Mallory persisted.

"The peasants come back, minus a good part of their livestock. They're fined for letting the Home Guards in. They know one thing: It's death to mess with us. We can't protect them from the VC's."

"What's next for Hieptre as far as we're concerned?"

"Damned if I know right now. We can't leave the VC in possession. We've got too much prestige invested, even if it weren't on the border. Relocation, burn the village maybe. I just don't know right this minute."

Harkness shrugged his shoulders and pulled himself erect. His walk was lighter and he carried his head with some of his old jauntiness. As they passed the sentries on the wall, he nodded to each and made the thumbs up sign. "I wish I could talk to them. Wish I could find out what they're thinking. But even Tuey says he doesn't really know."

Approaching the square, they passed another blown-out hut. Mallory noted the crude Confucian altar below the lithograph of the Buddha tacked to the wall. Two red wooden tablets stood on the altar, stylized Chinese characters painted in gold upon them. On one side of the Buddha hung a portrait of the young general who headed the government in Saigon, on the other was a portrait of the Communist chieftain, Ho Chi-minh.

"They play all the angles, don't they?" Mallory observed.

"These poor bastards don't know what's hitting them. Hell, I've seen the same set-up with a crucifix thrown in too—and once Mao Tse-tung alongside Lyndon Johnson."

They had come to the lane that opened onto the square.

90

Tuey was crouched on the sentry platform beside the radio, talking to Gould. Levoncier was aiming his camera at one of the soldiers, a tall, thin man carrying three rifles in his arms. The Vietnamese dropped one of the rifles and stooped to recover it, hiding his face from the camera.

Harkness paused indecisively at the edge of the square. He turned to Mallory, saying abruptly, "Look, Mr. Mallory, if...."

"Call me Gerry," Mallory interjected.

"Yeah, Gerry. Look, Gerry, you're not going to quote me. If you do, I'm finished."

"Of course not, Jack. I probably won't use any direct quotes at all. And if I do, I'll pin them on someone else—a diplomat, a European military attaché, someone like that."

Gould was semaphoring with his arms. He shouted, "The choppers'll be here in five minutes. They're bringing in a couple of platoons to comb the jungle."

Three black specks appeared in the bright sky to the southeast, rapidly resolving into light helicopters. They were followed by three heavy passenger craft. As the big craft set down, a swarm of little men in green uniforms tumbled out and disappeared into the grass. Mallory smiled broadly for the first time that day. The unloading was like the circus turn when two dozen clowns pile out of a miniature car.

"No catch," said Tuey. "VC go way long time."

"The lesson," added Levoncier, "it is over."

A melancholy procession wound its way through the bamboo spikes of the glacis and across the muddy field. With one man at the head and another at the foot of each of the stretchers the helicopters had brought, there were barely enough able-bodied men to carry away their dead and injured fellows. The dead lay on their backs, faces waxy yellow and the flies frolicking in their wounds. The wounded lay limp on the canvas, their bandages and tunics black with encrusted blood. Not quite two hours had passed since the arrival at Hieptre.

As the helicopter rose into the naked sun, Levoncier offered a bottle of red wine. Most of the soldiers took long draughts, acknowledging the gift with brief smiles of thanks, but each man had withdrawn behind his own moat. Harkness slept, and Mallory, beyond exhaustion, wrote up his notes.

They came back to Tonsonnhut a little after high noon.

Harkness led them to a waiting jeep. He apologized. "I'm sorry you didn't get a chance to talk to any of the villagers."

10

Mallory closed the crimson curtains, pleating one edge over the other to keep out the sun, with the intensity of a surgeon drawing the lips of a wound together. He squatted before the chattering air-conditioner to adjust its clumsy controls.

The succession of gurgles and wheezes was unaffected and the weak air stream moved irregularly. It was clammy and barely cool.

Frustrated, he turned away. But his body took control, his bare foot drawing back to kick the old, gray machine. He commanded his foot to return to the carpet. Reluctantly, it obeyed, and he allowed his palm to slap the cabinet. The machine responded instantly, subsiding to a gentle hum and pouring a torrent of dry, cold air past its battered grill.

Mallory chuckled, hitched up his sarong with self-satisfied bravado, and lay down on top of the sheets. The curtains parted to admit a shaft of light. The air-conditioner returned to its asthmatic lament, and the torrent of air gave way to feeble gusts.

He grinned broadly, running his hand over his crewcut. He could still laugh rather than storm over the perversity of the inanimate world. But he felt himself slipping back toward the black caves of despair.

Too tired to contemplate the gargantuan lunch Levoncier proposed, Mallory had asked room service for a large martini and a small omelette. The tremors of his arms had subsided into an occasional fluttering of his fingers. But the shock was still working inside him. Blanketed in hopelessness by the clammy air, he watched with dull eyes the smoke serpents rearing from his cigarette tip.

Sudden death in the morning could never become a commonplace. There was an awful clarity in men dying one by one, rather than in mass carnage—almost companionable —wrecked by heavy bombardment. These deaths, in their terrible isolation, were without purpose; neither side had gained a substantial advantage. Soldiers and partisans alike had stumbled under the Juggernaut of guerrilla warfare, which moved just fast enough to crush the sacrifices as it inched toward an unknown goal years away. Meaningless death was a commonplace, the essence of the new sub-civilization that had appeared in the jungles and swamps of Vietnam.

But the roots of his own despair were deeper. He had felt such utter darkness of the spirit only once before, when he realized that divorce was unavoidable because Laura would no longer endure the erratic, drifting life which had fascinated her when she married a young correspondent. He had recoiled from the routine comfort of an editorial job in Washington, London, or New York. For her, the glamor had evaporated; for him, it had become a drug.

Now his manhood was diminished by the demonstration that his reserves of physical courage were seeping away. That morning he had been frightened far beyond the normal gaping emptiness and the painfully intensified vision. His entire body had revolted. Perhaps fear enhanced one's humanity, but the world should grow more orderly as one grew older, not merely more beastly.

He stubbed the cigarette out and lit another, seeking a transition in the small gesture. He summoned up Harkness' comments on John Humboldt. It was during the ride from their helicopter landing to the parking lot and the Major's taut face had clouded when Mallory asked whether he had known Captain Humboldt.

"Yeah," Harkness had replied. "I knew him pretty well. He was a good kid."

"What kind of an officer was he, Jack?"

The red handles of the spring-exerciser had paused in their rhythmic motion. "It's hard to say. He did a good job—and it was a tricky job. He was eager, though not more than a hair too eager. But, for Chris' sake, the kid was an intellectual."

"What do you mean?"

"Gerry, I told you I do a lot of reading here. Partly just to pass the time, but I know you can't be a blood-and-guts leader anymore. You can't just scream follow *me*! War's too complicated, especially this kind. But you can overdo the reading and the thinking."

"You mean Humboldt was beginning to have doubts?"

"Not exactly. You can't fight this war without doubts—about tactics, even about strategy, which means politics. But I had the feeling his mind was going around and around in his skull like a red squirrel on a treadmill. He wasn't getting anywhere, just making himself dizzy."

"You didn't think much of him then?"

"Gerry, you're getting what I say backwards. Matter of fact, I liked Johnny a lot. You could always talk to him, try out ideas and know someone was receiving you. Not like those retread cavalry officers that clutter up headquarters. He was a tough man in the field, and he got along with the Vietnamese—not just the simple, decent kind like Tuey, but the complicated, over-subtle types we have to live with."

"Then what was your objection, Jack?"

"Maybe we're both too tired to make sense. I knew this boy well. You get to know a man in the jungle. And we could talk about everything you could think of. He never spared words, never worried about being safe or how his words would strike me. But, somehow, I felt I was talking into a vacuum...."

"I think I'm beginning to understand," Mallory had urged. "Go on, Jack."

"Yeah. Somehow there was an emptiness inside him. He was intelligent, and he was honest, and he cared a lot. But

95

right at the center there was nothing. So everything else was built up around nothing."

Harkness had paused to tuck his hand-exerciser into his pocket and to light a cigarette.

"Gerry," he had continued, "I'll try to make it clear, but it's a job for a writer not a soldier. He was thirty, thirty-five or so. But everyone called him Johnny. Somehow you always thought of him as a kid. And in a way it was like talking to a kid, a monstrously clever kid. He had everything it seemed, even conviction. Dedication, too. But it was like a ventriloquist's trick in reverse. There was this little child, understanding nothing and caring for nothing, sitting inside the man and pulling strings."

"I think I've got it. He was," Mallory had interrupted.

"If you understand, it's more than I do," Harkness interjected, embarrassed by his own rhetoric. "Is there any more cognac in that flask?"

Musing on the conversation, half-asleep, Mallory was wrenched by the telephone's shrilling. A youthful American voice rang in his ear.

"Hello, Bob, I've got a couple of chickens lined up for tonight and. . . ."

"I think you've got the wrong room," Mallory said.

"Oh, isn't this Lieutenant Wald?"

"Sorry, I'm afraid not."

"Are you sure? You sound just like him."

"Sorry, I can't oblige, but I'm not."

"Well, if you're sure. . . ."

Hanging up, Mallory felt his contact with the world outside abruptly severed. Recollecting the bizzare conversation with Harkness had actually intensified his dislocation. Humboldt and Mallory, two psychic casualties of the war in Vietnam, poor bastards.

Reaching across a chasm for communication with the human race, Mallory lifted the black telephone that stood six inches away.

96

"Can you," he asked slowly and distinctly, "get me Miss Vguyen-lee in the Ministry of Information?"

When the phone rang after only ten minutes, he was mildly astonished to hear the cool voice saying, "Allo."

"Tuyelle," he said.

"Yes."

"Tuyelle, this is Gerry Mallory."

"Yes?" Was it a faint glow of warmth or merely the interrogative tone?

"I'd like to see you tonight."

"Why?" It was definitely not warmth.

"I'd like to ask you more about Humboldt. I have some ideas about him," Mallory began. "Oh, hell, I just want to see you and talk to you. Do you find that odd?"

"Perhaps not, but I'm sorry. I cannot see you tonight."

"Why not?"

"I am invited to a party and I must go."

"Take me with you and we'll have dinner afterward."

"I do not understand this sudden urgency, Mr. Mallory."

"Neither do I," he admitted. "But I do really need to see you."

"Well," she conceded, "if it is so important, perhaps I should."

She rejected his offer to collect her and gave him an address in the middle-class western district. "I'll be there after seven," she said. "Good-bye, Mr. Mallory."

He lay back on the bed, wooing sleep by casting his mind free to drift as it would. Instead of the succession of pleasant, unrelated tableaux he had invited, the mental screen displayed the scenes of the morning in brilliant detail. Vietnam, Humboldt, and his own predicament became inextricably tangled in his revery. What would be his next stop if this story did not jell? "Solid but a little past it!" If that tag were attached to his name in editors' simple minds, instead of "brilliant, penetrating, and iconoclastic," the future would be bleak indeed.

Sleep was still far away. Herding his mind from the side paths, he concentrated upon Tuyelle, not as a captive in the brutal enclosure called Vietnam but simply as a woman. Surprised at the feeling awakened by her image, he finally fell asleep.

11

Mallory extracted himself from the minute Renault taxi with the protracted anguish of a boa constrictor struggling out of his old skin. Lighthearted after his bout with despair, he had ignored Rosen's warning against taxis.

A peaked red roof perched above a high wall of pale yellow. The red wooden gates displayed a card reading Dr. Van-quoc Thau and a metal plate bearing the silhouette of an Alsatian's head, black fangs bared.

An elderly maidservant stared hard at the wiry figure in suntan slacks and checked sportshirt before stepping back to admit him. The graveled courtyard was dominated by a single palm growing out of a circle of grass. As Mallory followed the maid toward the porticoed doorway, a plump spaniel puppy, all long ears and brown-and-white spots, played at his heels.

Tuyelle was waiting on a bench in the doorway. Her blue long-gown was brilliant in the fading sunlight, and the sweet-pungent smell of jasmine rose from the circlet of white flowers in her hair.

"Good evening, Mr. Mallory. I'm glad you found the way." She did not smile and her hand was cool in his own.

"Good evening, Mademoiselle Tuyelle. I'm delighted that you let me come."

"There seemed no reasonable alternative," she fenced. "Come and meet my friends."

In the shadows of the room—narrow, constricted, and bare after the spacious ease of the Hooghlys'—Mallory had a kaleidoscopic impression of simple uniforms, glowing silks, and green plants. A second room, painted in the same neutral beige, lay beyond an archway. The rectangular table on a square of coconut matting in the far room was heaped with books. Massive bookcases covered the far wall.

Tuyelle clapped her hands together gently and the hum of conversation receded. "This is Mr. Mallory," she said. "He has come to Vietnam to write about our—our war. I believe you can speak freely with him. Dr. Thau agrees."

A heavy-bodied man in a white sport's shirt rose from a wooden settee and extended his hand. His broad face, dark beneath a stubble of coarse, white hair, crinkled into a thousand creases when he smiled. He was at least twenty-five years older than anyone else in the room.

"Dr. Van-quoc Thau," said Tuyelle.

"How do you do, sir," Mallory said. "I have long wanted to meet you. Your reputation, of course, I know."

"Good or bad?" asked Dr. Thau in a sighing, old man's voice, the heavy French accent almost obscuring his meaning.

"Both, sir." Mallory grinned. "Depending on the source."

"And what do you think, Mr. Mallory? Good or bad?"

"I don't know, Dr. Thau. That's why I'm here."

"Oh, to examine me," the old man said. The old rebel had lost none of his acerbity. He had fought the French and then the Communists, choosing exile in England, instead of the more fashionable France or the United States, when he found it impossible to live under the Diem regime. Returning after Diem's death, he had been given a vague position as senior advisor to the foreign ministry.

"No, sir," Mallory answered. "I've come to listen, not to judge."

"You are welcome, Mr. Mallory, as Tuyelle has told you. A few of us come together from time to time to discuss our predicament. We also try to make some—ah—meaningful connections with the foreigners in our midst, outside the official realm."

100

"Meaningful?" asked Mallory.

"That is your American term, is it not?" Dr. Thau asked. "I mean, human and intellectual contacts. We do not presume to solve the problems of the world—or even Vietnam. But we do exchange opinions. Sometimes we are gay."

Mallory moved around the room, directed by the light pressure of Tuyelle's fingers on his arm. Knowing he would not remember names, he accepted confusion gracefully. A plump woman with an innocent face was introduced as Dr. Buey. He met a dark Frenchman, M. Andre Something. Two young Vietnamese lieutenants, one Army, the other Air Force, pumped his hand. A raw-boned Sergeant named Perkins or Jenkins or Jurgens hailed him in the accents of Tennessee, "Right proud to make your acquaintance, Mr. Mallory." A startlingly thin girl of about twenty-five, with a serene white face, smiled up at him, exposing a jagged purple scar under her chin. He nodded to Vao, Tuyelle's cousin and protector, who was arguing with a dapper Chinese in a sharkskin suit. A stout, boyish naval officer in immaculate whites was Lieutenant-Commander Huey or, perhaps, Tuey. The twanging sounds were beginning to run together. An American Army Captain wore wings and a clear name plate declaring him to be Roberts. Two brothers, probably called Nan-do, were almost indistinguishable in appearance and both were from the Ministry of Foreign Affairs. One was on leave from a post somewhere in Africa; the other was stationed in Saigon.

They returned to the group around Dr. Thau, who asked, "Why have you come to Vietnam, Mr. Mallory?"

"I hope it's not presumptuous to say I'll try to find out what's really happening here and to estimate what will happen in the future?"

"Not presumptuous, Mr. Mallory, just very brave. How much time are you giving to these researches?"

"About a month this time, but I'll be back again and again. Just as I've been here many times before," he answered, uncomfortably aware that Tuyelle was looking up at him through her lashes and that the corners of her crimson lips were curved in a secret smile.

"Look, Dr. Thau," he said, eager to justify himself, "I visit wars. I know that sounds strange. But your family doctor will sometimes call in a specialist. Well, I visit crises, as a consultant of sorts."

"And is your diagnosis always correct, your so quick diagnosis?"

"Not always, but often enough to make editors want to call me in again.

"What is your diagnosis here, Mr. Mallory?" Tuyelle asked.

Mallory paused, nonplussed by the swift question. It was hardly remarkable that all the Vietnamese he met were so gripped by the war, the single overwhelming factor in their lives, that they could talk of little else. Nonetheless, normal Occidental courtesy, not to speak of Oriental punctiliousness, would have suggested a somewhat less abrupt confrontation. He glanced around the room at the streamlined descendants of Vietnamese Mandarins who, more Confucian than the Chinese, would never have discussed business before at least a half-hour of tea-sipping. Yet, for all their surface shine, he had an uneasy impression of indecision and bewilderment. Finally, he answered, "If I knew, I'd probably be writing it. What about your diagnosis, Dr. Thau? More important, what about the prognosis?"

"Ah, if the government would only ask me, I should at least feel useful," the old man said. "But I must admit I find it hard to say."

"Dr. Thau is too polite," the young woman with the purple scar interrupted in rapid French. "Our men are dying and our state grows ever worse. Only China and the United States benefit. But Vietnamese die." She flushed when the young Army Lieutenant placed a restraining hand on her arm.

"You are over-simplifying again," he said.

She turned on him. "I am not over-simplifying—and before

102

you begin talking about feminine logic, listen to what I have to say."

"Ngyuen, you promised me," the Lieutenant began, but abruptly shrugged his shoulders in elaborate disregard and gazed down into the red pool of Dubonnet in his glass.

Dr. Thau leaned forward and laid his plump hand on the girl's shoulder. "Go on, my dear," he said.

"You've confused me," she resumed, still sulky. "Oh, yes. I do not want the Communists, the Chinese, but not this either."

"Ngyuen is at it again!" Mallory heard the feminine whisper behind him. "She'll just get herself excited and end up with a weeping fit. If only she'd have a drink and relax."

"Then," Mallory asserted, cutting into her continuing flow of words, the Vietnamese *are* served by the resistance."

"No, they are not," the thin girl replied passionately, "because the resistance is a fake."

"A fake? The Americans are fighting more than we should —and helping you fight as much as you'll let us," the tall Sergeant said in fluent French, the Tennessee drawl even more pronounced.

"You're a little late." Tuyelle laughed. "Like the aging lady who tells her fifth husband she is giving him her best years."

"Yes, you're fighting, Teddy," the girl with the scar declared, "but not to win. You're fighting just enough to keep the others from winning, but not enough to defeat them. . . ."

"Would you have the Americans risk a general war?" Dr. Thau asked gently.

Mallory was amused by the skill with which the old negotiator guided the conversation between the two extremes of a bitter quarrel and trivial cocktail-party chatter.

"Ngyuen is right." The Army Lieutenant lunged into the conversation before the girl could reply. "Dr. Thau, you can't fight a war without risks. This is a phony war."

"Here we go again," the plump lady doctor protested.

103

"And I thought tonight we'd just gossip and dance."

No one paid her the compliment of a reply.

Dr. Thau smiled, swinging his big head to include the entire group in his gnarled radiance. "Mr. Mallory, you Americans stand accused of bleeding Vietnam in a struggle you have no intention of winning."

"Dr. Thau, why should we be fighting without meaning to win? God knows, we don't want to be here."

"If I may, M. Mallory," said the dark Frenchman waspishly. "There are, of course, many motives—commercial, imperial, internal politics, even a kind of perverted idealism to stop, to contain the Chinese. But it is, I'm afraid, unfortunate for the Vietnamese."

"Would it be better to turn them over," Mallory began hotly, but he was interrupted by the girl with the scar.

"It is immoral, immoral I say, to pay in lives and misery for time."

Someone started a phonograph in the next room, and a few of the debaters drifted away. To Mallory's surprise the music sounded like Beethoven's Ninth.

"Would you rather the Communists?" asked the American Sergeant, in the center of the remaining contenders.

"No," the Lieutenant answered, "but they will—unless we all fight to win. It would be better to save lives."

The Lieutenant-Commander spoke from the eminence of his superior rank and his few additional years. "You are all hysterical. We have dealt with the danger from the north in the same way for two thousand years—we fight and then negotiate, bend a little and then snap back again. So we have survived."

"Not this time," the Lieutnant said bitterly. "You can't resist the Communists with subtlety. Once we start negotiating, that will be the end. A coalition government and then—poof—all is over."

"Not that." The Lieutenant-Commander laughed. "Not, at least, till we get our promotions."

"Then the war will go on forever," the Lieutenant said ironically.

The conversation was becoming general. Relieved to find himself no longer the center of attention, Mallory felt the pressure of Tuyelle's hand on his arm.

"Come and have a drink," she whispered. "They're good for the evening."

"But," he protested, "I want to hear this out. This is what I came for."

She pouted, astonishing him, the cold, marble Artemis reaching for an ice-cream cone.

"I thought you wanted—needed—to see me," she said, as he marveled. "Anyway, you can come back any time. They'll still be going around in circles."

He followed her through the dimness and the throng. Out of the corner of his eye he saw that Vao had broken off his animated argument with the Chinese and was watching them fixedly. Among the bottles set out in the dining room, he saw a bottle of scotch.

"We have no gin for martinis," she said. "What about a whiskey."

"No thanks," he said, arresting her motion. "I'll have plain dry vermouth. For some reason, it seems, I'm feeling too good to spoil it with whiskey."

Again she surprised him by responding to the compliment with a smile. They took their glasses to the bench in the door-way. The twilight air was warm and fresh after the clouds of smoke and the talk within.

"Now," she said, "please ask me your questions about Johnny quickly. I do not want to talk about him too much."

"It's really the same question, Tuyelle. What kind of guy was he? Why did he crack? I don't want to keep picking at this, but I've got the crazy idea that his tragedy was not just personal."

She paused to sip a pale, straw-colored liquid he did not recognize. "What more can I say?" she asked. "I've told you

I had the feeling he was in many ways a child. Maybe that's why I came to him. . . ."

"Did he believe in this war?"

". . . maybe that's why," she mused, ignoring his question. "Our Vietnamese men are too much of a piece, too self-contained and intent on themselves. They need no one. Johnny needed me desperately. Maybe Vao is right."

"What does Vao say?"

"That I have turned in my mind against my own people," she continued in the same low voice, almost as if she had not heard the question she was answering. "Vao says I turn to white men, to Americans, because they represent an escape, another world. . . ." She paused abruptly and looked down at the ground, her ear lobes blushing pink.

"Did Humboldt believe in this war?" Mallory repeated harshly. He was surprised at his own irritation; he had invited confidences, but he realized that he did not at all like her treating him like an ancient father confessor. But her candor, like his own annoyance, might be the beginning of something.

"We all believe and we all do not. He, at once, believed more and doubted more. He was a kind of holy fool."

"Then his sympathies were with the government?"

"Sympathies? His sympathies were with the people," she answered. "You are not subtle, Mr. Mallory. No, he was not a Communist sympathizer. He had seen too much in Korea, and here in Vietnam, to be a friend of the Communists."

"I'm not trying to be subtle, Tuyelle. I'm really interested in Humboldt. It's not just an excuse to see you, though that too. . . ."

She did not smile, but asked gently, "What else can I tell you?"

"Can you think of anything else, anything that might tell me why he did this thing?"

"I can remember nothing. All I have left of him is a small

106

box of poems, stories, and fragments. He didn't want his wife to see them ever, he said, so he left them with me."

"Could you look them over and see if anything might help answer the question?"

"I may look," she said, "and I may not. But I don't think I'll tell you anything I find. Believe me. He was just a fool, a holy fool. For such there are no explanations."

The subject was banished. For the next hour they talked of Paris and Hanoi, of the sun setting over the Inland Sea of Japan and over the island rocks of the Baie de Leong, of the ballet in London and New York. Despite the disapproval of her strait-laced father, who still lived in the old style in the old capital of Hué, she told him, she had made two trips abroad with official delegations—once to Europe and the United Nations, once to Tokyo for a conference.

"I was cold all the time," she said, "but it was always exciting. I should like to go again."

"And I'd like to show you some of my favorite places—Kyoto, Munich, Salzburg, Carmel." The words slipped out without any thought as to their effect, he was so caught up. Did they sound like a bald suggestion?

She was formal again, brushing aside his further trifling compliments without a smile. The flirtation, it appeared, was over. Nonetheless, Mallory found himself strangely exhilarated. He was startled and annoyed when Vao appeared and she rose calmly, saying, "Good night, Mr. Mallory. Vao will see me home."

12

Euphoria lingered long after she had had swayed down the
path into the dusk with Vao glowering at her heels. Mallory
sat on the hard wooden bench, still sipping his dry vermouth,
until he could no longer conjure up the lingering scent of
jasmine amid the waves of ginger from the hedges. Then he
strolled reluctantly back into the smoke of the room, where
the riot of conversation had hardly abated. The tall American
Sergeant intercepted him.

"Sir," he said, "I've been hoping I'd meet you since I heard
a couple of weeks ago that you were coming. I've got some
questions. . . ."

"How did you know I was coming a couple of weeks ago?"
Mallory asked. "I hardly knew myself then."

"Well, sir, I work in the G2 section and we hear things.
The Colonel doesn't care, but the Major says it's important
to know about correspondents' coming. He says we're fighting
this war with words, not just guns."

"I'm flattered that the Major considers us so important,"
said Mallory.

"Yes, sir. But I wanted to ask you something. You said in
Asia at Dawn that we could never hope for success as long as
we supported old-line despots—Chiang Kai-shek, Syngman
Rhee, Sukarno. You also said we couldn't create democracy.
I'm still not sure what you meant."

Mallory grinned and ran his hand over his short-cropped
hair. It was always a delight to find a real reader.

"Well," he began, "if there were any easy way, even Washington would have found it by now. Not democracy—that's an unattainable ideal. But something to make men feel they're building their own lives by their own efforts. Make them feel it was worth resisting the Communists, because they could attain more in their own way. Then, perhaps. . . ."

"I'm still not sure exactly what you mean," the Sergeant insisted.

"Yes, Mr. Mallory," Dr. Thau's voice interjected. "What would you do here? What is the magic formula for my own unhappy country?"

Finding himself once more at the center of a group, Mallory paused before answering slowly, "I don't know exactly, Dr. Thau. The military problem seems to come first, and then. . . ."

"But how can you expect to solve the military problem when the people won't fight? How can you expect simple efficiency when the government is cut off from the people? How. . . ."

"How can you expect efficiency," the girl with the scar took up the litany, "when our leaders come to power by internal intrigues, when they know nothing of the will of the people, when newspapers are censored or closed, when even discussions like this are frowned on?"

"I don't know," Mallory admitted. "I said I was here to try to learn, not to give answers. But the General seems to be trying to get closer to the people. Maybe he needs more time."

"That's what Diem used to say," said Thau. "And the repression went on for years, and things got worse all the time—but we did not ask you here to harass you. Come back any time with any questions you may have. I shall always be glad to see you."

Dismissal or reprieve, Mallory accepted it gratefully. Outside he hailed a *pous-pous*, despite the informal interdict. Seated alone and unprotected in the open front of the three-wheeled vehicle with the driver astride a bicycle seat over the fuming engine behind, he cringed each time they ran a six-inch gap between cars. Fifteen minutes later, damaged only in his nerves, Mallory was seated at a table at the sidewalk café of the Majestic ordering a martini. Sid Rosen had said he might stop by.

The scene was unchanged, as if the same actors took their appointed places at darkness each day. American soldiers and raucous Vietnamienne flirted demonstratively. A pair of Frenchmen at a corner table comiserated with each other in low, conspiratorial tones. An earnest German correspondent was speaking guttural French to a portly Vietnamese at the bar. Levoncier had already identified him as the "independent source" all visiting German correspondents quoted as their final authority. His chief source of income was imports from Germany, his chief business to convince the Germans that the time in Vietnam was five minutes to twelve—if not, actually, five minutes past. Doleful reports in the German press fully bore out his demands for an even higher percentage to his already exorbitant profits.

A deep voice rumbled above Mallory's head, *"Permittez-vous, Monsieur?"*

Nodding automatic approval, Mallory glanced at his un-chosen companion. Although dusk had passed into night, dark glasses, oversized and curved, concealed half his face. A thin black cigar bobbed between startlingly red lips, and a jet-black bush of a mustache shone against a sallow skin. A half-caste, Mallory decided, as the waiter returned with the newcomer's *citron pressé*, a Eurasian, sprung of one of the Orient's innumerable mixtures of blood.

"The heat has abated somewhat, but it is no weather for traveling," his companion said. Except for a barely percep-tible alien rhythm the accent was pure British—good, middle-class British. Mallory groped for an answer, something ap-propriate to an English garden party.

But the cultivated tones continued, "And how did you enjoy your trip to Hieptre, Mr. Mallory? A bit grisly, was it not?"

Mallory was suspended between alarm and fear of embarrassment. The mission to Hieptre was, in theory, still secret. The man in the sunglasses should not have known, but Saigon was, after all, a sieve.

Mallory replied cautiously, "It was interesting."

The bright red lips pursed, and a throb of irritation marred the suavity of the voice.

"Interesting? That's a strange term for an encounter in which ten men died. Even the French would never have been so cavalier. But I have not come to discuss semantics with you. Mr. Mallory, I have a proposition for you."

"What is it?"

"Mr. Mallory," the tone was once more bland and persuasive, "you have seen a little of the struggle here, but always from the viewpoint of the oppressors. Would you like to meet a man who can tell you what it is really like?"

"Who is that?"

"Let us not go quite so fast, if you don't mind. First, are you interested in hearing about—perhaps seeing—the other side? You bourgeois newspapermen pride yourselves on getting both sides of the story, don't you?"

"Yes, of course," said Mallory. "But who's going to give me the other side—the Communists? If you're proposing a trip to Hanoi, of course I'm interested. But I'm dubious too."

"Nothing quite as dramatic as that. It is merely that I could arrange for you to talk with a man who knows the people's struggle well."

"Who is that? For that matter, who are you?"

"It is not important that you know who I am," the man smiled. "Indeed it could be quite inconvenient. But the man who wants to talk with you is a leader of the National Liberation Front."

"In other words, the Communists."

"No, not the Communists as such," the messenger inter-

111

rupted. "Just a group dedicated to ending the struggle for the people's benefit."

"Well," Mallory wondered aloud, "it's an interesting proposition. But you've got me tabbed as a lackey of the Imperialists. If I do meet your man, how do I know I'll get back alive?"

"You don't, Mr. Mallory, you don't." The man in the dark glasses smiled broadly, his smile sliding into a rumbling laugh. "You must excuse me, but it is funny."

"Maybe to you, friend. Perhaps if I were more detached about my own life, I'd laugh too."

"I beg your pardon. It's not that at all. But we do not war against the press. You are not valuable to us dead."

"Maybe so, but why go to all this trouble?"

"Precisely. If we wished to injure you—just think, I have five men out there." A grand sweep of the hand indicated the darkness outside the café. "And I have three more in the hotel. Not to speak of your carefree jaunting around in taxis and *pous-pous*. No, if we wanted you removed—or abducted —it would be simple."

"What do you want then, if I'm such an easy pigeon?"

"We want not merely your co-operation, but your willing interest. We want you to listen, not to sit in resentful silence, as you would if we abducted you. We want you to give the truth a hearing."

"Why me?" asked Mallory. "And why this sudden passion to tell the world?"

"You, because we have reason to believe you are honest —by your own lights. To tell the world—you might say that we are so strong that the truth, once known, can lead to only one conclusion. That conclusion would bring peace and prosperity to Vietnam."

"Well," Mallory began, wondering how he would finish the sentence, "it's interesting. But I'd like to think about it."

"By all means, Mr. Mallory, by all means."

112

The emissary laid a hundred-piastre note on the table and began to rise. He checked the movement to lean across the table, saying, "Someone will get in touch with you within the next forty-eight hours. He will say, 'The heat has abated somewhat.' If you are interested, you will reply, 'But it is no weather for traveling.'" And you will be prepared to follow him. There might be an even more interesting proposition afterward."

"And if I don't choose to play?"

"You would be missing an opportunity, but there would be no recriminations. By the way, Mr. Mallory, please do sit absolutely still for ten minutes after I have gone. My men outside would not hesitate to fire. Good evening."

The man in sunglasses twisted through the tables and disappeared into the darkness outside.

Strange emissaries in improbable disguises were commonplace in Asia at war. Mallory remembered the crippled Irishman who was public relations officer in Singapore for the fanatical Indonesian Moslems, the Darul Islam; he recalled the soft-faced students the Chinese Communists had used to make contact with the American press before they decided that they wanted no contact with any American. But he could not recall such daring disregard of the normal subterfuges beloved of conspirators. The Vietcong were unquestionably confident. Could they know of his involuntary secondary role? If they did, a quick thrust in the dark would suffice, rather than this elaborate invitation. He began to consider the prospect seriously, not merely as a fantastical device appropriate to this Oriental Graustark. An interview with one of the underground leaders of the Vietcong would certainly add distinction to his story. It could provide just that spectacular and illuminating insight which editors expected of him.

He ordered another martini, resigned to conforming to the stereotype defined by Levoncier: "It is very sad about American reporters in Vietnam. Between alcohol and dysentery

113

they never seem to sleep." When a smooth brown hand placed the clear goblet before him, Mallory looked up sharply. Was this waiter one of the "men inside" reporting to the man in the sunglasses?

Mallory fiddled with his glass, then checked his watch. He gazed at the vendors and listened appreciatively to the rich mixture of accents around him. He made a few notes.

But it was no good. If he could defer decision on the strange invitation, he could not evade another problem. There was Jenkins or Perkins or Jurgens, the Tennessee Sergeant, and the pilot called Roberts. They were probably innocent of anything except a laudable desire to learn more about the country for which they fought. But he was not innocent. He was committed by Gilroy's ten thousand dollars. If he turned their names in, that would be a sop to Gilroy—and it would get him off the hook or partly off the hook. If they were not innocent, then all the more reason to turn them in. Let Gilroy have his rubber bone.

He began composing a letter in his mind. He had to clear his skirts so he could concentrate on his own work, that was more important than temporary embarrassment for a pair of GI's.

A hand touched his shoulder and he instinctively covered the imaginary letter in front of him. Rosen sank into the chair beside him, at once sleekly dapper and comfortingly commonplace after its previous occupant.

"What are you hiding?" he asked.

"Nothing," Mallory said, lifting his hands from the table.

"Well, that's good," said Rosen, looking at him intently. "And I've got just the prescription for your troubles, a little touch of home."

"Where's that?"

"You'll see, my boy, you'll see. First a martini for the gentleman from the New York *Times*."

"Not Madame Jahn's again," said Mallory. "I'm hungry."

"Certainly not. I said a little touch of home. And you shall

114

have your chow." Rosen laughed. "It's been a big day. Nearly a battalion of paratroops tangled with a couple of battalions of Vietcong outside Bien-hoa and came off best. But it's a much bigger night. At the American Officers Club of Saigon there's bingo tonight!"

13

The swirling marble staircase encapsulated a narrow elevator, stained glass above shoulder level, and polished wood below. The tattered velvet of the ceiling exuded the acrid stench of black French cigarettes, though the stale smell of the milder American variety floated in the air as well. Twice the elevator stopped abruptly between floors, gears grinding and relays clicking. But Rosen, imperturbable, leaned on the button marked *ascendé* until the upward struggle began again.

The gilded gate on the top floor yielded to Rosen's persistent tugging, folding into a tangle of metal rods. The broad reaches of the pale blue foyer were reflected from a series of mirrors framed by chains of pink plaster roses.

"This," Mallory objected, "is a touch of home? What did your mother do for a living?"

"Patience, my old one, patience," counseled Rosen, opening the quilted velvet door.

An American MP in a shiny black helmet-liner scanned their identification cards before opening an interior grill.

"Things have deteriorated," Rosen observed. "Time was a white face was the only identification you needed."

They stepped into a wave of sound held in suspension in a mist of stale cooking oil. On their right a narrow room was almost filled by a bamboo bar. The expanse of blue-tinted mirror reflected an array of bottles. The mirror was sprinkled with hand-drawn signs: TODAY'S SPECIAL: VIETNAM LIBRÉ—15¢; a printed placard reminded in large letters: HAPPY HOUR EVERY WEDNESDAY AND FRIDAY: 1815 to 2030.

"What's a Happy Hour that lasts two hours and fifteen minutes?" Mallory asked.

"Drinks at half-price," Rosen answered. "What better reason for happiness."

"Good God, why? Half of fifteen cents is seven and a half."

"In this case, seven. They're not allowed to make a profit and business is so good they've got to cut prices or struggle with a surplus."

"Why don't they just give the stuff away?"

"They tried it," Rosen answered. "But some stuffy colonel objected that that was too, too much of a good thing. Even at seven cents a drink it can get pretty hair-raising."

Mallory chuckled into the martini set before him by a chubby Vietnamese bartender in a blue mess jacket. Mallory began to sort out the different elements of the overwhelming din funneled into the room by a long corridor. The crash of dishes and the shouts of irate cooks echoed from a kitchen nearby. A heavy brass section, contending with a set of drums and an electric guitar, was savaging the "Hong Kong Cha-Cha-Cha" like a fox worrying a rabbit. A high-pitched male voice floated across his eardrums in a stream of continuous patter. From time to time a phrase was clear: "Clickety-clicks . . . shut the door . . . road to heaven."

But he could also hear the pounding of a mechanical surf. The metallic waves broke in an irregular tempo after brief crescendoes. Smaller crests sounded like random wavelets slapping the sand between breakers. Above the surf he heard the shrill cries of children building sand castles.

Fascinated, Mallory slid off the stool. The corridor was full of men and women, all facing a blank wall and all uttering grunts and squeals of triumph or disappointment. A new Buddhist rite spawned by Vietnam, the land of eclectic religions?

Mallory elbowed his way through the group that clotted the entrance. Thirty slot machines stood against the wall, six

117

inches apart, each tended by a figure that fed coins into the maw and pulled the lever in an obsessed rhythm. Most were older women in backless sun dresses. Behind each principal stood four or five spectators. Whenever a player relinquished his position, two more jostled to reach the handle.

As Mallory watched, an imposing matron in a green silk dress, her hair coifed into tight blue waves, whooped shrilly. Tears cutting a path through her pancake make-up, she stooped to sweep a torrent of silver dollars into her skirt. From the worshipers arose the chant: "Jackpot . . . jackpot . . . jackpot."

At the bar Rosen was talking to a tall man in a white dinner jacket, his gray hair cut short and his eyes bloodshot.

"How are you, Jim?" said Mallory to Hooghly, the Director of the United States Information Service.

"Fine. Good to see you, Gerry. I was just saying to Sid here that Martha and I had stopped in for a bite. Another damned cocktail party. How about joining us?"

Rosen slid off his stool to stand like a sleek, black bantam between the two taller men. They skirted the edges of a large, bare room where a throng was frantically twisting. Three Filipinos in ruffled yellow silk shirts and tight red trousers were chanting, "Yeah . . . yeah . . . yeah . . . she love me." Separated from the dance floor by a palisade of rattan screens, a group of older officers and women, silver hair gleaming above silver eagles and oak leaves, was engrossed in square cardboard cards held in their laps. A willowy Captain with a hairline black mustache was reading off numbers drawn from a spinning cage. He intoned, "Eighty-eight, there's the gate. Who can make it swing?"

Rosen nodded at the intent heads, stage whispering, "Guardians of empire, suffering nobly in exile. It's only fair to give them some diversion. And there are plenty here to be diverted—more than half our sixteen thousand people are in Saigon."

118

Hooghly led them through a side door onto a terrace which was enclosed like an aviary by wire mesh at the sides and above. To the north the Saigon River gleamed the oily black of a dragon's spoor; to the east the sober dimness of Saigon melted into the pool of colored lights that was Cholon. Halfway down the long terrace Martha Hooghly, an overblown daffodil in a strapless yellow dress, was seated beside a Major whose short-cropped white hair matched his white dress uniform.

She offered her hand languidly. "Jim usually comes back with someone, but his luck isn't usually as good as this. It's nice to see you Gerry, Sid."

Hooghly introduced the Major as "Dr. Calaveri, call him Vince." He swayed infinitesimally as he rose to shake hands.

"We've been having an argument, Vince and I," Martha said.

"Nothing serious, I hope." Mallory smiled.

"No, don't worry, Gerry. It's not that sort of night. We were just wondering why they've wired the terrace. I say it's just because everyone in this town is grill happy and no one ever bothered to think that even the Vietcong can't toss grenades up eight stories. Vince says it's to keep his brother officers from trying to fly without helicopters."

"Actually, you're both right," Rosen declared. "I got curious and checked. Somebody could get up on the roof and toss something down. But the fellow I talked to finally admitted it was also a good idea to guard against sudden impulses."

"Sid's always got the answers," said Hooghly lightly. "I don't know why we bother to have political and economic sections in the embassy. Personally, I always go to Rosen for hard facts and to Levoncier for the latest intrigue."

"With that visitors' bureau you have to run, that's not a bad idea," Mallory said.

"Oh, it's not so bad. Only one senator, two congressmen, and five special investigators this week."

Mallory toyed with the two squeeze bottles—red for catsup, yellow for mustard—flanking a silver-colored napkin holder. A tiny waitress, wearing a brown checked apron over a white dress, presented a mimeographed menu which ran to such items as "Special Today: Meat-packed Ravioli with Special Sauce of Sun-ripened Tomatoes and Fresh Herbs, Our Famous Chicken in the Basket with Healthful Corn Bread and Farm Honey."

"They're out of almost everything," Martha offered. "I guess the can opener's broken. We're thinking of hot dogs or hamburgers."

"See how we fight the pernicious French influence," Rosen said, slurring the initial consonants. "No devilish degenerate dishes drenched in delicate, decadent sauces, but wholesome American hamburgers and hot dogs. I wish they had some nice pastrami like Ma used to buy from Goldberg's Delicatessen."

"Ignore him," Hooghly advised, "or we'll be getting a lecture on gefüllte fish next."

"That's not fair," the Major spoke up, suddenly assertive. "It's anti-sem—anti-semt—racism. If he wants to he can talk about—about—that fish. And I'll tell you about Mama's spaghetti bolognese. They dare call this stuff ravioli, why...."

"Can we order?" Martha asked abruptly.

The pair emerged from the caves of national memory into the bright moonlight of Saigon.

"Scotch and soda first, two hamburgers, no onion, with a Budweiser," Rosen said crisply.

"Same for me," Calaveri added. "But first Scotch on the rocks. Make it a double."

The order for hamburgers went around the table, only the drinks varying.

"Americans all, after all, and all united," Mallory said into the silence that followed the waitress's departure.

"Yeah, real united, and united with our gallant allies,"

Calaveri said with heavy sarcasm, a scowl twisting his tanned, heavily modeled features.

"Now, Vince," Hooghly said, "let's not knock the Viets."

"It's all right for you, Jim. You deal at a high level where everything's real political—cocktail parties, kiss your hand, madam, of course, General. But I've got to work with them down at the low level. And the daily mani—manif—ma-ni-fe-stations. . . ." He broke off and drained his glass to celebrate his triumph over the word.

"Christ, I used to think Sicilians were tricky, but these boys make the Sicilianos look like kids on Halloween. Nothing ever goes straight and you can't believe a word they say—or a thing they do. Drugs disappear in carloads. . . ."

"Now, Vince," Hooghly said automatically.

A memory was fighting its way to the surface of Mallory's mind. "Haven't we met before, Vince?" he asked.

"Maybe, I meet a lot of people."

"I seem to have a memory of you in a crowd out in the sunlight. Maybe at an airport. . . ."

"You're thinking of what I'm thinking about—the day Johnny Humboldt checked out."

"That's it," Mallory said. "You pronounced him dead, didn't you?"

"Yeah, that was all I could do for him. Poor, mixed-up bastard was shy. I wonder how he'd feel if he knew everyone was talking about him."

"Oh, are they? I didn't know."

"Yeah, there's a lot of talk. It's shaken everybody up. Stopping a Vietcong's bullet's one thing. But suicide or—suicide, that's another," Calaveri answered. "Bright young guy like that, too. Lucky we don't believe in om—om—omens like my Roman ancestors. But it's cast a shadow."

"It's nothing to write about," explained Hooghly primly. "But there is a feeling going around that this kind of sacrifice is pretty bad."

"Yes," said Rosen. "I've heard."

121

"Don't pussyfoot, Jim," Martha snapped. "People are saying that when a guy like Johnny Humboldt quits, things have to be worse than they look."

"Now, Martha," Hooghly said.

The waitress arrived with a laden tray. She slid drinks, hamburgers, and beers onto the middle of the table and flounced away.

"Well, Jim," Martha said patiently, "suicide isn't pretty. Just think of his family—even if that chit Tuyelle...."

"*If* it was suicide," blurted Calaveri. He drained half his new drink.

"What do you mean?" Mallory asked.

"Oh, nothing. Just maybe that this place drove him to it."

"But you said 'suicide or...'" Rosen persisted.

"Well, could be . . . Aw, it's nothing," Calaveri cut himself off, looking appealingly at Hooghly.

On the edge of speech Hooghly drew back. He kneaded his forehead with the side of his hand, a cigarette still burning between his forefinger and his middle finger. He stubbed the cigarette out decisively and spoke. "Look, Vince, my friends won't drop it now. Why don't you just tell us what you're getting at?"

"All right, Jim, you asked for it," Calaveri said sheepishly. "Somebody ought to know and I can't get the Army interested.... But you'll cover my flanks?"

"Sure," said Hooghly.

"Tham, the Vietnamese escort officer, died this morning," Calaveri began. "Nobody can question him now, but it looks simple. Humboldt grabbed Tham's pistol and shot him in the struggle. Then he ducked into the sentry box, put the muzzle in his mouth, and pulled the trigger. Simple, isn't it?"

"Seems so," said Rosen. "What's wrong with the picture?"

"It's full of versi—versim—ver-si-mi-li-tude," Calaveri said. "But Humboldt was full of sedatives. You can never tell about the mind, particularly a high-strung guy like Humboldt. But I'd say he would've been more interested in

122

sleep than in suicide. It does require a certain active decision, you know."

"And what else?" Mallory prompted.

"Well, this sounds a bit crazy, even to me, but his front teeth were shattered."

"What's that to do with anything?" asked Martha.

"People are funny," Calaveri said. "They like to be comfortable, even when they're killing themselves. I've seen maybe a dozen suicides—muzzle in the mouth. Never saw one with broken teeth before. Guy puts the muzzle between his teeth, not in front of them. But Humboldt's teeth were clenched tight. It's more as if he were fighting the muzzle off."

"Couldn't the recoil have smashed his teeth?" asked Rosen.

Disgust drew down Calaveri's beautifully formed lips. "Naw," he said. "I'm maybe not as bright as a new intern, but the fragments were driven inward. The bullet went through those teeth."

"Wasn't anyone interested?" Mallory asked.

"Naw, and I don't blame 'em. It's just a crazy idea of mine. And there are no rules about suicide."

"Maybe they're right." Hooghly reverted to his soothing role. "Why pursue this? All it can cause is misery and doubt."

"And murder would be even worse than suicide from the official point of view," Mallory said.

"That's true, too," said Hooghly. "And from yours as well. You've got a stake in this fight, too."

123

14

Mallory woke in the red room at nine—late for the tropics. Like a complacent tom cat's, his gray eyes slit and then widened under their black brows. His depression had dissipated. Gerald Mallory, by the grace of God and the skin of his teeth Bachelor of Arts of Yale University, by act of Congress and a general's whim sometime lieutenant in the Intelligence Department, Army of the United States, a former bestselling author on his way back up, was content with himself and the world. He revelled in that moment of clarity which comes early in every major story before the reporter's vision clouds again. He knew exactly where he was going and exactly how he would get there. Even circumstances were smoothing his road—as they always did as such a time.

Three points would carry his story: Dietrich, the American loyalist; Dr. Thau, the Vietnamese skeptic; and Johnny Humboldt, the man-in-between. Everything else would fit into that broad framework, even the talk with the Vietcong leader, if it worked out.

With his *café complet* the waiter had brought him not only a telegram from McAllen at *Quest,* dropping the deadline back a week, but also an invitation to lunch at Dietrich's penthouse. Scrawled across the back of the white cardboard rectangle in a heavy, backhand script was the message: "I'd like you to meet some *real* Vietnamese—G.D."

The first point: Humboldt—murder or suicide? In either case, why? His approach must involve no emotion beyond cool compassion, no identification with Humboldt. But he would, somehow, find out exactly what had happened.

Dietrich and his friends he would see that day, and there was, finally, Dr. Thau. If that redoubtable rebel despaired, then it was indeed hopeless. So far he had not appeared wholly despairing, but neither was the old politician far from it. The standing invitation would enable him to pursue the question of Dr. Thau and his strange circle.

Besides, there was always Tuyelle as a reflection of Thau. On her own, she would make a few paragraphs of color, rounding out the story nicely. What do the modern girls of Vietnam feel? He made a note—he would need a country-woman to balance her. He hesitated in his planning, unwilling to break the clarity of his mood.

The frown disappeared, and he ran both palms over his scalp, linking his fingers behind his neck. He leaned back with a grin, and, his right eyebrow cocked high, reached for the telephone.

"Hell," he said aloud, "let's not complicate things any more. I want to see her again—soon. We'll just see what develops."

The instrument shrilled before he could lift the handset. "Mr. Mallory?" asked a female American voice. "Just a moment, sir. Colonel McGuffey calling."

"Gerry?" the light Irish voice asked. "Gerry, why the hell haven't we gotten together?"

"McGuff. Good to hear your voice. I've been meaning to call you, but. . . ."

"The hell you have," insisted the Colonel. "I can tell when you're in one of your I-never-talk-to-the-PIO moods. But come and have a drink or coffee with an old friend, anyway. I'll send. . . ."

"Not really, McGuff. Just awfully busy. And many thanks for sending Lieutenant Gould to meet me. . . ."

McGuffey ignored the interruption. ". . . my car to pick you up in fifteen minutes."

"Make it half an hour."

"Okay. See you then."

He had, almost unconsciously, reached another decision while speaking with McGuffey. Getting the operator back, he asked for Mlle Vyugen-lee in the Information Ministry and, simultaneously, rolled a sheet of paper into his rickety Smith-Corona. When the instrument rang again after five minutes, he had finished writing and was addressing the envelope to "Mr. G. H. Simmons, American Embassy, Saigon." The letter to Gilroy was short and clear: the names of the two Americans, obvious habituées, whom he'd met at Dr. Thau's. He'd drop it off on his way.

He picked up the telephone. "Mademoiselle," he said, "I did enjoy last night. Pity you had to rush away. How about that dinner we discussed—alone, tonight."

"Well," she began, but her hesitation yielded to his insistence. "All right, Gerry. What time?"

"I'll pick you up at seven. Where do I come?"

"No," she said, "I'll meet you at the hotel."

"If you insist. Till tonight then."

"Till tonight," she answered slowly.

His buoyancy survived the long drive in the khaki sedan all the way across the city onto Boulevard Gallieni on the way to the Military Assistance Group. He was stimulated by the broad, asphalt streets, the hosts of cars, trucks, *pous-pous*, and bullocks swimming in the morning's heat. His mood was curiously intensified by the long, white-washed corridors of the MAG building, awash with filing cabinets, typewriters, adding machines, duplicating machines, and steel desks. He was, he knew, on the verge of mastering the intricacies of both worlds and displaying them, with quiet lucidity, to several million readers.

Colonel McGuffey looked up sharply when Mallory strode into his office with springy steps and subsided onto the cane couch.

The face of a debauched leprechaun foreshortened by the

domed bald brow, grinned a puzzled welcome. "Good to see you, Gerry," McGuffy said in a light tenor with a whiskey dressing. "And what's the occasion for joy this morning?"

"Shure, Mac, it's just the pleasure of seeing yourself again," mocked Mallory, "the wit of your conversation, the warmth of your coffee, and the coolth of your air-conditioning."

"If that's all it takes to make you happy, a fine spalpeen like yourself, why we'll...."

"No, McGuff, fine as it is, that's not all," interjected Mallory, his tanned face relaxing. "I'm finally breaking a block that's nearly three years old. I can see this story, just waiting to be taken like an eager virgin."

"Congratulations," said the Colonel dryly, pressing a button on his desk. "I thought this mess might stimulate your perverse tastes. Coffee ready?" he asked the redheaded Sergeant who poked his head around the door.

"Yes, sir. Just coming up."

As the door closed on the Sergeant, McGuffey reached into his desk drawer for a bottle of Johnny Walker Red Label and poured a dollop into the white mug marked McG. He waved the bottle suggestively over a mug marked VIP.

"Freshen your coffee?" he asked.

"Fine, Mac—no, no thanks. I'll skip it. But tell me what I'm going to find in Vietnam. What shall I write?"

The small humorous face disappeared behing the mug. When it reappeared, the spiderweb of wrinkles was doubled. "Christ, Gerry," McGuffey said, the light tones dropping to a melodramatic baritone, "I'm damned if I know what to answer. You'll write what you damned please; you always do. Anyway, I don't know what to tell you myself."

"What's wrong, Mac," Mallory asked. "The situation? Your job?"

"Nobody's pushing me around. But you could say my job stinks because the situation stinks."

"What do you mean?"

127

McGuffey pushed himself away from his desk and walked across the grass mat to the door. His emaciated body looked more like that of an Indian coolie than that of a Colonel in the stout-feeding United States Army. His narrow shoulders seemed to bow under the bright metal insigniae on his collar.

"Dick, keep everyone out for a while," he said through the open door. He turned a dial on the air-conditioner, which responded with a whirring blast, and flipped on a transistor radio, which responded with a lilting chanson.

"What are you afraid of, Mac?" Mallory asked, grinning. "The Soviet KBG, the Chinese Special Service—or your own home-grown spooks?"

"We've been over the place with a fine-toothed electronic detector, Gerry," the Colonel answered, forcing a smile. "But the walls are too damned thin. I like to keep my personal opinions personal."

McGuffey poured whiskey into his cup and bit the end of a black cigar. When the walnut-sized coal was glowing red, he spoke from a fog of greasy smoke.

"Thank God we're still friendly with the Philippines. My grandfather, Sergeant Major Patrick Doyle of E Troop, finished his service there. Before that, he fought on the plains. He used to tell me one story over and over again. It always ended: 'And there we were, Clarence, my boy, log fort aflame from fire arrows and more coming in. All of us hopping around like a young widow at a wake, so busy putting out the fires we couldn't sally against the Blackfeet. All we could do was pray and wait for C Troop to come up.' "

"How'd the story end, Mac?"

"Oh, C Troop finally arrived. But Goddamn it, Gerry, we *are* the United States Cavalry here—and all we can do is try to put the fires out."

"Pretty hopeless?"

"Did I say that? We always fall over our own feet at the beginning, but we always come through in the end."

"Why so melancholy then?"

"Well," McGuffey answered, draining his cup, "there's just too much stumbling around right now. I've never seen so many chiefs. The Ambassador, my General, Special Forces, the CIA, Army *and* Navy Intelligence, the bright boys from Washington. And the whole confusion duplicated on the Viet side. No time to deal with the Communists. Just barely time for cocktails and intrigue."

"We've seen all this before, Mac."

"Yeah, maybe—but never as crazy as this. And, Gerry, we're making it worse, ten times worse."

"I thought the Ambassador had a free hand, was ending all that."

"Don't you believe it. His name's not Hercules. As long as you've got semi-independent empires in Washington, you're going to have them feuding out here."

"Mac," asked Mallory, casually lighting a cigarette, "did you ever hear of a captain called Humboldt, John Humboldt?"

The Colonel's high forehead furrowed in irritation. "Chris' sake, Gerry," he snapped, "don't be so damned smooth. How could I help hearing? If you mean what do I know about him, I can tell you quick: bright boy, too damned egghead for my taste, but good at his job. He got trapped in the meat grinder, somewhere in the meat grinder I was telling you about. So help me Christ, that's all I know. I can't even find out enough to dream up a good cover story."

He took a long drag on his cigar, intently watching the cigarette smoke spill out of Mallory's nostrils. "Another coffee?" he offered. "A drink now?"

"No, thanks. I've got to get along."

McGuffey walked to the door with Mallory, resting his hand on the correspondent's shoulder. "Look," he said, "let's have dinner. I'll call you. Maybe you'll call me. . . . And, Gerry, I'd take it as a personal favor—lay off Humboldt if you can. The thing's sealed so tight, you'll never find out what happened anyway. Wish I knew, but I don't."

"Sure, Mac—if I can," said Mallory, his hand on the knob.

"And, Gerry, it'll take time, but we're going to lick this one. I'm not crapping you. This I believe."

"It's hard to keep the faith right now, Mac."

"Yeah, I know, Gerry. Harder maybe where I'm sitting. But I believe it."

Mallory's mood was a little worn but still intact as he watched the young Vietnamese driver striving to solve Asia's over-population problem. Never had he seen McGuffey, the professional optimist, so low, so strident, and so desperate in his affirmation of faith. Clarence McGuffey, spokesman for a confused policy, undoubtedly believed what he said. But it was hard for Gerald Mallory, brevetted impartial observer, to go along.

He clasped his hands comfortably behind his neck and leaned back against the hot fabric of the car seat. It would in the long run be a pity—no, a catastrophe—if the situation in Vietnam were hopeless. But his immediate worry was getting the story and writing it; he'd worry about the funeral later.

The shopkeepers were putting up their wooden shutters against the post-noon heat and locking their steel gratings for the long siesta when the Chevrolet stopped in front of the green-and-white apartment house. After the elevator ride to the sixth floor, Mallory was admitted by a slender *boyess* whose single thick plait of black hair gleamed against her white tunic. She offered him a green leather chair, poured a martini from a crystal shaker, and departed with the murmured assurance, *"M'sieu, vite arrivé."*

Air wafted dry and cool and slightly scented from louvres set into the dark-paneled walls. The glare was broken by the awnings above the broad terrace, even before the light entered through an expanse of green-tinted window. A cushioned Tientsin carpet was deep green, contrasting with the filmy green band of glass tanks set at eye level in the book-

130

cases that lined the far side of the room. The brilliant colors of tropical fish darting amid the water plants were the only touch of brightness. There were no flowers. The leather-and-wood furniture clustered on the veined malachite floor was all green or deep brown, and the books had been stripped of their dust jackets. Mallory gave himself to the cool embrace of the room. A sandstone Buddha stood in a high niche between the bookcases, its voluptuous lines a hectic memory of the abandon of ancient India. On a broad teak coffee table, stained a lustrous brown, lay a wholly incongruous copy of *The Vietnam News,* its headline screaming NEW DEFEAT FOR VIETCONG. The translucent green of a thumb ring lay next to a tiny bear carved of apple green jade. A pale pink Kwan Yin stood beside a Chinese ink box, and, in the center of the table, reared a bull that could only be Tang or a magnificent copy. The delicately rounded legs were almost too slender to support the straining muscles of the rump and the great horned head above the silken hump.

Squashing out his cigarette in a capacious onyx ash tray, Mallory picked up the Kwan Yin. The statuette of the Madonna of Asia bore no markings, but the ink stone, in its azure box, displayed a gilt inscription which he recognized as a conventional exhortation to learning and ambition. When he turned it over to find the hallmark—*The twentieth year of the Great Ching Emperor Chien Lung,* that much he could read—the cover sagged into his palm and he saw that one of the minute gilt hinges was broken. He put the box down and took up the bear. No bigger across than a fifty-cent piece, the curled-up cub needed no seal to identify it. Only the Han Dynasty, almost two thousand years earlier, could have produced that blending of delicacy and crude strength in such a small compass.

Lighting another Camel, Mallory marveled at this sea grotto suspended six stories above the slumbering, sun-parched streets of Saigon. Aside from the carelessly displayed copy of *The Vietnam News,* the room offered little indication of its owner's nature. Only three attributes were obvious: the compulsive sense of order, the wealth necessary to furnish this refuge, and the determination which compelled Saigon to deliver both the current and the maintenance necessary for a central air-conditioning plant.

"I am sorry not to have been here to welcome you," piped the owner's voice. Hand outstretched, Dietrich rolled from the foyer into the living room, a ship of the line under full sail of double-breasted, paunch-swelled sharkskin. The attendant *boyess* darted frigate-like behind him. "Others not here yet? They'll be along soon. A bit shy, I'm afraid. Another drink? *Boyess*," he said, pointing to Mallory's glass, and the crystal shaker appeared within an instant. *"Pour moi aussi."*

The pink fleshy face beamed on Mallory as if his mere existence conferred great pleasure on the publisher. The wintry blue eyes, usually so remote in their padded sockets, showed a touch of spring.

"What a sensible costume," said Dietrich, indicating Mallory's white linen safari jacket and slacks with a sweep of his pudgy hand. "I'm imprisoned in this Somerset Maugham garb by business conventions. The Vietnamese are even more formal than the French, and the tieless, short-sleeved, short-trousered American military are uncomfortable dealing with a civilian in deshabille. Representation, representation is all. The same holds for this rather gaudy establishment."

"Gaudy?" answered Mallory. "I'd call this anything but gaudy—a haven, a sea grotto in Saigon. I'm awed by your jade."

Dietrich's eyes kindled. "I'm so glad you find it pleasant. A bit elaborate for my taste perhaps. But one must be comfortable if one can. And the old pieces do recall the heritage of a city now detached from its past."

Feeling the incandescent breath of the true collector's passion, Mallory bit back the observation that Han and Tang objets d'art were hardly in the direct line of descent of the Vietnamese. He touched the pink Kwan Yin, about to ask

132

its provenance when the *boyess* glided in to announce, *"Messieurs est arrivé."*

"Splendid, splendid," piped Dietrich, pushing himself out of his leather chair. "The Dong-ninh's have arrived. You must, by the way, excuse my *boyess'* fractured French. She is quite admirable in other ways."

Dietrich returned from the foyer shepherding two dapper Vietnamese. The elder, a man of about fifty with a broad, good-natured face that was completely unlined, was thin except for the watermelon potbelly his double-breasted sharkskin suit could not quite disguise. The younger was somewhere between twenty-five and thirty and a near-perfect reproduction of the other facially. He was equally thin, though four inches taller. Under his narrow-lapeled, blue-and-white Dacron cord suit, his body moved like an athlete's, but the violet rimming his eyes was even deeper than the older man's.

"May I present," said Dietrich in surprisingly unaccented French, "the Messieurs Dong-ninh? We usually call them M. François and M. Richard to distinguish the father from the son. I'm sure they will not mind if you do the same. M. Gerald Mallory."

The elaborate, Continental hand-shaking and the murmurs of *"enchanté"* over, the four settled into deep leather chairs.

"I have," Dietrich continued in French, "deliberately refrained from telling the Dong-ninhs with whom they were to lunch. I thought we should avoid any preparation for this encounter. I should like you all to feel that our discussion is quite spontaneous."

"Of course," murmured Mallory against the older man's whispered, "We quite understand!"

"But I shall now allow myself the pleasure," Dietrich went on, "of making three distinguished gentlemen known to each other. M. François is my closest and most valued business associate, a man of much experience of life and the vagaries of events in his beautiful but troubled country. M. Richard, a scholar and a sportsman—did you not drive magnificently in last year's Macao Grand Prix, M. Richard?"

"I should not call it magnificently, though the Ferrari did come in third," lisped the son.

"To resume, M. Richard is a scholar, the Sorbonne, and a sportsman in his own right. But, if I may presume, M. Mallory, he can best tell you of the educated, honorable Vietnamese of a generation slightly younger than our own."

"I'll do my best," interjected Richard, "but I have been away a lot lately."

"Nonsense," said Dietrich amicably, "born of modesty. There are few who can speak with such authority as yourself. But I must apologize. What will you drink, gentlemen?"

When father and son were sipping whiskey sodas, Dietrich resumed. "M. Gerald Mallory is the world-famous author, the most distinguished correspondent in Asia. He is here to tell the world about the struggle of the Vietnamese people for freedom from Communist domination—and the inevitable victory over the Vietcong. You will appreciate that he must be given all the facts without hesitation or prevarication when I tell you that he is writing a major article for *Quest* magazine."

Simultaneously, two broad mouths pursed into gravity and four delicate ochre hands were spread wide.

"*Quest*," said Richard. "It has a fine sports section. Very good on racing, but sometimes they mix things up."

"Oh," said François, "a thorough business section, very thorough."

"The Dong-ninhs," interjected Dietrich, "of course read English well and follow *Quest*. M. Richard, I often—indeed, customarily—find myself in disagreement with *Quest's* so-so, so liberal line; and I'm sure M. Mallory does not agree with everything his magazine publishes. But M. Mallory and *Quest* together—they are formidable."

"How magnificent, how fortunate," murmured the father

and son in chorus, their eyes slit and each smiling mouth revealing exactly the same number of stained teeth.

"M. Mallory, the pulpit is yours," said Dietrich abruptly.

Mallory preferred to let a conversation develop naturally. Taken aback by Dietrich's directness, he was searching for an opening question, when the *boyess* entered, followed by the largest Vietnamese Mallory had ever seen.

Almost as tall as Dietrich and appreciably heavier, the old man advanced slowly into the room, leaning heavily on a gold-banded Malacca cane. With astonishment, Mallory saw the hornrimmed glasses, too small for the great moon face, the frizzly white hair under the round, black mandarin's hat, the slack lips working to some internal rhythm. If the great Dr. Samuel Johnson had been resurrected in Oriental guise, so he would appear. The black damask long-gown, stretched tight over the pendulant stomach, was greasy and pocked with particles of food.

Dietrich uncoiled from his chair with that swift grace he could display on occassion.

"Ah, Dr. Ty, we are honored by your presence."

"I am, as always, delighted to join you, my dear Dietrich. You have not changed cooks, have you?" the old man inquired anxiously, his French impeccably Parisian, though his words emerged with difficulty after long pauses.

"No, my dear Doctor, be assured that I have not." Dietrich smiled. "May I present M. Gerald Mallory, the distinguished American journalist whose reputation you know. He is here to write the definitive article on Vietnam. M. Mallory, I am sure you know by reputation Dr. Ai-ngoc Ty, Professor Emeritus of Oriental Philosophy at the University of Hué."

"Of course," said Mallory, shaking hands and automatically marking the pinpoint pupils of the opium smoker framed by the hornrims. The Dong-ninh's sprang to their feet and elaborate formulas of respect sprang to their lips.

"Since there is no need for further introductions," Dietrich resumed, "we can plunge straight into the river of our conversation."

"Good," rumbled Dr. Ty. "Conversation always gives me an appetite."

"Well, Mr. François," Mallory asked lamely, "what are the prospects for Vietnam?"

"Excellent, M. Mallory; I can assure you that the prospects are excellent. Investment is already piling up in Saigon. As soon as the rascals are under control, the countryside will provide vast new opportunities for profitable expansion."

"M. François, of course, has in mind the enormous opportunities for fulfilling the great role of the entrepreneur under private enterprise," Dietrich interjected. "Making his honorable and essential profit while bringing new goods and services to the people."

"Of course, of course," said François. "With the support of your excellent Agency for International Development we find great prospects for profit. There are so many things in the countryside the people need and want."

Mallory protested. "That is fascinating, but I meant the general prospects."

"Is that not what we are talking about—the general prospects?" countered François.

"And, M. Richard, do you agree that there are great prospects in the countryside?" asked Mallory, for the moment giving up his attempt to make the discussion more concrete.

"Well, you see, I really can't say. I haven't actually been in the countryside much lately—too busy racing, keeping up our interests in France, and so on, you know."

The father took the conversation back. "I know the countryside, M. Mallory. I know our good, simple country people. My roots are with them. And I can assure you that the prospects are magnificent, never better. You can assure the American businessman that he will find a warm welcome here, and a magnificent opportunity once our valorous armed forces have cleared out the rascals."

"And you, Dr. Ty? M. François seems to feel it's very simple—just a matter of clearing out what he calls the rascals. Do the people really want the rascals cleared out?"

"Eh?" ejaculated the old professor, levering himself to an upright position with his cane. "What was that? What rascals?"

"The Vietcong," said Mallory sharply. "Do the country people really want them wiped out?"

"Oh, the Vietcong. Why yes, yes of course. There is no question. The entire spirit of Vietnam, our true Confucian heritage . . . How can you doubt that the good and simple farmers want anything else but?"

"And how long will it take, getting rid of the Vietcong?"

"That's hard to say," answered Dr. Ty. "Matter for the military really. But the spirit is the important thing. The spirit of Vietnam will triumph."

"How long would you say, Mr. Richard?"

The son came to attention in his chair. "Hard to say. As Dr. Ty says, it's really a military matter. But six months, maybe a year. You Americans are giving the push. Then there will be spendid opportunities. Splendid shooting in the hills, too, you know."

"What's your judgment, Mr. François?" Mallory persisted in his uphill work.

"Military matter really, I agree. But the first thing to do is open the channels. Reopen the channels of economic life. Once goods start flowing and people get the benefit, it will all be over but the mopping up."

"Isn't there a strong feeling for the Vietcong? Don't they dominate some areas so that no government authority and no goods can get through? Don't they have a strong network of agents and spies even in Saigon?"

"Nonsense," answered François angrily. "Just nonsense put out to deceive gullible Americans. Aside from a few malcontents and a few misguided youths, maybe a few fanatics, there's no sympathy for the rascals."

"Are the youth really for the government, Mr. Richard?"

"Oh, yes, of course. No question about it. Only one complaint—the government should be quicker about getting things back to normal so people could lead normal lives, enjoy themselves."

Mallory persisted until the *boyess* announced lunch, bringing Dr. Ty to his feet with the first vigorous motion he had displayed. Between the snails and the lamb chops Mallory gave up, letting the conversation wash around him. Aside from Dr. Ty's appreciative comments on the food, the talk was chiefly devoted to new American contracts for airfields. M. Richard also alluded enthusiastically to the new Go-Kart Club at Tonsonnhut Airport.

As his guests left, Dietrich acknowledged that the conversation had been somewhat less than helpful to Mallory. "They're not articulate like you and me," he said softly. "But they're the backbone of the country. Solid, unimaginative types—they'll stand forever against the Communists. And Dr. Ty, perhaps he's a bit past it, but he stands for the old values and the old virtues. They are shared by the common folk."

The elevator whisked Mallory back to the reality of Saigon —heavy, odoriferous, and silent at siesta time. One thing, at least, he had learned from the old professor. Despite the popular impression, it *was* possible to combine the vices of opium-smoking and gluttony.

15

When Mallory strolled into the sidewalk café, his hair still glistening wet from his post-siesta shower, he found Rosen and Levoncier, lounging in cane chairs. Glasses of cloudy-yellow Pernod stood before them.

"Ho, he comes," trumpeted Levoncier. "The man of affairs —great affairs."

"Have a drink, Gerry," Rosen offered.

"Thanks, Sid. Why didn't you tell me you were waiting for me?"

"Because we were not," Levoncier answered. "Though in our hearts there beat the tremulous hope that you might reveal yourself."

"We came here to escape," Rosen added.

"Escape what?"

"Jack Martin, the world famous TV personality, just blew into town direct from Washington. He's sitting in the Caravelle bar dispensing limpid drops of wisdom from the President's own brow. He's also telling the local peons exactly how the war will be won—decisively and within ten months!"

The dapper, self-contained *Times* correspondent was as bitter as Mallory had ever seen him. He was normally tolerant—as only a man who feels he has seen almost every variety of evil and almost every manifestation of foolishness can be tolerant. But he was viciously contemptuous of any reporter who, he felt, juggled the facts to swell his reputation, to pad his bank account, or to feed his ego.

"I can't stand that fat slob," Rosen went on. "Men and

women are dying, even the sybarites of the press are sweating to do some good reporting. And Jack Martin turns up to inform us, with heavy condescension, that he and the President have settled the whole bloody mess over a couple of cocktails in Georgetown."

"So much wisdom makes my head ache," Levoncier said. "So the gracious Sidney consented to accompany me here for treatment. He walked slowly by my side all the way in case I fainted en route."

"Pierre, I just couldn't take any more. I had a note from Washington a couple of days ago saying the exact opposite."

"Martin'll be back next year saying exactly the same thing," Mallory consoled them. "Where've you been? You both look beat."

"Out for a little helicopter ride and a stroll to watch resettlement in Quang-ngai Province. Very efficient, lots of troops, lots of American advisers, and hordes of bulldozers."

"How did it go?"

"Fine," said Levoncier, "perfectly co-ordinated. Except the peasants they had all run away and there was no one to resettle except three dogs, an old grandmother, and a blind man."

"Not quite so bad, you evil Frenchman," Rosen said, his literal-minded good humor restored by Levoncier's extravagance. "They did get one whole village and a few families from a couple of others. But almost everyone had taken off."

"Was it old style or new style?" asked Mallory.

"New style," answered Rosen. "No advance preparation till it actually started."

"Nontheless, the sturdy peasantries knew all about the blessings planned for them by the government. And they all ran away. Thinking that the simple and direct Vietcong might also have prepared a little welcome, a *feu de joie,* for the troops, Sidney and I left the camp before the shooting commenced."

"It was pretty sad," said Rosen.

140

"But we have not asked after your day—and, tragically, I have not been there to record all on film." Levoncier's glance swept over Mallory's dark suit and striped rep silk tie. "Yet it is obvious—after many high-level consultations and the siesta hours spent reflecting upon them, Mr. Mallory is to dine with the Ambassador. Or is it the General?"

"Jack Martin'll be there giving them both their instructions," said Rosen again unsmiling. He would, Mallory knew, brood at odd intervals for days at the perversity of a television commentator who based his conclusions on his own wishes rather than on facts.

"I shall leave Martin to it," Mallory said, ruffling his damp brush cut to make it stand up. "I, gentlemen, am taking Mademoiselle Tuyelle to dinner alone, *à deux, tête-à-tête.*"

"If you will forgive me, Gerry," Levoncier said, grave when discussing a serious topic, "I simply am evaded by Tuyelle's attractions. Perhaps she appeals only to a certain type. . . ."

"Yeah," Rosen interrupted, the compliment falling oddly from his tightened lips, "the male type."

"Is that sure," Levoncier continued. "There were some who said that Johnny Humboldt was not entirely the male type."

"That's a lot of crap," Rosen said angrily.

"How do you know?" Levoncier insisted.

"Well, for God's sake, you can tell." Rosen paused, then added with a conciliatory smile, "anyway, he never made a pass at me. Not even when we were drinking."

"Perhaps you were not his type, *mon cher* Sidney. You must not be so vain of your beauty."

"About Humboldt," Mallory put in hastily, "is there anything new?"

"Not a thing," answered Rosen. "I tried again, after what Calaveri said, but couldn't turn up a thing. I think Vince was really reaching. I figure this was the hundred and first case—and he didn't put the muzzle between his teeth."

"Are you still following it?"

"I can't waste any more time on a cold story." Rosen

brushed Humboldt aside with the unthinking ruthlessness of the daily newspaperman dealing with yesterday's story. "You still interested?"

"If I could get any more," answered Mallory cautiously.

"Are we interested professionally or personally, *mon general?* Are we, perhaps, just ever so little touched by the tragic Mademoiselle Tuyelle?"

"Professionally, Pierre, damn it." Mallory laughed. "It would make a damned fine allegory. . . ."

"When you magazine guys begin to talk literary," said Rosen, "it's almost as sickening as Jack Martin unveiling the Tablets from the Mount."

Jack Martin, Mallory reflected, must have been even more insufferable than usual. Rosen, after all, was an affable Broadway character who always insisted that he was merely on "out-of-town-assignment" and who believed passionately in only three things: the facts, the New York *Times*, and the stern God of his nomadic ancestors—perhaps in that order of importance.

"But, hark," whispered Levoncier, "she comes."

Mallory felt his breath catch in his throat, and a rush of pure joy dilated his nerves. He watched Tuyelle approach with that perfect clarity which excludes everything but its object.

She wore an *ao-dai* of lustrous, deep blue silk, and her pantaloons, flirting above her silver sandals, were the pale orange of a budding tiger lily. A deep orange bracelet of baroque stones encircled her left wrist. She clasped a small, black-beaded purse and a packet wrapped in a pale blue scarf shot with silver. Her face, framed by the straight black hair that hung to her shoulders, was raised as if in anticipation. Beneath the pale cream skin of her narrow, high forehead, her green-lit eyes were aglow and her lips were parted. Her face closed and a line intruded itself between her black eyebrows when she saw Levoncier and Rosen.

"Good evening, gentlemen," she said, ignoring Mallory. "Do correspondents always travel in packs?"

Only when she had punctiliously shaken hands with his companions did she turn to Mallory. Once again he saw that eager, yet self-contained expression, a small girl going to a party, confident that she will savor all its anticipated pleasures. Slowly she extended her hand to him. *"Bon soir,* Gerry," she said, slurring his name.

Realizing with delight that her head was tilted to offer her cheek, Mallory leaned forward and brushed the soft skin with his lips. The sweetness of jasmine, tinged with the heaviness of musk, was still in his nostrils as she laid her hand on his arm.

They walked in silence through the faded red and gold of the lobby. She spoke only when they approached the open doors beyond which taxis waited.

"Gerry, I have brought you something," she said, unwrapping the silvery-blue scarf to reveal a heavy brown-paper envelope.

Mallory took it automatically, murmuring, "Thank you." He was too absorbed to wonder what it held.

"It is," she continued, "everything I could find of Johnny's writings. Perhaps you will find what you seek. When you give them back, seal them well. I do not wish to read them again."

They were almost out of the gates before she broke the spell. "Gerry," she asked smiling, "don't you think you'd better leave it in your room?"

Too impatient to wait for the elevator, Mallory ran up the narrow marble steps two at a time. He laid the package next to his brief case on the blond table amid a welter of cups and glasses. Time's passage seemed to have been abregated. He found Tuyelle still gazing entranced at a calendar advertising Air France.

In the taxi he said crisply to the driver, "Guillaume Tell,

s'il vous plait." Turning slowly, he saw her slender hands bright against the blue silk.

"Bon soir, Tuyelle," he said joyously, *"bon soir."*

"Lean over, Gerry," she whispered, "I want to tell you something."

Her lips brushed against his ear and his nerves tingled. Her breath played against his skin. She murmured, "It is a beautiful evening. The swans are playing on the river. And I do not wish to talk of politics this beautiful evening."

"Yes," he said, "yes, Tuyelle, it is a beautiful evening. And, no, Tuyelle, no, we shall not talk of politics." He lifted her hand and touched her palm with his lips. "Perhaps we shall never talk of politics again."

"It is not that bad—yet." She laughed, withdrawing her hand.

They sat in silence, but the fraction of an inch that separated their arms might not have existed. He was completely enveloped by her scent and her nearness. . . .

The tiny hot sausages served on the dark wooden table of the Guillaume Tell had never been so crisp and piquant. The martinis had never been so like an astringent nectar, and the cold crab vinaigrette never so like ambrosia. He couldn't afterward remember what they talked about. But it was the best talk he had ever heard—witty, mocking, and tender all at once. He could only remember that they had not once mentioned the war in Vietnam.

He did remember that once she raised her glass of champagne and whispered, "Gerry, it will be good, will it not?"

"Yes, Tuyelle, it will be good—tonight and tomorrow and in a year, and forever."

She shivered. "Not forever—don't say forever. It would be what I wish, but to hope for next year is already to defy fate."

"No, Tuyelle, we have both propitiated fate," he insisted, suddenly aware that he had to believe what he said. "This time, fate will yield to our desires."

144

He emptied his glass and tossed it gently into the ornamental fireplace. When Tuyelle's followed, the bespectacled French proprietress looked up quizzically but did not protest. The glasses would appear on the bill, their value enhanced only slightly in tribute to sentiment.

Tuyelle drew his hand across the table and pushed back his cuff to look at his watch. "It is still too early to go home, Gerry," she said. "It is impossible before eleven."

"Tuyelle, I've waited so long, I'm in no hurry now, but, for curiosity's sake, why impossible before eleven?"

She smiled, then suddenly giggled. "It sounds terrible. It is never the same with others as with one's self, is it? But my brother is leaving tomorrow for a course at Fort Benning. I told him he could have the flat to say good-bye to his fiancée. But not—I was very stern—after eleven."

"You do organize things well. You mean you knew?"

"Ever since the party at Dr. Thau's—but I shall organize things no more. You must order everything, and I shall obey."

"First I want to be completely alone with you. And I know no better way to be alone right now than amid a throng of people. We shall go to the Baccarat."

A frantic Filipino combo was beating out a twist when they found a miniscule table in the far corner of the night club. Through the smoke stabbed by hot, white spotlights, they could see the outlines of dozens of small tables crammed together. Overladen waiters handed glasses and bottles to a clientele half Vietnamese and half foreign.

Mallory leaned over and spoke softly when the combo paused. "Could you find a better place to be alone?"

Her crimson lips parted in a smile, and he noticed with fresh delight that one of her front teeth was slightly crooked. Tuyelle saw that for the first time since she had met him, his wide gray eyes did not brood, nor did he run his palm over his hair in dumb anxiety.

Without warning the room went black. A waiter's white

145

jacket, glowing pale violet, floated disembodied through the darkness. Violet collars and the vees of shirt fronts glowed across the room from them. The combo began a fox trot, arms flailing in ruffled violet shirts but heads and legs invisible. Slowly the dance floor filled. White collars cavorted madly, and an occasional violet-white *ao-dai* cast a faint glow on the face above it.

"I don't know why this ultra-violet trick always tickles me." Mallory laughed. "Shall we join the choir invisible?"

"First some repairs," she answered. "I think I can find my way."

He heard her chair scrape and felt her withdraw, but saw only a hint of light from her silver sandals. A waiter's white coat leaned over him deferentially, and Mallory began, *"Bon soir,* bring me a bottle of Krug, extra brut. . . ."

"Mr. Mallory," a sibilant voice interrupted from the darkness above the jacket, "the heat has abated somewhat."

Mallory's mind went blank with shock. It was fully thirty seconds before he remembered the courier in sunglasses. "Yes," he replied, the decision solemnized by the words, "but it is no weather for traveling."

"Come then," said the voice.

"But, I can't right now. You saw. . . ."

"Either immediately or not at all," the sighing whisper insisted. "We must be sure you are not followed. Come now."

Mallory wrestled his notebook from his pocket, noting gratefully that the white paper gave off just enough light to write by.

"Can I leave a note?"

"A short one. And I must see it."

Hastily he scribbled: "Tuyelle, I must leave. I'm desperately sorry, but it's essential. Wait for me at home. I love you."

"All right," said the voice, and Mallory, hating himself and the unseen censor, tucked the note under the ash tray.

He followed the glowing jacket into the vestibule, which

was dimly lit. The waiter had disappeared, but he heard a voice in his ear, "Straight ahead, Mr. Mallory. The taxi in front of the door. And don't look around."

As he stepped into the taxi, he saw a figure huddled in the corner of the seat, but it vanished when he closed the door. The windows and even the glass partition cutting off the driver's compartment had been painted black.

"Good evening, Mr. Mallory," the cultivated English voice with the nearly imperceptible lilt spoke out of the darkness. "I am glad you have decided to come and hear our tale."

The pause was broken by the flare of a lighter. The emissary, still wearing his sweeping dark glasses, spoke again from behind an orange cigarette tip. "Please smoke, if you wish. The journey will take a while I'm afraid. I'm sorry about the melodrama of these blacked-out windows, but I assure you it's more comfortable than a blindfold."

"How long will this take?" asked Mallory. "You snatched me away from an important occasion."

"Yes, I'm sorry about that. But we had to be reasonably sure you weren't planning to pot us. Besides, we must all make sacrifices for our art mustn't we now?"

Mallory smoked three cigarettes in silence, squashing the butts out on the floor. The taxi proceeded jerkily, the noise of traffic outside rising, then subsiding and rising again. Brief bursts of speed were succeeded by long waits, and twice the unmistakable double jar of railroad crossings shook the seat. Finally they accelerated and ran smoothly for ten minutes before coming to an abrupt halt. A shutter rattled closed and a ray of light broadened as the taxi door opened from the outside.

"Here we are. If you'll just let me go ahead."

Moving fast to keep up with his guide, Mallory had no more than an impression of a corrugated-iron garage with a workbench at one side. He went up a flight of narrow wooden stairs, treading carefully in the dim light, and suddenly smothered a grin. His hosts could have spared him the elaborate ride around. He smelled the mingled odors of soya sauce, vinegar, boiling rice, and hot oil. He knew they must be above a Chinese restaurant because he did not catch the penetrating odor of fermented fish, the unmistakable *nyuknam* sauce which was the essential condiment of the Vietnamese cuisine. He heard the low throbbing of traffic outside and the rattle of a mah-jong game. He had to be in Cholon, probably no more than ten minutes' ride from the Baccarat and probably somewhere near the river, to account for the clear road that had allowed the last burst of speed.

A door opened at the head of the stairs and the courier flattened himself against the wall. Mallory heard the door close behind him and the courier's feet departing. Brilliant fluorescent light revealed a gaudy wall calendar advertising a Hong Kong ship's chandler, a pile of rice sacks in one corner, and, in the other, a small table heaped with cigarette tins, ash trays, small tools, wood and jade carvings, and books.

At the far end of the whitewashed room a man sat behind a rough wooden table. When he rose, Mallory looked into an unmistakably Caucasian face. There was nothing Oriental about the full ruddy cheeks, the powerful hooked nose, the wide dark eyes, and the full red lips beneath the sweeping white mustache. Incongruously dressed in black Vietnamese tunic and trousers, the man's body was too slight for the full face.

"I must apologize for my appearance." The heavily accented French boomed oddly behind the "foreign devil" mask Mallory now recognized as a staple of Hong Kong toy shops. "We don't move in the same circles, but there could be an accidental meeting."

"It is startling," Mallory admitted.

"We also thought it might give you some—'color,' do you call it—for your blasé readers. Will it help, do you think?" the Communist leader inquired anxiously.

"Perhaps." Mallory couldn't help grinning. "Thanks for taking the trouble. But our meeting itself is quite enough."

148

"Good. We hoped you'd realize that we move at will through Saigon. We see all and control much. If I gave the word, thousands of workers would strike tomorrow and paralyze the city. If my superiors gave the order we could take the city. We are more powerful than the so-called government."

"Why don't you, then? Why not take the city if you can?"

"The bloodshed and the anguish, Mr. Mallory. We hope to avoid it. We would rather see you Americans withdraw sensibly. Then there would be no bloodshed, for the people would come to us openly and freely."

"And the present government?"

"A joke, a farce!" A thin edge of contempt cut across the hollow booming. "If the rapacious American Imperialists withdrew, the so-called government would not last twenty-four hours. It would disintegrate."

"And what would take its place, a Communist government?"

"By no means, Mr. Mallory. I am, myself, it happens, a Communist. But the majority of my co-workers are not. They are interested—as are we Communists—only in ending the present struggle, in destroying foreign influence, in freeing the people from exploitation. The National Liberation Front would form a government."

"And the Communists?"

"The Front might ask us to assist them. We have had more experience of organization."

"Then you're saying that your aim is not a Communist government?"

"That is correct. We are anxious only to establish a peaceful and prosperous Vietnam. Once the present oppression ceases, the spontaneous resistance movement would end, and the National Liberation Front could attack the country's pressing economic and social problems."

"Under the guidance of the Communists?" Mallory persisted.

149

"I am speaking to you as an official of the National Liberation Front. But, of course, we Communists should be glad to provide guidance," the voice boomed. "We do not, however, seek power now. We are but part of the Liberation Front."

"And ultimately?"

"Ultimately, I personally believe that a united Vietnam would move toward socialism and, eventually, Communism. It is inevitable that the people will see the necessity. But we will not use coercion."

"Any more than you are using coercion now," said Mallory dryly.

"That is correct, Mr Mallory. The present resistance is a popular movement to which we Communists provide some assistance. Any decision to move toward socialism would be spontaneous."

"Can you tell me more about the military situation?" asked Mallory, fighting the sense of unreality evoked by the contrast between the words and the Colonel Blimp mask.

"If the American people could force their madly ambitious rulers to withdraw, the National Liberation Front could begin its task of reconstruction within a week. Otherwise, it will take longer, since we wish to avoid bloodshed."

"How long?"

"I do not know." The slender figure sketched a broad semicircle in the air with a nicotine-stained forefinger. "We shall not move so fast as to offer the mad-dog generals of the Pentagon an excuse for spreading the conflict. But we already control—we, the Liberation Front, that is—seventy per cent of the country's land and fifty per cent of the population. We have our friends in every ministry and in every unit of the armed forces."

"Just to help me in my writing—how can I describe you?" asked Mallory, lighting a Camel with great deliberation and blowing the smoke out in a long stream. He felt a malicious pleasure when the set mask leaned forward to sniff the smoke and the wiry hand instinctively reached toward the table for the cigarette the disguise denied him.

"As I am. I hope this farcical mask will not detract from my complete earnestness."

"I wouldn't worry about that." Mallory smiled. "You'll come through strong. But I meant to ask what is your job!"

"You may call me the Saigon District Co-ordinator of the National Liberation Front. I am really the shadow mayor of Saigon. I have my counterparts, all wielding great power, in every district, county, and village."

"Tell me, why did you invite *me* here?"

"Quite frankly, Mr. Mallory, it was not altruism. We want you to hear for yourself, and then tell the American people, that the struggle will be won by the Vietnamese people. America is merely wasting blood and treasure in an ignoble cause. Tell the American people it is time for them to rise and say to the Pentagon and Wall Street, 'Get out of Vietnam. Stop sacrificing our sons in the hopeless cause of oppression.' "

"Do you really think I'll write that message?"

"Yes, Mr. Mallory, if you put aside your prejudices. We know you are less biased than most Capitalist writers. We shall give you all possible facilities, but more of that in a minute. . . . And, Mr. Mallory, I am authorized to say that later a trip to Hanoi—would that interest you? There is, if things go well, even a strong possibility of a visit to People's China. We could say a word to our friends, the Chinese. That would be a plum, a very profitable plum, for you, would it not?"

"Could be," grunted Mallory.

It would be a plum indeed, with American correspondents banned by the Communists from both North Vietnam and Red China. Bribes proferred by the CIA and the Vietcong all within the space of a week; Mallory was in a seller's market.

"You see," the voice was booming again, "we are asking you

to do nothing against your conscience. We merely wish you to describe the real situation. If you can refrain from calling us bandits and murderers, we should be grateful. But tell the American people we shall prevail—regardless of anything they can do."

"You spoke of further facilities?"

"Oh, yes." The figure sighed. The long fingers could no longer resist the temptation. They took up a round tin of cigarettes, stroking it caressingly. The tin's removal started a minor avalanche on the littered table. A magazine called *Révolution* slid against a tiny gilt Buddha, knocking the statuette on its side. Two .45 cartridges clattered against a blue Chinese ink box with a broken hinge, and an open map fluttered gently down to cover the debris like a blanket.

"Yes, Mr. Mallory," the masked voice continued, "I could tell you many things. Some American officers, moved by true patriotism, are already helping us indirectly, and. . . ."

"American officers helping you? That's fascinating. Can you tell me more?" interjected Mallory.

"I'm afraid not. It's obvious why. But we have already talked too long for tonight. If you wish, I can arrange another talk. Perhaps you could spend a few days with one of our units in the field. Then you'd see how things are going, how inevitable is the people's triumph."

"I think I'd like that," said Mallory slowly. "But I'll have to think about it."

"Do that, Mr. Mallory, do that. We'll talk again in any event. I'll be in touch with you. Or you might leave me a note."

"How could I get a note to you?"

"Oh, very simple," Mallory heard a chuckle behind the mask. "Very simple. Just write a note to yourself and leave it on your desk. My messengers will pick it up."

"You're not that efficient," Mallory taunted.

"Are we not?" asked the masked man, reaching into his pocket for a sheaf of papers. "Your telegrams, Mr. Mallory, every one you've sent since you've been here. We didn't choose you without evidence about you."

Mallory leafed through the papers, confirming his boast.

The man in black, standing erect, was speaking again. "And just one more thing, Mr. Mallory. Do not try to betray us. You yourself might be able to escape our vengeance for a time. But we should put our hands on Mademoiselle Vguyen-lee at the first suspicion. We do not shrink from violence— when others make it necessary."

While the taxi retraced its circuitous path, Mallory brooded unhappily. At Tuyelle's name he had almost said, "Forget the deal. You've got nothing to offer me that's worth your threats."

But not quite. A first-hand account of a Vietcong unit in operation would make his story, not to speak of possible trips to Hanoi and China. The man in the Halloween mask had too much to offer. That was the trouble. He wondered just how far he could go without imperiling Tuyelle—or compromising himself irreparably.

The taxi stopped and the man in sunglasses opened the door, saying, "I think you can find the Baccarat from here. Have a good evening."

Mallory walked slowly toward the night club, reflecting gratefully that one fear, at least, had not troubled him. Neither during the interlude nor pondering the future had he wasted a moment's thought on his own physical safety.

Finding that Tuyelle had left the Baccarat, Mallory flagged a taxi. "Drive to," he began and stopped, realizing he did not know her address. ". . . the Majestic," he finished glumly.

The sidewalk café was closed. Swearing at Tuyelle's coyness, Mallory trudged dispiritedly up the marble staircase. It seemed incredible that only yesterday her caution had still withheld her address from him—and almost as incredible that he, scribbling a note under the waiter's eyes, had simply forgotten his ignorance of it.

The day that had begun so well and had risen to such

153

heights was dying in a muddle of frustration and indecision. The Vietcong offer was infinitely tempting. But a counter-temptation was urged by caution and by whatever he could discern of duty in the tangled web of Saigon. He wondered if Gilroy would feel his ten thousand dollars were well-spent if they helped him take the shadow mayor of Saigon. But the threat to Tuyelle and his own hopes for the story held Mallory back from that sensible course.

Tuyelle, too, must be placated. It surely had appeared deliberate desertion, but, hell, she'd have to get used to a correspondent's life. If only it hadn't happened on this first night!

He noted with irritation that the dishes had not been cleared from the table, though one glass lay broken on the floor. His brief case lay nearly at the edge of the table, yet he had left it among the debris. The brown envelope containing Humboldt's manuscripts had been neatly slit open. But he was too dispirited to concern himself with the threat implicit in the disarrangement.

Automatically he picked up the fragments, and, automatically, he took a sleeping pill. Despite the drug he lay awake, alternating between elation at the promise of the story and the promise of Tuyelle—and fear of the decisions he must make.

16

Tuyelle's voice was cool and more distant than the bad connection justified. "No, Gerry, I wasn't very happy. And I'm still not very happy."

"My darling," he said, savoring the endearment, "you know it was something unavoidable. I want this as badly as you do."

"I cannot," she said, "imagine anything of such importance in Saigon at 10:30 in the evening."

"I'll explain, full detail, when I see you."

"You do want to see me then?" The tone was a degree less frosty.

"Don't be idiotic. How otherwise? I'd have battered down your door last night—if I knew where it was. I couldn't even call you. This secrecy of yours—that didn't help either."

"Gerry?" her voice was hesitant, the Gallic slurring more pronounced. "Did you mean what you wrote in your note?"

"About it's being essential? Of course. Only that. . . ."

"No," she interrupted, "I didn't mean that part. What you said at the end."

"Of course." He smiled. "Even more now."

"Then say it," she asked.

He did. "I love you, Tuyelle," he said, "even more today than last night."

She paused, sighed, then giggled. "I'm glad," she said. "But we can't tie up the Ministry's phone for this sort of talk."

155

"When can I see you?"

"Well I could have a headache...."

"Have a headache then. When and where?"

"Two o'clock. Ground floor, 23 Rue Trongkyi."

"Till two then. I'll love you even more after six hours."

Mallory ordered breakfast and sat down at the desk, promising himself a full morning's work. The fragments of glass in the waste-paper basket recalled the intruder of the preceding night. Perhaps the man in the mask was just rubbing in his point. But the display of telegrams had really been effective enough.

He kept coming back to one fact. The broken glass, the envelope slit—he was undoubtedly intended to know that his room had been entered. He would, he concluded with a show of equanimity he could not have mastered twenty-four hours earlier, just have to live with the knowledge that someone was trying to warn him off something. Whoever it was would have to make the point a lot more clearly before he could even react. He smiled crookedly; elucidation would certainly come.

He worked steadily for two hours typing up the notes and impressions of the preceding four days and, occasionally, making a handwritten notation on a separate sheet. The pattern of the story was emerging clearly. He'd start, logically enough, at the beginning, with his own arrival and Humboldt's suicide. Next, the over-all situation, primarily through George Dietrich and Dr. Thau; they agreed that the crisis was grave, one holding that it could be salvaged, the other too shrewd to offer any flat prediction. He'd definitely need more color and fact from the field, though this was no blood-and-guts story.

Above all, Humboldt's death required full explanation—or the most dramatic point would be lost. Was he a suicide, a casualty because he cared too much? Why had the Army wanted to rush him out of the country? Was he betraying his oath? Or, as McGuffey had hinted, was he trapped between contending factions? Could Calaveri's suspcions be dismissed completely?

Mallory began to leaf through the sheaf of Humboldt's manuscript with distaste. It was obvious that Tuyelle did not want to talk about Humboldt again, but he'd be forced to press her. He simply could not sacrifice the impact Humboldt's death would give his story. Besides, there was a nagging sense of affinity—not only because of Tuyelle, though it began there. Whatever he'd done, Humboldt deserved a better epitaph than silence. He had had the courage to become involved, and that was more than Gerald Mallory had ever done.

He glanced through a long essay entitled, "Americans and Guerrillas." A page of verse headed "Tuyelle by Moonlight" he pushed aside without reading. A short story, untitled, yielded nothing to a quick reading. It told of the shock of an American sergeant, assigned to a Vietnamese Ranger Company, at the casual brutality of his allies under their martinet captain; his growing sympathy with the Vietcong; his final revulsion from the Communists' calculated viciousness; and, finally, of his death in a vain attempt to save the captain from an ambush. Nothing there, obviously.

Mallory went through the rest of the material methodically —another short story, fragments of poems, and notes for other stories. But nowhere an indication as to why the young Captain had put a bullet through his head.

He sighed and lit a cigarette. There was a certain amount of meat for the story, but he felt like a Peeping Tom. Idly he ruffled the sheets, straightening them before putting them away. When he tapped the bundle of paper on the table to align the edges, two single sheets fell out. One was the poem, "Tuyelle by Moonlight." Stuck to the back by a red stain that looked like wine was a closely typed page filled with interlinings in blue pencil. Mallory was arrested by the strange language.

157

"He was a taught man," it began, "needleskin and tacilturn. His face was taut to play the jests and prey for rain. Armageddon on and on, deeper and deeper, nearer, my guard, to see. . . ."

The Joycean mélange, so completely different from the careful if often purple prose of the other manuscripts, puzzled Mallory. Just playing with words, he wondered, a mere cry of despair, or was there a meaning in the broken sentences and half-puns? Why else the careful corrections in pencil?

The first two sentences did yield some sort of meaning to free association. The words "taught" and "taut," so obtrusive in their closeness, could, be reversed. That gave a "taut man." Taut could mean tense, thin, slender, nervous, and the unknown was also "needleskin and tacilturn." Thick-skinned or thin-skinned—what would "needleskin" mean? Or might it just be "needlethin," referring once more to his figure? What about "tacilturn"? A man who spoke little, taciturn, or a man who hated to be touched, a man who was withdrawn? He went through the rest of the passage, guessing somewhat wildly at the meanings.

Mallory checked himself. It was an interesting game, but the chances were slender that it had anything to do with Humboldt's death—except, of course, except for the note of desperation. Yet, not knowing the significance of the "he" so elaborately identified—or concealed—there was little the conundrum would tell him even if he did succeed in disentangling it. He put the paper in his pocket, meaning to ask Tuyelle about it.

Ordering a mushroom omelette and half a bottle of white wine to be served in his room, he was interrupted by a phone call from Levoncier, who insisted that he must meet Colonel Danh, chief of the Vietnamese counterintelligence services. After fifteen minutes of argument, Levoncier hung up, muttering about "pundits." He was not placated by Mallory's pleading that he had a throbbing headache.

With two bottles of chilled Krug from the Majestic's stores

tucked under his arm, Mallory rang the bell of the yellow villa at 23 Rue Trongkyi at five past two. Tuyelle herself answered, all in white like a schoolgirl, her lips just touched with pink lipstick.

"Good afternoon, Gerry," she said, extending her hands.

Mallory took them in his free right hand and brushed her cheek with his lips. Today there was only the faintest scent of jasmine.

"Good afternoon, Tuyelle," he said, offering the champagne. "Could you check these somewhere? Or, better still, let's check one and open the other."

When she returned, carrying a tray with two glasses and one bottle, he was seated on the cane couch between two bookcases. The plain furniture and the straw matting were enlivened by bright vases filled with purple and pink flowers. A half-dozen photographs of Vietnamese faces hung on the walls.

"A present from Pierre," she said.

He felt a stab of anger. Tuyelle was just too friendly with too many people.

She laughed. "No, Gerry, it's not what you're thinking. I'm not that active. It's just a kindness to let Pierre give you a few portraits. He's really a good photographer, but no one, he's always complaining, no one wants anything except his gory pictures."

Feeling relieved and foolish, he extended his hand to pull her down to the couch. She evaded his grasp, smiling. "No, not so fast, my friend. First I want to hear about your desertion of last night. What was this urgent business?"

Mallory calculated for about thirty seconds, reluctant to tell her the entire story. Then he began, convinced that there was no harm in her knowing. She laughed once during the account of taxi ride, then her face grew grave.

"Gerry, it's all so improbable, it must be true. But please be careful. I don't want—not now—after. . . ."

"I will," he promised. "I will. I'm not feeling nearly as

159

carefree as I did when I got to Saigon. But this story is going to put me back where I was. It's worth the risk, if—and now the champagne?"

She sat beside him, her hand resting lightly on his knee. When the shallow goblets were foaming with pale gold, he said softly, "To the future with hope—and peace to the past."

She drank quickly and turning like a cat laid her face against his chest. "Oh, Gerry, I do so hope that. . . ."

"It will, darling, it will. This time will be right."

He cupped her shoulders with his hands, feeling the smooth cool skin and the delicate bones under the thin silk. When she turned her face up, he kissed her gently and touched her eyelids with his lips. Her arms tightened around him and her lips came up to his again. He tasted perfume and champagne and her pointed tongue, and they were on their feet pressed together. The soft weight of her breasts pushed against his chest through the silk, and her hips pressed hard against him. Her hands were on his neck. He ran his palms down her smooth back, feeling the intricate delicacy of her waist and the taut fullness of her buttocks.

She broke away suddenly, holding him at arms length. "This will be good, Gerry?"

"Yes, Tuyelle, yes," he reassured her. "This will be good—for you, for me, for both of us, forever, if we are fortunate."

"Come," she said, taking his hand with both of hers and leading him into a room dominated by a low bed.

She was against him again. Suddenly she was smaller, for she had kicked off her sandals.

"Gerry, I want you. Make no promises—no need for promises."

He drew the diaphanous white pantaloons down from her waist. She stepped out of the froth of white and pirouetted, the broad panels of her skirt swirling. She pressed against him, and his hands went to the catches in her high collar. He fumbled, unable to find their secret, until she stepped back.

160

"Like so," she said, flipping the hooks and eyes open. "Next time you'll know how."

The white *ao-dai*, with its trailing panels and broad sleeves floated to the grass mat. He held her away for an instant, marveling at the upturned breasts and the secret curve of the waist above her swelling hips. Her eyes were wide and her lips drawn back, and her voice was husky. She slipped off her remaining garments with hurried grace.

"Now you," she said urgently.

When her hands plucked at the buttons of his shirt, he realized that he was still fully dressed.

She stepped backward, falling softly when the edge of the bed caught her knees. She lay, white and cream, against its rose spread.

"Now, Gerry, now," she breathed. . . .

Smoking a cigarette and sipping champagne afterward, she said pensively, "a proper Vietnamese maid, a good Confucian girl, is not even supposed to *see* her husband before they are married. But I wanted to seal this pact—whatever it is—and you did not think I was a virgin."

"I didn't think about it," he laughed. "But—the French should say it, if they don't already—a woman without a past is like champagne without bubbles."

"Not so many bubbles," she flared, half-laughing. "A very, very slight past. Never anything like this. Never before. . . ."

"Nor for me . . . Never anything like this before. Not ever through the years."

"But," she said gravely, "it's all right for a man to have a past."

"And for a woman to have a very slight past," he teased.

"Do you really feel so?" she asked.

"Yes," he reassured her, laughing, "as long as it's very, very slight. But the future must be. . . ."

She laid her palm against his mouth, whispering. "We'll talk about the future another day. For this moment, the present is enough. The future? Who dares to pretend he knows?"

"No politics today either," he insisted.

"No, none. No politics—at least until this evening. You said you wanted to see Dr. Thau again."

"Yes, I suppose so. This evening perhaps. But now I want to see and feel and taste only you."

Later, they made love again slowly and languorously. It was relaxed and sweet and, somehow, innocent, after the hectic fire of their first encounter.

In the broad tiled bathroom, naked except for a beflowered bathing cap, she laughed as she threw water at him from a chest-high earthenware jar. Later, lying on the bed, a towel around his waist, he watched with delight as she brushed her hair and touched her face with lotions and powder. She shrugged into a fresh brassière and wriggled into a tiny latex girdle before drawing on nylon stockings.

"What's all this?" he asked. "You're not wearing that gear under an *ao-dai*?"

"I don't feel like an *ao-dai* girl." She smiled, unhooking a green Thai silk sheath from a hanger in the cupboard. "I feel modern and gay and Western. I know the stockings will be hot, but I can't wear this dress without a girdle, and I can't wear a girdle without stockings."

"You'll be sorry later," he warned.

"Probably, but I don't care. I want to pretend I'm in London, Paris, or New York—and I can't do that in an *ao-dai*."

"Shall we go then and see Dr. Thau in Saigon?"

"Dr. Thau, by all means. But not in Saigon. Let's visit him in London."

17

Sipping his Campari and soda, Mallory felt infinitely distant from the throng of young Vietnamese and foreigners. With delicious smugness he watched Tuyelle across the room, remembering the hours past and knowing that they would be together again in a few hours. He would not think beyond tonight and tomorrow. The future must remain in its own keeping.

"The mixture as before," wheezed Dr. Thau in his ear, indicating the crowded room with a sweep of his hand. "Except for young Sergeant Jurgens. Captain Roberts tells me he has been 'shipped out'—that is your American phrase? Suddenly, only this afternoon."

Mallory felt a stab of self-accusation. Had his report produced such quick results? "Was he due for reassignment? Did Roberts know?" he asked.

"No, it was all very sudden. No one seems to know why," answered Thau. "It will make him unhappy. He was writing his master's essay on the power structure in Vietnam. I was able to help him a little. Now he'll not be able to finish it."

"No idea at all why?" persisted Mallory.

"No, as I have said, no real idea," answered Thau, looking at Mallory sharply. "But I can guess. Your military do not approve of men who get too close to the natives. But, tell me, Mr. Mallory, have you made your diagnosis?"

"Just a preliminary one." Abruptly, he decided to be

brutal. "Frankly, I can't see how we Americans can possibly salvage your country."

"Why do you say that?"

"Because you seem unable to do anything for yourselves. Governments come and governments go, but the decay goes on forever."

"Your diagnosis is probably correct, if a bit banal," murmured Thau. "Your prognosis—about that I do not know. But what doctor expects a patient to heal himself after nineteen years of grave illness?"

"A realistic doctor may not expect self-healing, but he must have some co-operation."

"Perhaps, Mr. Mallory, perhaps. Or perhaps his medical knowledge is inadequate."

"It is," stressed Mallory, "good enough to know when a case is hopeless—beyond the reach of medical science or political and military science."

"And what would you advise the American people to do?"

"I don't pretend to have the answer," Mallory said, suddenly chastened. "But I'd say take the National Liberation Front into the government, guarantee neutrality with American air and sea power. Tell the Communists: This is the end. One step further and you will have to deal with our full might."

"Mr. Mallory, are you an admirer of John Foster Dulles?"

"Not particularly. Why?"

"You never advocated a policy based upon massive retaliation?"

"No—and I still don't. But we don't need the big bombs. . . . Blockade, conventional bombing—those threats would restrain the Chinese."

"Hardly." The old man smiled. "A defeated power can hardly expect a victorious enemy to shrink from new threats. You'd rapidly come to nuclear bombs—or nothing. Mr. Mallory, you must either fight it out on the ground or get out, cut your losses."

"Then," said Mallory, pursuing the logical thread, "I'd say get out, cut your losses."

"Mr. Mallory, we Vietnamese risk our liberty, such as it is, and our lives, such as they are." The old man's wheeze sank to an anguished bass. "But the American stake is the greatness of a nation—the pride, perhaps the existence, of a civilization."

"I cannot," said Mallory stubbornly, "see that the stakes are that high."

"You know the Chinese. Their civilization presses ever outward. Now, under the impetus of communism. If it wins here—and it is close, very close—it will continue to press outward. It seeks your destruction."

"Vietnam may be vital to you, sir," Mallory retorted. "But we can stand elsewhere."

"Mr. Mallory," Thau snorted, "you know Mao Tse-tung's tactics too well to talk nonsense. Violent guerrilla revolution everywhere in the underdeveloped world. Vietnam, the ingestion of South Vietnam, it will prove to Mao—and the peoples of the underdeveloped world—that he is right, that his revolution will win everywhere."

"We could," repeated Mallory, "take our stand where the odds are better."

"Where, Mr. Mallory, where in Asia? Encircled, isolated, your communications lines impossible, with the Communists to the north and Indonesia to the south? Each step back makes the next stand a hundred times more difficult."

"We can fight on terrain of our own choice," said Mallory stubbornly.

"Drawing strength from your defeats?" asked Thau.

"Not a defeat, a sensible accommodation to reality."

"That is all Mao wants. He is not seeking mere territory but to discredit your promises. Still, leave aside the native peoples. Do you really believe that America, once having made sweeping concessions, can fight effectively again?"

165

"Of course, Dr. Thau, of course. You don't know the American people."

"Perhaps that is fortunate," said Dr. Thau sharply. "Mr. Mallory, if your are right, my only hope is to flee again—and I am too old. The Communists might still have me. And the attraction of their coming victory becomes well nigh irresistible."

"Then you, too, believe it is inevitable?" Mallory attacked.

"If most Americans think as you do, yes," said the old man wearily. "But I must sit down. Come and talk to our French friend. He thinks as you do—all the French think as one, and all think as you do."

"And why do you think we are wrong? How can you still cherish hope?"

"I do not know that I can," sighed Dr. Thau, the rough vigor gone from his wheezing voice. "Perhaps I do not. Analysis is easy—in the abstract. But against reality, human perversity, I cannot tell."

His mood darkened, Mallory side-stepped the French diplomat. The old man might be right. The catastrophe in the making might be much greater than he had imagined. But for Gerald Mallory there was only one answer: Don't get involved; get what you need out of this mess and get out—the story he needed so badly; Tuyelle, perhaps. Then, get out. He was no Johnny Humboldt to leave his broken body, or even his emotions, bleeding on the soil of Vietnam.

Tuyelle and her cousin Vao, he saw, were standing face to face. Her smile was fixed and she was not drinking from her glass. Vao's lips were drawn back and his eyes smoldered beneath the errant lock of hair. They were arguing; their Vietnamese low, but staccato and quick.

When Mallory joined them, Vao turned away. *"Putain,"* he spat over his shoulder, *"putain Americaine."*

"Gerry," said Tyuelle, clutching his arm. "Let us go. It is not amusing here tonight."

Her heels clicked on the pavement, too fast for the evening's heat. She held her head stiffly on her slender neck, and he saw that her eyes were bright with anger and unshed tears. Except to reject his suggestion that they find a taxi, she did not speak until they had walked several blocks.

"Gerry," she finally asked, "you heard what he called me?"

"Yes, I did. Under other circumstances. . . . But I didn't think you'd welcome a demonstration."

"No," she half-smiled, "that wouldn't have helped."

"What brought on the outburst? My fault?"

"Obviously, in part," she answered impatiently. "But also this dress, the past. So many things. You see, Vao wants to marry me."

Mallory was dismayed at the anger he felt at her flat revelation. Finally he asked brusquely, "And you?"

She glanced up at him, a twisted smile on her lips. But her voice was grave when she answered. "Well, I've thought about it. I like his spirit, his stubborn independence. But a man is what he is, and Vao is a muddled Vietnamese patriot trapped in the crazy maze of Vietnam. There would be no future—even if I wanted him. So, I've never said yes or even maybe, but he won't believe my no."

"Oh," said Mallory without expression. "I see."

This time she laughed aloud. "Don't be a fool, Gerry. If I wanted Vao, I'd have taken him, long before I ever heard of you or Johnny." Her amusement vanished. "But it still hurts. I'm fond of Vao. And it hurts when he calls me an Americans' whore, almost spoils what we have. I told you how he argued before, said I was fleeing myself. Maybe he's right."

"Tuyelle." Mallory spoke urgently. "It may be true, may have been true originally. But what we have—it has nothing to do with race or countries or different cultures."

"Perhaps not," she said slowly.

"Tuyelle." The part of him that always remained an observer was increasingly astonished at his own words. "Tuyelle, he's wrong—and you're wrong. I don't know what Vao wants you to do, perhaps sacrifice yourself nobly. But in this mess, there's only one thing an individual, a person like you, *can* do. Salvage what personal happiness she can. Don't throw yourself into the fire. Don't commit *suttee* on the pyre of Vietnam—or for Vao's violent frustrations. Tuyelle, I love you, and I think I want to marry you."

When her lips parted to speak, he stopped her. "Don't answer now. Don't give me an answer out of bitterness and confusion. I haven't asked you now. I'll ask you again later, when you can think clearly."

"All right, Gerry." She laughed. "It's a strange proposal—reeled back like a trout on a line. All right, Gerry, I haven't heard. You're right; you don't know yet yourself. But you've made me much happier."

Her hand moved down to rest in his, and they walked in silence until they reached her flat. Inside the door Mallory drew her to him. She returned his kiss, at once limp and urgent in his arms, but then pushed him away.

"No, Gerry, not right now. Not yet. I'm hungry and you should be after your exertions and all the emotion. I've got some paté and some cold ham, and some red wine."

With his second glass of wine Mallory spoke hesitantly, his words stilted with embarrassment. "Look, Tuyelle, I hate to bring this up. Humboldt's always been between us. First, he fascinated me; then I half used him as an excuse to see you. Now I don't want to talk about him, but I must."

"Yes, Gerry, go on," she said evenly, but unresponsively.

"Until we know what happened, really happened, to Humboldt," he went on, damning himself for his need to know, "I'll not be free of him. Nor will you. Somehow I have an image—Humboldt wandering beside the Styx unable to go in

168

peace to Hades. We've got to let him in—and free ourselves."

"I don't know. But if you feel that way—it seems we must.
What can we do?"

"The only way, the only thing is to find out. The only
service we can render is to find out exactly what happened.
Is there in truth a villain? Why was Humboldt railroaded
out of Vietnam? Did he shoot himself? Was he murdered?"

"Why do you say that—murdered?" she interrupted.

Mallory told her of the nature of the wound and Calaveri's speculation.

She shook her head, bewildered. "It didn't make sense
when they told me he'd shot himself, but then it did. Now
it doesn't make sense to think he was killed. Who would
want. . . ."

"That's what I'd like to see. If there's really no one, we
can put aside the question of murder and just assume he
was pushed beyond endurance at that moment and killed
himself. That will lay the ghost. . . ."

"Gerry," she said quickly, "I want you to understand one
thing. You may think me heartless, may feel differently about
me. I know now I never loved Johnny, but he needed me,
and I guess I needed him. But not love. I know now. . . ."

"Why so sure?" he asked as gently as he could.

"You see, I never felt for him what I feel for you, and
I don't know if I love you yet. But if we must pursue this,
it doesn't disturb me any more. I can see, we'll have to do
it for your sake, or you'll become as obsessed by Johnny
as he was by Vietnam."

"Whatever the reason, then, let's go on. . . This is what I
know. Humboldt was drinking too much, seeing too many
Vietnamese, and, above all, talking too much. The Army
decided to ship him out. Depressed, perhaps feeling dis-
honored, he snatched a gun and shot himself. That's the
official version, and it makes perfect sense, except. . . ."

169

"Yes," she prompted.

"Except for one thing. Why quite so much fuss and mystery? Why a cover-up job so quick even the PIO knew it would arouse suspicion? And why wouldn't they even listen to Calaveri when he claimed Humboldt might have been murdered?"

She shook her head decisively. "Now, when I think, Johnny would not have committed suicide. He was depressed and worried those last few days, but suicide, never. He seemed to be working himself up to an important decision. He talked always of finding himself—finally."

"Suppose they'd threatened to tell his wife about you? She's supposed to be a bitch, and she controlled the money."

"No, that wouldn't frighten him. I did not tell you, but I must now. He had asked me to marry him."

"What did you say?" His tone was not detached.

"I said I did not know. But he had already written her, telling her they must divorce."

His voice was under control again. "Suicide to escape blackmail—that's out. And you hadn't said no, not definitely?"

"Gerry, you flatter me. Johnny would not have suicided because I said no. It is a nice-eerie thought for a girl, but not true."

"Then we'll say no suicide. But how could it have been murder? According to Calaveri, Humboldt and this Vietnamese officer were alone together for about three minutes. Somebody must have grabbed the officer's gun, shot him when he resisted, and then Humboldt. But there were guards all around. No one could have escaped."

"It could have been one of the guards," she said. "What does the Vietnamese officer say—or couldn't you find out?"

"I couldn't—and no one can. Tham died in the hospital."

"But one of the guards, the MP's around, might have. . ."

170

Her voice trailed off. Abruptly she asked, "What did you say the Vietnamese officer's name was?"

"Didn't you know? I've got it here somewhere," he said, turning over the pages of his notebook.

"No, I was told nothing, except not to inquire too closely."

"Here it is. Tham, Pham-quot Tham."

"Pham-quot Tham . . . Was his father? It must be the same. Look, Gerry, Pham-quot Thai was an important man in Hanoi. He had a son named Tham, who was in the Viet Minh Regular Army. They both deserted—I don't know exactly why, but it was something to do with a purge. They defected, and the father became an adviser to Ngo-dinh Nhu's secret police. He was killed when Nhu was killed. The son was a strange man. He believed in nothing, but he had a brutal mind, a Marxist mind. Does this mean anything?"

"It could mean a lot," he said. "Tham is really the only man who could have done the job. We never throught—because he died. But he could have forced Humboldt into the sentry box so they'd be unobserved. A struggle for the gun—Humboldt was much bigger—Tham shot and Humboldt recoiling in shock. Tham picks up the gun again and does the job he was ordered to do."

"But if Tham killed Johnny—why? Why? Even if he were working for a faction or even the Communists. What had Johnny done to them?"

"I don't know, Tuyelle. I'm stuck. Maybe that's where you can help. Perhaps—but, no, that's too ridiculous. No, we'll have to see if you know anything more."

"What's too ridiculous?"

"Well," he began sheepishly, wondering how he could tell her enough without telling her too much about his own weakness in allowing Gilroy to blackmail him. "I knew when I came down here—I can't explain exactly how—but I knew the Americans were very disturbed. Maybe it's what Humboldt *could* have done, not what he *had* already done."

"You started to tell me," she reminded him.

"Yes, I'm sorry. . . . Well, the Americans were—are—disturbed. There have been too many operations ruined because the Vietcong got the word long beforehand. The Americans naturally say it must be a Vietnamese source. But, privately, they think it could be American. . . ."

"So?" she prompted. "What's that to do with Johnny."

"You said he was on the verge of a major decision. Could he have been suspicious of some American but afraid to talk? Was he brooding, and did someone discover it and decided to get rid of him?"

"I don't know. All I know he was brooding about some decision. Look here, Gerry, we'll never get beyond this point. Can't we drop it for a while?"

"No," he shook his head, "we can't. We've got to go on, even if—I thought my Vietcong leader was bragging when he said American officers were helping him. But, if they were, if Humboldt knew, then it would make perfect sense to sacrifice Tham to protect the sources."

"I suppose so," she said crisply. "But finish your paté. At least that's real."

"Bear with me a while longer, please. There must be some way."

"Did you read his papers?" she asked. "Was there anything there?"

"No, nothing," he answered—except a fragment. I'd like you to have a look. But it's more material for a Ph.D. thesis. . ."

She smoothed the crumpled sheet out on the table and shook her head. "No, I don't recall this sheet. But two nights before his death he was a little tight, and he worked for an hour on something he said I couldn't see. Not much typing, but lots of correcting—maybe it was this."

She read carefully, then shook her head again decisively. "Gerry, this is just a garble to me. Why can't we forget it? We're not getting anywhere. And it's becoming too much for me."

He was contrite. "I'm sorry. I've pushed you too hard. Let's stop—for a while at least."

Mallory knew he was treading the edge of an emotional chasm. He had been foolish—even brutal—to accept her assurances that the examination would not distrub her. Nonetheless, when she left the room to make coffee, he spread the single sheet out again.

He was a taught man [the words, now familiar, sprang out at him], needleskin and tacilturn. His face was taut to play the jests and prey for rain. Armageddon on and on, deeper and deeper, nearer, my guard, to see eternity in an upturned howl or, beside the flowing Babylonian, hands sans skill to sit. He props a coin into an eerie and up comes Jack potted, Joe potted, Tham potted, all potted they. Pease potted hot or cold? Hot, I say, but hot to do? And how? Emeraldcund, oh thy jacket others for, to cross or not to cross? Double-cross, iron-cross, knight's cross, criss-cross. But how? Wrapped in coins, dispensing coins, stealing coins, coining coins, and living coins that he should live.

Mallory shook his head wearily. The passage made a certain wild sense, if he assumed that it was a description. But who could it be? Was his spy theory in any way compatible with this twisted verbiage? He read it through again, rubbing his hand across his head in perplexity. Among the interlined and crossed-out typescript at the bottom of the page, a handwritten scrawl stood out: "Rarely such betrayal, but can I be sure?"

Tuyelle's voice broke his train of thought. "If you must. I suppose you must, or you'll become as driven as he. Oh, God, not another holy fool on my hands. I thought this was a man. But, if I must, how can I help?"

"Just hear me out, Tuyelle. I promise I'll drop it soon."

"All right," she conceded.

173

"I've already worked out part, the first part. I'm assuming he's describing our putative spy. The first part anyway: A thin man, who is very quiet and aloof. You see, he's taut or thin, thin as a needle, and quiet, taciturn, but aloof, not wanting to be touched; therefore the tactile or tacilturn. It's ingenious enough."

"If you say so." Her voice was dull.

"Then, substitute 'taught' for 'taut' and you get a man skilled at concealing his emotions, a man 'taught' to live a jest or a role, while he preys on those around him and prays—for rain? That makes no sense. But reign, power—yes. Armageddon, a moment of decision, or the Apocalypse, besides the obvious pun 'I'm a gettin' on and on. And he, Humboldt, is getting deeper and deeper, working toward his decision. It must lead—but where? Oh, I think I see. He'll be guarded or, alternately, if he howls—speaks up, presumably—he'll meet eternity, be destroyed. And otherwise? 'Beside the flowing Babylonian, hands sans skill to sit.' That's easy."

"I'm glad *you* think so," observed Tuyelle. "Your nonsense is beginning to be as nonsensical as Johnny's."

"Yes, it is easy," he insisted. "The 'flowing Babylonian' must be the waters of Babylon, and to sit beside them without skill. Do you remember: 'And if I forget thee, Oh Jerusalem, let my right hand forget its cunning.' The alternative to possible death is a betrayal and the moral punishment: to do nothing and live, punished by conscience. I'm sure he's stating his own dilemma here. And you see what it means— he expected death for speaking up."

"Then," she offered, "it must have been murder."

"If he spoke up, yes. It could have been. Certainly there's no evidence that he was thinking of killing himself."

"Go on, Gerry!" She was anxious now. "This is beyond my English. But maybe you are making sense."

"The next sentence still mystifies me. 'He props a coin into an eerie and up comes Jack potted, Joe potted, Tham potted, all potted they.' A coin is a coin, and the reference

174

appears to be to a slot machine, but I can't see how that works in. What about 'potted'? Let's see the dictionary."

She handed him the familiar, blue-covered Concise Oxford Dictionary.

"Here it is," he said with excitement. "I'm sure we're getting his meaning. 'Pot, v.t. & i.'"—we'll skip the first part—'bag (game), kill (animal) by potshot; shoot. . . Jack, Joe, and Tham—Americans and Vietnamese shot because 'He props a coin into an eerie.' What could the coin be?"

He ran his hand through his hair in perplexity. Lighting a Camel, he leaned back and said, "Tuyelle, maybe we ought to take a break."

"No," she said, "you're getting it. Don't stop. You know I've heard the English say somebody 'potted' somebody else, when they didn't mean shoot or kill."

"Of course." Mallory grinned. "It means to reveal wrong-doing, to inform on. The coin in the eerie—whatever it may be—is the information that gets the Americans and Vietnamese shot. A spy again. Coin must be information, popped into an eerie—eer. . ., ear. That's it—an ear, a mysterious ear, an eerie, in short. But 'coin'? Let's look in the dictionary again, maybe. . . ."

"There is," she offered, "also 'coign,' meaning 'place affording good view of something.' Does that help? A spy would need a coign."

"The person who gave him the information could be his 'coign.' But that doesn't explain all the coins later. What does it say for the ordinary spelling?"

She skimmed through the entry, muttering, "No, not that. Not that. But, here, it has something to do with words, making words. Words are information, aren't they?"

"Yes, indeed. Yes, they are. So information into a mysterious ear and men get killed. That's what an informer sells. Besides, words are the coins of communication. Let's take it at that."

"The next, I do not understand," she said.

"But that's the most obvious. 'Pease potted hot or cold? Hot, I say, but hot to do? And how?' Don't you know the old nursery rhyme: 'Pease porridge hot, pease porridge cold'? He was hot to do something about the spy, but wondered how. No, that's easy; but the next three sentences evade me. 'Emeraldcund, oh thy jacket others for, to cross or not to cross? Double-cross, iron-cross, knight's cross, criss-cross. But how?"

"Skip them and come back later."

"All right," he agreed. "What do we make of this, 'Wrapped in coins, dispensing coins, stealing coins, coining coins, and living coins that he should live.'?"

"You said coin could mean 'word.' Try it."

"All right then. We have a man who is wrapped in words, dispenses words, steals words, coins words, and lives words. A man who makes his living by words. That would fit me, a correspondent, a newspaperman, or a politican or a teacher—even a PIO. It's too broad, but we do know it's someone who lives by words."

"Maybe that passage we skipped—maybe that would help."

"I'll try, but it's got me stymied, I'm afraid. 'Emerald-cund.' An emerald is a jewel, a stone, a gem. But how does 'cund' work in. We've got to assume a direct meaning or else it's all gibberish. We've found direct meanings else-where—jewelcund, stonecund, gemcund—that's meaningless. What about other stones. Diamondcund, sapphirecund, ruby-cund, pearlcund . . ."

"There's a word there," she interrupted. "I heard a word. Do it again."

"Diamundcund, sapphirecund, rubycund, pearlcund—ruby-cund, rubicund. Let's look at the dictionary again. 'Rubi-cund, (of face, complexion, or person in these respects), ruddy, high-colored.' It's another word describing the in-former. We're moving Tuyelle; we're moving. And look, just before it, rubicon. . . 'to cross or not to cross?' He's mixing *Hamlet* and *Julius Caesar*."

176

"Read me those sentences again," she asked.

"Here you are: 'Emeraldcund, oh thy jacket others for, to cross or not to cross? Double-cross, iron-cross, knight's cross, criss-cross. But how?' It does make sense, it does. Here, look—'oh thy jacket others for,'—did you ever read Caesar? After he makes the decision to cross the Rubicon, he says, *Jacet alea est,* the die is cast. 'Jacket'—it must be cast, and he makes decisions for others as well. And all that cross business, I'll take it as fairly straight. 'Double-cross' is straightforward in this situation. 'Iron-cross, knight's cross'— maybe just playing with the words, maybe some sort of German connection."

He put the paper down and spoke, suddenly subdued. "Tuyelle, we've got a message, but Johnny was too clever. It's still concealed."

"Why don't you write the whole thing down according to your guesses? Maybe when we see it all together. . . ."

After working for twenty minutes, Mallory produced a curious document.

He (the informer) a thin man, very quiet and aloof, skilled at concealing his emotions, playing a role, and victimizing others in his quest for power. The moment of decision or revelation is approaching, because I (Humboldt) am getting deeper and deeper into this business. I'll either end up guarded or dead, if I speak up; or live the rest of my life with a burden on my conscience, if I do not. He (the informer) passes information mysteriously, and Americans and Vietnamese, informed upon, are shot. I (Humboldt) am wavering, but I think I know and I want to speak up. My problem is how? [Why is this a problem?] The spy is ruddy of complexion, and he decides the fates of others, but I (Humboldt) must make up my own mind to reveal this double-cross and confusion. Finally, the spy is deeply involved with words, living by them, not only as a spy but in his public character.

Mallory pushed the paper away in disgust and asked, "Tuyelle, have you got some cognac? Let's go to bed with a bottle of cognac—and to hell with this."

177

"That's an abrupt proposition." She smiled. "Will champagne do?"

"Yes," he answered, rising. "But—wait a minute—let's take one more crack at this. Let's put together all the descriptive material and leave out Humboldt's own dilemma."

After five minutes Mallory had another sheet of paper before him.

A thin man, very thin, but ruddy of complexion. Very quiet and aloof, playing a public role involving words. His information leads to the deaths of men.

"Do you," he asked, "know anyone who remotely fits that description? I don't—except for my old friend, Colonel McGuffey. But that's ridiculous."

"Why ridiculous?" She bridled. "Just because he's an old friend? Don't dismiss him so quickly."

"All right," Mallory agreed. "But who else? Or maybe we could reason backward. . . . Whom was Humboldt interested in?"

"Dr. Thau," she said hesitantly, "who was almost his mentor. And, who else? Well, of course, Colonel Taylor, his commanding officer; Jim Hooghly, with whom he worked; and George Dietrich, who fascinated him. A living fossil, he used to say. Also Vao. But that's ridiculous."

"Don't rule out anyone," he reminded her. "So we have McGuffey, who fits the physical description; and Thau, Taylor, Dietrich, and Vao, who do not. Shall I denounce McGuffey tomorrow morning?"

She did not answer immediately, for she was musing. "Backward, backward reasoning you said. . . ."

"Yes," he jumped in, "and emeraldcund was backward, green for red. Then the spy might be noisy and fat, as well as thin and quiet. That would fit Dr. Thau or Dietrich. But the way they talk—it's inconceivable."

"They would talk that way, wouldn't they?" she asked tartly.

178

"All right. McGuff, but there's no corroborating evidence. Thau, a perfect choice. He's fat and highly articulate. He associates with American and Vietnamese officers. He's convinced the Communists will win, and he knows everyone. Thau fits best. Hooghly and Vao—you'd have to wrench the facts to fit either one, but let's include them. And, finally, Dietrich."

"What about Dietrich?" she asked.

"Well," he answered, "he's fat and outspoken. There's your opposite; there's the twist. But he's committed up to his neck to the status quo. I can't imagine Dietrich and the Vietcong leader I saw sitting down to a cup of tea or a chat about objets d'art."

He paused to light a cigarette, then resumed. "But Dietrich—he doesn't quite make sense. Those objets d'art, those objets d'art . . . Tuyelle, it's crazy, but I'd swear I saw the same Chinese ink box at Dietrich's in the morning and the Vietcong leader's that evening. Light blue, an odd light blue, one hinge broken—what a wonderful way to pass a message. Repair me this box, master craftsman, do. And, inside, a slip of paper."

"It must be Dietrich," she interjected. "It must be."

"Don't rule anyone out," he reminded her. "There are thousands of Chinese ink boxes in Saigon, dozens of bright blue ones, no doubt. Thau, Dietrich, McGuff, Vao, and Hooghly, maybe Taylor, in that order."

"Gerry," she asked abruptly, "what was your lunch with Dietrich like?"

"Why, I told you, pointless, unless he wanted to convince me South Vietnam couldn't survive. Yes, I see what you mean. If he were what we're thinking, that lunch would make sense. Not otherwise. Still, you're assuming that he controls people like a puppet master. I still like Thau—he fits best of all, it seems to me."

He folded the papers neatly and slipped them into his pocket. "Look," he said, "I'll write a letter to a guy I know.

I'll tell him what we've worked out—Thau, McGuff, Dietrich, Vao, Taylor, or Hooghly. Let him do the donkey work. Then we'll have done our duty and I'll have a hell of a dramatic intro for my piece."

"And now? The champagne?" she asked.

"And now, the champagne," he agreed, taking her hand.

18

The two yellow bulldozers, one enormous, the other smaller, sported on the edge of the clearing like an elephant dam and her calf. Roaring, sputtering, and whining, the big bulldozer knocked down scattered trees to enlarge the open space. The smaller followed, heaping the trunks and loose earth into rough defensive breastworks. The Vietnamese soldiers at their controls were sweating heavily, though it was only eight in the morning.

Mallory, watching, pulled his mind back to the present, still wondering if he had made a fool of himself. Early that morning, with Tuyelle's scent still breathing warmly from his own skin, he had sat down at his typewriter. He had ignored his own misgivings, suspending disbelief to state the varying cases against each of the six men: McGuffey, Thau, Dietrich, Taylor, Vao, and Hooghly. Copy-reading the typescript, he had half convinced himself, enough at least to scrawl broadly at the bottom of the last sheet: "Over to you, pal. The amateurs have done the groundwork. Let's see if the pros can finish the job." Then he had slipped Humboldt's obscure message into the envelope together with his own interpretation.

Smoking his last cigarette, he had wondered whether Gilroy would reject the entire hypothesis because of its mock-literary basis, or would, instead, be intrigued by the code. Well, he had concluded, crushing out the cigarette, he had done all he could. He was free, free of Humboldt and free of Gilroy. He'd actually done much more than Gilroy had demanded.

Levoncier had awakened him a few hours later, even his buoyant spirits burdened by the hour and the prospect of spending two or three days on the High Plateau.

"Still no sleep, Gerry? This is not recommended for a growing pundit."

Despite his own exhaustion, Mallory had felt renewed relief on dropping the letter off with the Marine guard at the embassy. Two hours' sleep in the light plane and then the helicopter had almost washed the preoccupation from his mind, and the dry air of the highlands was completing the catharsis, leaving him wholly detached from the perplexities and the joys of Saigon.

The bulldozers had almost finished their work when the helicopter landed. The trees were sparse, not like the luxuriant growth of the true jungle, and the bulldozers' job was just to tidy up. Aside from the scattered groves, the green earth stretched in a clean sweep, unbroken in a shallow bowl to the far horizon. After the fetid damp of the lowlands, it was a fresher world where hope did not seem quite so far away.

Vietnamese soldiers in dappled camouflage suits were staking out tents, assisted by a few tribesmen in breechclouts with blankets rolled around their shoulders. An American jeep, long aerial whipping, jounced up beside Levoncier and Mallory. A spare figure, wearing the silver eagles of a full Colonel, stepped out, and Mallory saw with surprise that it was Harkness, the Special Forces officer.

"Good morning, Jack," he said, "or do I call you Colonel?"

"Morning, Gerry, Pierre," answered Harkness, right hand working his red-handled exerciser. "Just call me Jack."

"I see," said Mallory, obdurately clinging to his question, "that congratulations are in order, really double congratulations. You seem to have skipped a grade."

"Not really," answered Harkness slowly. "My boss couldn't

make it today, but we thought we'd better have some rank around. This is going to be a big one."

"What's your rank, really, Jack?" Mallory persisted. "If it's all right to ask."

"Sure it's okay, Gerry. Light Colonel, really, but we go up and down as we need to."

From over the western horizon shots echoed, and Harkness turned abruptly toward the slight Chinese wearing First Lieutenant's silver bars, who sat behind the Vietnamese driver, a microphone in his hand.

"What is it, Lee?" he asked.

"I'm not getting anything yet, sir, but I'll keep on it," the answer came in the unmistakable accents of Los Angeles.

"Let me know as soon as you do," ordered Harkness tensely. He grinned, relaxed again. "Lee's a civil engineer by trade, but he knew a few words of Cantonese from his parents, so they decided to make him a Vietnamese linguist. Biggest surprise—he's turned out to be damned good."

"Is it not a bit early in the proceedings for the salutes of victory?" asked Levoncier, who had been crouching, focusing his camera on Harkness and Mallory outlined against the sun in the east.

"No, Pierre, we expected a little opposition. The net is flung . . ."

"Colonel," interrupted the Lieutenant from the jeep, "I'm getting something. Column B ran into a small ambush. It's all over now. Whole thing lasted about thirty seconds. They think they killed a couple, but they're not sure."

"Okay, Lee. Stay on the microphone," said Harkness. "No, Pierre, rounding up two to three thousand *montagnards* from maybe twenty villages, we were sure we'd run into a little opposition. But this time we've got surprise on our side, and the VC won't have time to position themselves. There'll be no big attacks, nothing we can't handle."

"But is it not a little early for the shooting?" Levoncier persisted.

183

"Maybe, Pierre, maybe. But I'm not worried. We're bound to get some. Still," Harkness broke off to shout at the Lieutenant, "Anything else, Lee?"

"Yes, sir. Doyle has just come through. Blood marks, but no VC bodies. And," the lieutenant laughed, "three casualties on our side."

"What's so funny about that?" demanded Mallory.

"Well, sir, one old lady was hit in the ass by a spent bullet. A bullock lost a horn, one horn. And Major Doyle's sore as hell because a burst messed up his knapsack. He's dripping wine all over, he says."

Levoncier was poised against the sky, right hand pointing west. "Look over there," he exclaimed. *"Mon Dieu,* the houses here, they are walking by themselves."

A dark column was spilling over the edge of the horizon into the bowl. The surrounding cloud of dust was pierced by the sun's brilliance.

"Our first guests," said Harkness with satisfaction. "Column A right on time. There, now—now you can see better. You'll notice each blob is a yoke of oxen and a cart, some of them carrying houses. This time we're doing it right. We've got to move them. But wherever we can, we're moving houses and everything. No reason to make them any sorer than they'll be anyway."

"Look, Jack," Mallory asked, "I get the general picture of a mass relocation, but could you fill in the details for me?"

"Sure, Gerry, sure." Harkness was completely relaxed again, the hand-exerciser working rhythmically. "But, first, how about a cup of coffee?"

He strolled over to the jeep and Lee handed him a basket, from which he drew four cups and a gallon Thermos jug. "We've learned one thing from the French," he said. "Any fool can be uncomfortable in the field, but the wise man is comfortable."

"And, perhaps, another contribution from France," offered Levoncier, producing his silver flask of cognac.

184

"With thanks, Pierre, *beaucoup merci*," said Harkness, spreading a map on the back of the jeep. "You really want a briefing, Gerry? There won't be much you don't already know."

"Yes, please," Mallory answered.

"All right. Here we go again. We're about here." The dark forefinger stabbed down on a red cross on the map. "About seventy-five miles northeast of Khonthum, maybe twenty miles from the border, the Laotian border. Up in those hills," the forefinger traced a semicircle to the west of the cross, "are the *montagnard* villages, little clusters of the Radhe and the Jerbrai, with a few Black Thais thrown in. At dusk yesterday paratroop sections hit every village. Right now the columns, six in all, are beginning to roll. By evening we'll have them all down here and in two other enclosures we're preparing."

"Won't the paradrops alert the VC?" asked Mallory.

"Oh, they'll know something's going on, but we have a pretty good idea how they're operating. Small units, ten to twenty men, not the hundreds they use in the Camau. This is primarily a supply area for them. It would take them at least thirty-six hours to put together a unit big enough to bother us. And we've got planes, helicopters, and a couple of Ranger companies in reserve over here on this airstrip. No, this time it's been well-planned."

"I'll take your word for it," said Mallory. "Now what's the point of this operation? How do I fit it into the over-all picture?"

"Simple. The tactical purpose is depriving the VC's in the hills of food, recruits, and intelligence—just like the Limeys did in Malaya. Food's short here and you can use food denial tactics. Then we get the *montagnards* in a huddle and they're protected. We can work on them, try to mellow their hostility."

"Hostility toward whom?"

"The Vietnamese, naturally, *mon cher*," interrupted Levoncier. "The *montagnards* hate the Vietnamese, and the Vietnamese treat them like pigs. When we ruled this country, we French, we would not let Vietnamese settle here on the High Plateau along the borders of Laos. I think we were not so wrong, Jack?"

"Well, it didn't do much good, Pierre. That's one reason for the hostility today. But the Vietnamese are pretty rough on these people, kick them around, try to get sky-high taxes, ban their liquor, take their women and goods. They despise them as *kha* or *kau*, whichever word you prefer, but it means savages anyway. You know, we've got a dozen Americans who can get along in a tribal language, but I know only one Vietnamese who can."

"Maybe you ought to be re-educating the Vietnamese instead of the *montagnards*," suggested Mallory.

"Maybe we should." Harkness grinned. "But we can only do what is possible. Anyway, the idea is to cut the underpinnings from the VC here by moving the people. Mao Tse-tung said, 'The guerrilla swims among the people like a fish through water.' If we take away the water, we hope we'll leave the VC high and dry."

"Why here? Why the concentration on a few thousand *montagnards*, when the real trouble is in the lowlands?" Mallory asked.

"Not a few thousand," corrected Harkness, "maybe seven hundred thousand in all. We can't handle them all now, obviously. But if we can clean up a few key areas, it'll go a long way."

"A long way toward what?"

"Gerry, that gets us into the strategic picture, the general picture. I'm sure you know—do you really want me to tell you?"

"Yes, please, again. I may have some ideas. But you know a hell of a lot I don't."

"All right." Harkness sighed. "If you want it. If you'll look at this large-scale map with the markings, you'll *see* why.

Guerrillas have never won in Asia except when they could resupply across a convenient border. You'll remember the Viet Minh couldn't fight the battle at Dienbienphu, which knocked out the French, till they had a road and rail network direct to China. But right now the fortifications along the seventeenth parallel, the armistice line, pretty much cut off resupply. Instead, men, equipment, everything the VC needs to expand, comes through these mountain passes from North Vietnam through Laos and into South Vietnam through these other passes and over the High Plateau. If we can cut off the help the Vietcong infiltrators are getting from the *montagnards,* the theory goes, we will have stymied them."

"Will it work?" asked Mallory.

Harkness looked at him quizzically, the green flecks glowing in his iodine-colored eyes. "Off the record?" he asked.

"Not for attribution," Mallory said automatically, closing his notebook reassuringly.

"Okay then. In my opinion—my *personal* opinion—no, it won't. There will still be plenty of empty space for the VC to come through, even if they can't drop into villages where the chief's daughters have married agents. Besides, we can't move all the *montagnards* in any kind of time. Now, if we could get their co-operation, it might, I said might, be a step toward sealing the border. But this way—no."

"What would help?"

"Again my *personal* opinion. The only way is to hit the routes, the routes and supply bases in Laos. That would really stop the resupply operation—and give the Vietnamese a hell of a morale boost. But that's outside my scope, that's high policy."

"Yeah, I can see why," Mallory agreed. "What about bombing North Vietnam or hit-and-run raids up there? Put the pressure on the Communists to stop pushing this action down here?"

"Bombings, no," answered Harkness. "Too public, too much chance of making this thing bigger. Counter-guerrilla

187

raids, yes. Weaken their hold on their own people, make them worry about themselves. If things got really bad, we'd have to think about bombing. But I, personally, don't like the idea. Too risky—and not very effective."

"Two questions, Jack: Could the South Vietnamese stage those raids in the North? And wouldn't any fiddling around in Laos also broaden the scope—or carry such a risk?"

"Question number one: I don't know, really. Maybe, with our discreet help, yes. Question number two: Small raids, even bombing targets in Laos wouldn't put Chinese prestige on the line like a concerted bombing of North Vietnam. I think even if we had to put a few of our own battalions into Laos, we could get away with it. But, hell, you've got to take some risks in war."

"And the way we're going? Where will we end up?"

"We'll get pushed out slowly," said Harkness decisively. "Lee here agrees with me—and he knows the Chinese."

"Yeah," said the Lieutenant. "I know my mom and pop. Me only humble coolie boy. But, Dad, this man's talking sense, real cool sense."

"You guys are close to insubordination, aren't you?" Mallory probed.

"For Chris' sake, no. We carry out orders, but we're allowed to think. Besides, I'm not MacArthur and you're not going to quote us—are you, Gerry?" Harkness' voice hardened.

"No, Jack, relax. I was just needling you. Let's have another cup. . . ."

The radio crackled and Lee leaned forward listening intently through one earphone. His face grew somber. "Boss," he said, "we've got trouble."

"What's up?" snapped Harkness.

"I'm not sure yet. Doyle's not sure. But he thinks they're getting hit by a big one."

"Send him a section for effect, but hold the rest back till we know."

188

"Yes, sir," said the Lieutenant. He spoke urgently into the microphone, giving the column's position in a series of letter-number combinations.

When the immediate tension had passed, Mallory said quietly, "I thought you guys were just advisors."

"Let's say," said Harkness, "that we're assisting the Vietnamese Army in its communications. Taking the load off their own facilities."

His hand-exerciser had disappeared in the sleight-of-hand trick now familiar to Mallory, and he was puffing heavily on a cigarette.

"Here's some more, Colonel," said Lee. "It's clear. Shall I put it on the loudspeaker?"

"Yeah, go ahead."

". . .estimate force of three to six hundred with mortars and machine guns," a metallic voice spoke out of the radio set. "We're not pinned down, but we could be soon. Forward motion slowing now."

"Doyle," Harkness spoke into the microphone, "do you read me?"

"Loud and clear," said the radio.

"Can you hold? How long can you hold?"

"Shucks, Boss, all day—if we didn't have these tribesfolk. But they're milling around like stampeding cattle. It's getting rough."

"Keep moving, Doyle, you've got to keep moving forward," Harkness ordered. "There's a clearing a couple of hundred yards ahead of you. Get behind the *montagnards* and drive them."

"Damnedest round up I ever saw," the radio grumbled. "But the Viets'll love that job."

"I've sent you a section. I'm coming in with the rest of the company. I'll speak to you again shortly. Over and out."

"Out," the loudspeaker crackled.

Harkness had already swung himself into the jeep. Levoncier and Mallory followed, as it bounced over the uneven field. Levoncier, who was checking his camera gear, pulled a .32 caliber revolver out of his leather bag.

"Here, Gerry, you'd better take this."

"Hell, no. What for? They're using big stuff, not pop guns."

"If they get close—you never know. Take it."

"Okay," assented Mallory reluctantly, and pushed the revolver into his pocket. He turned to Harkness, who was lighting one cigarette from the butt of another. "What now, Jack? How do you figure this?"

"They must have gotten word," Harkness said bitterly. "Somebody must've tipped them—again. They could never get that many men together otherwise."

"What are you planning?"

"The Viets'll co-operate, I'm sure. General Cao's a good man. We'll go in to the clearing and push up the trail, if Doyle's stuck. I've called in some air too, but the jungle's so thick over that ridge of hills they'll be firing blind—mostly to scare the VC. We'll just have to get Doyle and his people to the clearing. Take them out by chopper, if we have to."

"How many people?"

"I'd say about five, six hundred tribespeople—men, women, and kids. Maybe two fifty, three hundred Vietnamese soldiers and Americans. It's a fair-sized show."

"Just for clarity's sake, Jack," Mallory continued, "Isn't a column that size awfully vulnerable?"

"Oh, course, Gerry," Harkness said impatiently. "But we were playing it smart. Figured surprise would let us move the big groups. If we trickled it out over days, we figured, the VC would get to know. Damned smart, we've been."

"You're sure they were tipped? Where from?"

"Absolutely, damn it. And it must have been from Saigon. Nobody up here got orders till yesterday morning. And I know the VC couldn't—they just couldn't—have put a battalion together without forty-eight hours notice. Right smack on the trail—hitting the biggest column, too."

Lee cut in. "It's okay, Boss, General Cao's going along. Troops getting airborne. Some first-class bitching from the Viet Major commanding Doyle's column. Our chopper's coming for us."

"Thanks, Lee," said Harkness absently. "That son of a bitch should be fighting, not talking. Well, thank God we haven't screwed up the co-ordination this time."

The elongated HUEY took off as soon as the four had clambered into the cabin. Harkness leaned over the American pilot's shoulder, shouting, "Go low, get real low down and let me have a look before we go in."

As the helicopter, surprisingly noiseless, skimmed over the first ridge of hills to the west, Mallory saw two big passenger helicopters appear from the southeast.

"The lead platoon coming in," said Lee, nudging him. "They're really moving fast today."

"Don't they always?"

A broad grin cracked his small Chinese face, and Lee asked incredulously, "Man, are you kidding?"

Mallory closed his eyes, surrendering himself to the misery of exhaustion. He started upright when he felt a hard object digging into his ribs. Levoncier was smiling at him and pulling his elbow back for another nudge.

"Wake up, Gerry," he said. "We are about to land."

"Thanks, Pierre. How long was I asleep?"

"About fifteen minutes. I have a magnificent picture of the cool warrior going into combat. We got a little bit lost, but the pilot says he is sure we are right this time. The troops are already in."

Mallory stretched wearily, suddenly realizing with a rush of pleasure that he was no more afraid than he had a right to be. The HUEY was racing along, almost level with its vanguard shadow, about twenty-five feet over the top of an

191

irregular, wooly-green coverlet. Mallory saw a small opening ahead and heard the irregular crump of mortars, interspersed with the crackle of small arms and deeper, coughing explosions.

"Recoiless rifles," Levoncier explained. "Pray God they don't blow themselves up when the shells bounce off the trees."

"Doyle knows what he's doing," Lee interjected. "If he's using the rifles, there's a field of fire."

"And the Vietnamese, Major?" Levoncier asked with a grin.

The Chinese Lieutenant halted his struggle into a backpack radio to shrug his shoulders in a pantomime of despairing ignorance. Then he brightened. "But if they're just making a big boom, then the VC mortars can't be doing much damage either."

The helicopter circled wide, the explosions growing louder at a point almost due west of the clearing. Under that comforting coverlet, men were shooting at each other, but not a tree stirred. The helicopter landed heavily in the clearing and was airborne again before Mallory could regain his feet after jumping out.

"Let's go," Harkness shouted, starting at a jog trot after the heavily-laden Vietnamese soldiers who were just disappearing into the shadowed trail.

After the narrow jungle paths of the Philippines and Malaya, this trail was a broad highway. The vegetation had been crushed into firmness by generations of feet, hooves, and wooden wheels. But the space was no more than six feet wide, and the secondary jungle was dark green on either side, exhaling the fecund smell of decaying plants.

After fifteen minutes, moving toward the sound of gunfire, they met the vanguard. At the same jog trot, Harkness passed the apparitions that had materialized on the jungle path. The seven Vietnamese soldiers were soaking wet, their faces smudged, and their camouflage suits torn and discolored. A

192

shot cut the air near Mallory's shoulder and he threw himself into the mold at the edge of the trees.

Around the bend of the trail, over the gunfire, Mallory heard a baby cry amid the howling of dogs. The trail was blocked by a tangle of ox carts and animals and tribespeople, the men in breechclouts, the women in short black kilts, their pendulous breasts bare beneath broad necklaces of coins. The second cart, Mallory saw with rising incredulity, was pushed to the side of the trail, the oxen dead in the traces and a thatched hut with soaring eaves sagging at a crazy angle from on top of the cart. A handful of soldiers urged the tribespeople forward. A crackle of gunfire rose and fell within the jungle.

"It is moving day on the *Haut Plateau*," shouted Levoncier over his shoulder, as he dived into the tangle, meanwhile unscrewing his telephoto lens. Mallory followed Harkness and Lee, clinging to the cover of the trees. On a cart in the center of the trail, a tribesman sat on the body of another, urging a pair of maddened oxen on. On another cart, stalled amid the turmoil, a woman wept over the body of a man without legs, heedless alike of the throng pressing behind her and of the cries of a boy of about seven who pulled at her kilt with bloody hands. Two smaller forms lay in a pool of blood where the green-brown floor of the trail was littered with broken earthenware cooking pots. The dirty pink hide and the patches of yellow fur mingled together had been a dog and a pig, apparently destroyed by the same explosion that had killed the man. A cock, hanging head down from the leadpole of the next cart, crowed in a mindless wail of terror.

Harkness was talking to a tall figure with a black face. Only when Mallory came close enough to smell wine fumes and see the red hair beneath the shapeless jungle hat did he realize it must be Major Doyle.

Lee pushed his earphones away from one ear and said, "Lead elements of the reinforcements coming up the trail."

Harkness snapped, "Tell them for God's sake not to come up four abreast singing the *Marseillaise*. How bad is it, Doyle?"

"Pretty bad, Jack, pretty bad," drawled the red-haired Major. "Most of my boys are off in the jungle. The VC—they've drawn back. But I'm figuring they'll be on us again soon. Maybe those reinforcements ought to make a lot of noise."

"What about casualties?"

"Military, not so bad. Few wounds, maybe couple, half-dozen dead far as I can see. But the poor damned Indians—they've caught it."

"I saw," said Harkness shortly.

"You ain't seen nothing yet. The Viets did almost as good a job on the stragglers as the VC did on this gang up here."

Something whistled through the growth at the edge of the jungle exploding with a flash of red light and tossing up clods of earth and a fountain of wood splinters. A tribesman, pulling at the bridle of his recalcitrant lead ox, dropped silently. A splinter a foot long protruded from his back.

"For Chris' sake, Lee," said Harkness from a crouching position, "tell the HUEYS to go away. They can't see what they're doing. Do us more damage than the VC."

Harkness grinned at Mallory, who felt strangely lightheaded and detached. "This," said the Colonel slowly, "is getting to be a mess."

Levoncier, pausing to change film, crouched beside them. "Gerry," he complained, "they are making a party whenever you are coming. Do you have a friend in Hanoi?"

"No, only in Peking," Mallory shouted back, realizing suddenly that he was stimulated by the danger. His weariness had dropped away, and only when he looked at the packed tribespeople did his stomach turn over. But, he realized with a small shock of shame, the contrast between the panic of the *montagnards* and the calm professionalism of the American officers heightened his sense of the battle.

194

A few minutes later he could not even see the suffering *montagnards*—except as a mass that must be moved. The rattle of fire in the jungle had grown sharper and faster, and he had followed Harkness a few feet deeper into the trees, closer to the actual fighting where they were, paradoxically, safer. A severed branch dropped on his shoulder, numbing it.

"You all right?" asked Lee, continuing at his nod. "Damned fool VC's. All these poor bastards of savages want is to fade into the jungle. And the VC firing keeps them on the trail."

The firing rose and fell again as the hours wore on. Occasionally a Vietnamese soldier fell, and the keening of the *montagnard* women became a continuous, piercing wail. Once Mallory stumbled on something soft and, looking down in the half-light, saw the yellow oval of a contorted face, thin lips drawn back to reveal a snarl of blackened teeth. The rusty black tunic of the Vietcong was stained across the chest with a deeper black.

Mallory hurried on, dodging fallen trees and swearing at the creepers with their two-inch thorns that impaled his clothing, keeping him unmoving till he had laboriously worked himself free. Absently he saw that fresh Vietnamese troops had come up and blended into the jungle. Finally the end of the column appeared, a single house on a cart, still miraculously intact, followed by a few dozen stragglers. A squad of Vietnamese soldiers filled the path driving the *montagnards* forward with their rifle butts. Behind them another squad faced the other way, firing into the jungle on either side and into the darkness from which they had come.

Mallory, close behind Harkness, reversed his direction, following the column. His elation had deserted him and he was conscious only of an immense weariness that blotted out both fear and hope.

"There's nothing I can do now, but follow them in," Harkness shouted over his shoulder. "Might as well be running an action before radio—hell, before bugles."

195

When they stumbled into the clearing again it was almost two in the afternoon, six-and-a-half hours since Mallory had landed at the resettlement area, about five-and-a-half hours since he had been deposited in the jungle. The hike from the clearing to the column, which seemed days ago, had taken fifteen minutes, the return under fire more than five hours.

Helicopters were lifting the tribespeople out of the jungle clearing, though they protested bitterly at leaving all their possessions, some of the squat, dark men defying the rifle butts and bayonets of their Vietnamese guards.

"Go on. Get on that chopper," said Harkness, pushing Mallory's shoulder.

"No, I'll see it out," Mallory protested.

"The hell you will. I've got to stay. But it's all over, bar a little shooting. You'll see more at the resettlement camp."

"No, I'll stay."

"For Chris' sake, Gerry. I shouldn't have brought you and Pierre. Get out while you're still in one piece—or you'll have my ass in a sling."

"All right, Jack. If you want it that way. But, tell me, is it always such a mess, such complete confusion and futility in the jungle."

"No," said Harkness, grinning through the mud and powder stains, "only when we've got civilians to deal with. Otherwise, it's only desperate. But, you know, we always seem to have civilians to deal with."

19

Mallory could never remember the next forty-eight hours with any clarity. Twice day ran into night and back again, but there was no real distinction between the two states. He did not sleep at night, nor was he fully awake during the day. He dozed for an hour or two whenever the noise of the encampment and the stabbing pain of his bruised shoulder permitted. Twice at least he found himself leaning against a tentpole half-asleep until a passerby jostled him.

He came to hate the blinding sun of the day because it parched his throat and dazzled his eyes, and raised battalions of flies to settle in the raw wounds of the soldiers and *montagnards* who lay baking under the canvas of a make-shift field hospital. When the helicopters landed, the flies settled greedily on their blood-smeared undersides, a black, pulsing curtain, glittering green and gold in the cruel sunshine.

Harkness and Lee stepped out of the last helicopter to arrive from the jungle clearing, the Lieutenant still chipper, the Colonel moving stiffly to avoid jarring the left arm he carried in an improvised sling that cradled a stained field dressing. The silent officers watched diminutive stretcher-bearers edge Doyle's bulk out of the door. His red hair shone in the sunlight, but his arms and legs lolled, and the waxy yellow carapace of death mantled the bare chest where the shattered ribs gleamed wetly pink through torn flesh. Mallory could still smell the wine fumes.

The moonless dark of night was kinder to the observer,

for it veiled the suffering and the turmoil. But the splendor of the stars in the southern sky was far away, and the darkness made the confusion greater. Men stumbled over tent ropes or the wounded, swearing monotonously and wearily in Vietnamese, English, and a half-dozen tribal tongues. The keening of the women, the wailing of the babies, and the howls of the dogs rose to a crescendo at night. But it was cool, and the glutted flies disappeared to their own rest.

After the first night Levoncier put his cameras away and asked, "Is it not time to go? There is no more here for us, *mon cher*."

But Mallory answered impatiently, "No, not yet, Pierre. We saw the beginning. We might as well see the end."

Above them the helicopters still came and went, enormous intrusive flies themselves. Vietnamese generals appeared and flew way again, brisk in their knife-edge uniforms, silver stars, and rainbow decorations. A planeload of correspondents was disgorged on the nearby airstrip to spread over the encampment, prying, probing, questioning, and making bitter jokes. They left after five hours, urging Mallory to come with them. But he remained, still doggedly speaking to whoever would speak with him and totting up the casualty figures, a begrimed recording presence. Levoncier hovered near, his round, baby face growing ever more disturbed, until finally he pleaded, "Gerry, you are killing yourself to no purpose. We have seen all we can. The figures we can get later in Saigon. Even I am a little tired."

"Go back then, Pierre," Mallory answered gently, wondering at his own words. "There's no need for you to stay. I'll be back when I'm finished."

"No, I'll stay too," answered Levoncier, puzzled. "You need someone to look after you."

Finally, on the morning of the third day after their arrival, order was beginning to appear in the enclosure. Mallory entered the last figure and stared aghast at the totals:

montagnards—killed: 78–96, wounded: about 170; Vietnamese—killed: 54–63, wounded: about 105; Americans—killed: 2, wounded: 5. He was ready to go, his notebooks full and his emotions scarified into numbness.

Harkness, himself walking heavily with weariness but still erect, accompanied them to the helicopter. Mallory shook hands ceremoniously and said, "Jack, we'll see you again. But, please God, not like this again. How can anything except hatred survive this?"

Harkness summoned a smile. "We don't look very good, do we? Even to ourselves? I'm getting tired of these defeats."

"So long, Jack," Mallory said from the top of the loading ladder.

A flush of anger mottled the Colonel's haggard cheeks. Even his low-pitched voice lost its habitual calmness and he shouted jaggedly, "We're being sold out. If I could only get the man who did this. . . ."

Saigon was unreal, the palm trees leaning into the noon's heat and the houses shuttered. Aware only of his weariness, Mallory did not linger over the thought that came unbidden to console him. He had not been afraid.

He answered only with an exhausted smile when Levoncier said, "Well, *mon cher,* you cannot make a revolution without breaking heads, as Bonaparte said."

The battered black Citroën wheezed through the somnolent streets toward the river. Eyes closed, Mallory slowly became aware of a prolonged, irregular humming, like the sea beating on rocks. As they approached the Boulevard of Independence, the humming resolved itself into strident shouting and a white-painted barrier barred the road. Levoncier spoke with the attendant policeman in a mixture of broken French and Vietnamese, which Mallory could not follow.

"It is," he said wheeling the car around, "either the Buddhists demonstrating against the Catholics and the government or the Catholics demonstrating against the Buddhists and the government. The *flic* is not sure. But they want, as always, more freedom of speech, more participation in the government, more eggrolls in the sky."

When the car reached the Majestic, through back streets and fetid alleys, Mallory shook hands with Levoncier and walked slowly through the open glass doors. Along with his room key, he was handed a wad of blue telegrams and a bundle of white message forms. The telegrams he stuffed into his pocket after reading the top one, which said: URGE YOU UNFORGET WE NEED GRAPHIC ONSCENE COLOR ORDER SUSTAIN DOUBLEDOMING STOP HAVE EVERY CONFIDENCE THIS WILL BE SMASHER STOP BEST REGARDS MCALLEN. The top message form noted that Mademoiselle Tuyelle had called, and, leafing through the remainder, he found that half the twenty forms carried the same message.

The air-conditioner was chattering away in the red room and the water was hot in the basin as Mallory washed the first layer of filth off his hands. He gave the telephone operator Tuyelle's number and an order for a double cognac before scrubbing his hands again. The change from activity to quiet, from squalor to luxury had been too abrupt, and he could not sit down, but prowled around the room smoking a cigarette until the phone rang.

He snatched up the instrument to hear Tuyelle's voice. "Oh, darling, you're all right? Darling, darling, I was so worried...."

"I'm fine. Just tired, but not scratched—I missed you—I love you."

"And I love you, Gerry," she answered, her voice hovering between tears and laughter.

"When will I see you? Why were you so worried?"

"When you wish. I knew you were going up to the Plateau—and then we began to hear. Then, all the correspondents came back, but not you."

"I'm sorry," he said, feeling a pang of guilt. "I'm sorry.... It was so much, I didn't think."

"It doesn't matter now. Was it very bad?"

"It wasn't pretty. I'll tell you when I see you. Tonight?"

"Tonight. But, are you very tired?"

"A little," he conceded.

"Then I shall hang up and you must sleep," she said severely.

But they talked for another fifteen minutes.

Too tired to sleep, Mallory let the bathtub fill with steaming water. He scrubbed himself thoroughly, using a brush on his arms and legs. He filled the tub again and lay back with the double cognac and a gaudy paperback to follow the adventures of a private detective in Chicago. The hero's chief problems seemed to be a surplus of blondes, the effort required to acquire hangovers, and the burning question of whether his ultimate fee would be fifty or seventy-five thousand dollars. Finally beginning to nod on page thirty-five, Mallory washed himself again and stood under the hot shower for five minutes. Finding a fresh sarong, he gulped down half a sleeping pill. When he lay down, the screen of his mind immediately began its display of unrelated pictures, but he was asleep in three minutes.

He was wrestling with an ox, tugging at its horns to lead it to safety while the animal lowed miserably and the great brown eyes stared at him reproachfully. A series of explosions sounded and the head came away in his hands, blood dripping from the severed neck and the eyes still staring softly up at him. As he struggled out of bed to unlock the door, the knocking continued, and he reflected idly that the animal's head had been surprisingly light.

"Coming, Goddamn it," he shouted, angry at Pierre for the intrusion.

Gilroy's bulk stood in the doorway in a white linen suit, his round face glowing red against the chalky fabric, his mustache a brush of bristling gold. "I practically had to knock the door down," he complained. "Anybody'd think you were asleep."

"I was, Harry, I was," said Mallory.

"I'm sorry, Gerry," the sometime liquor salesman answered. "But I never thought you'd be sleeping now. What the hell have you been doing with your nights?"

"Working, Harry, working hard."

"Consoling the girls in the Embassy or exploring the local talent?"

"Folk-dancing on the High Plateau," answered Mallory. "It's a new figure called 'catch me if you can.' The side with the best information wins. We lost."

"Oh, I heard about that little mix-up," Gilroy said. "Well, we can't win them all."

A light knock on the door cut off Mallory's sharp reply. A waiter stood outside, his tray laden with a bottle of Dom Pérignon, a pair of glasses, and two covered plates.

"I thought you might like a drink," said Gilroy. "I'll have both the *croques monsieur* if you're not hungry."

Mallory bit ravenously into the hot, gooey mixture of bread, cheese, and ham, washing it down extravagantly with champagne. Mouth full, he asked, "What brings you down here?"

"This fracas isn't a blessing for the munitions boys alone. American armies can't fight without booze. I'm here to provide the needful. Fuel for victory. And I just thought I'd look you up and have a chat while I was here."

"I'm glad you turned up. I want to talk to you. Did you get. . . ."

"First drink, then talk," commanded Gilroy. "We'll go for a walk and have our chat later."

The streets were damp after the afternoon's rain, and Mallory's fresh clothing was cool against his body as they walked up Rue Catinat, which was just awakening from its siesta. His feet automatically took him past the bars and shops, across the corner beside the Caravelle Hotel and toward the cathedral. Gilroy was silent amid the afternoon throngs except to warn once, "If you go on this way, we'll

202

walk straight into a Buddhist barbecue or a Catholic auto-da-fé."

"Yeah," said Mallory vaguely, without slowing his pace, "heard something was going on. But I want to have a look —Harry, did you do any good with that stuff I sent you? I hope to God your people did. It's bad enough here without somebody feeding all our plans to the VC's."

The fat man turned down a side street that was free of the crowd before answering. "Did a lot of good. And we're grateful to you. In fact, we're so grateful, we're paying you off now. That's what you wanted isn't it?"

"Paying me off?" asked Mallory. "Yes, I guess that's what I wanted. You mean you're through with me? I can go back to being a plain reporter?"

"That's it, boy. And I'm hoping, personally, that this piece will set you up again. I know it will—and I'll be proud to have helped."

Through the surge of relief, Mallory asked, "And what about the people I mentioned? Have you got any results? Can you stop the leak?"

"Well, Gerry," Gilroy answered slowly, "I'm not really authorized to say."

"Oh, for Chris' sake, Harry. I've sweated for you, practically bled."

"Well, okay, seeing it's you. I can tell you a little," he said hesitantly.

"Who is it—Thau? Give."

"You know, I didn't say it was any of them. Just that your ideas were helping. We're looking into it."

"You mean you're not any closer?"

"I wouldn't say that. We're closer, much closer. But we still haven't got the guy."

"What are you doing?"

"That I can't tell you. Look, Gerry, why don't you just drop this thing? You've done all you can. We'll take care of it."

203

"How do you expect me to drop it?" Mallory flared. "I've seen too many people die just to walk away with a check in the bank and your thanks."

"I'm afraid you're just going to have to," said Gilroy tonelessly.

"Well, I won't. I'm not dropping it till you nail the bastard," Mallory snapped. "Besides, I've got a personal and a professional interest. I want to know—I've got to know—what the real story on Johnny Humboldt is."

"I said I was afraid you'd just have to drop it. Take my advice and let it go. I'm speaking as a friend, not officially now," said Gilroy implacably. He smiled, the blue eyes crinkling. "Gerry, I just don't understand you. First you didn't want in, now you don't want out."

"And first you were dying to get me in. Now you want me out. What's going on?"

"As I said, you'll have to drop it or we'll. . . ."

"Threats again?" Mallory demanded.

"No, not yet, boy. No threats. Simmer down," Gilroy answered. Pausing as a group of young students squeezed past them, he resumed slowly. "I was afraid of this. You hotheaded correspondents. All right, Gerry, I can tell you a little more. We've had our eye on a number of these birds—Thau and Vao particularly. We'll clean it up in due time."

"That's all?"

"Yeah, that's all."

"It's not good enough. I'm going to keep rooting around . . . I'm going to stir up enough dust so you'll have to move. Every day you fiddle around costs lives, and I'll. . . ."

"No, you're not, Gerry. You're going to drop it right now."

"Why?" asked Mallory, exulting at having an enemy he could strike out against. "Are you going to make me?"

"If necessary, yes. We'll make you drop it."

"How?"

"Since you ask, my friend, it's very simple. Somebody's paid ten thousand bucks into your account in Hong Kong.

That's a pretty heavy transfusion, and the money was paid through the Bank of China. You see how we can make you."

"To hell with it, Gilroy," Mallory snapped. "I'm not folding this time. Sure, you expose my fancied dealings with a Communist bank. But then I blow the whistle on you. You won't like that. . . ."

"We can absorb it better than you can, Gerry," Gilroy answered. "Who'll believe you against our pressure?"

"Lots of people. At the very least, if you break me, you're through in Hong Kong. They'll have to throw you out. And maybe you'll be through in the agency, too. Getting exposed with a big public scandal—your boss won't like that."

"I'll survive, boy, I'll survive. We'll use it if you force us to. But we'd prefer not to, so. . . ."

"You'll not interfere if I investigate quietly?"

"I didn't say that. Regardless of how I may feel, it's not my decision. But let me think what else I can tell you. How can I convince you it's for the best, without all this melodrama?"

"First time," exulted Mallory, "I've heard you turn aside from threats. Doesn't feel so good coming the other way, does it? Remember if you break me—and I know you can—then I've got nothing to lose. Watch out for yourself then. That's all I say."

The heavy-set man was silent, walking beside Mallory, his hand companionably clutching the correspondent's arm. Silent, they emerged onto the cathedral square where a pale student clutching in his right hand a microphone exhorted a crowd of about a thousand through a loudspeaker. As he became more heated, his Vietnamese became more staccato and louder, except when he waved both hands wide of his body carrying the microphone out of range of his mouth. Placards in English raised among the crowd read CIVIL LIBERTIES NOW! Police surrounded the square, their hands on their submachine guns, and an Army jeep with a long aerial was parked in front of the post office.

"Let's get out of this mess," said Gilroy. "Unless you'd rather watch than finish our talk."

"No, let's go," Mallory answered, turning back the way they had come.

"All right, Gerry. This much I can tell you. But you can't write it. You're all upset about Humboldt. Don't be. He *was* the American we were worried about. We know now that he was a neurotic kid who was passing information to the Communists. Probably thought he was helping humanity or something. So don't worry about him. Incidentally, we think maybe he was being blackmailed. He was AC-DC, you know. That's why we wanted to get him out of here, but fast."

"That's hard to believe, Harry."

"Truth always is, isn't it?" countered the fat man. "As for the rest of them—McGuffey, Hooghly, Dietrich—we know all about them. They're okay. Forget this. You've got enough for your story, anyway."

"Yeah, I guess so," Mallory answered slowly. "You're sure Humboldt was passing information?"

"Absolutely. No question about it."

"But somebody's still passing it. Who now?"

"Probably a Viet, as you guessed. We'll get him. But it'll take time."

"Look, Harry, it's a shock. I'm half-convinced. But you've got to move fast. You've got to stop this."

"We will, I promise you."

"In that case, I guess . . . But I still don't understand one thing. Why do you want me to drop it? Why can't I go on helping?"

"Let's just say you're crossing lines of communication, fouling up our effort. Okay?"

"Well, not quite," answered Mallory stubbornly. "I don't see why I can't go ahead. I want this finished."

"Just leave it—or I'll have to threaten you again. Nothing personal, Gerry, even if you are a stubborn son of a bitch. Just orders."

206

"What's the new threat?"

"No new threat. But we can break you if we have to, and we will if you force us. It's not only Laura and the kids—did you think of them if you can't sell your stuff—but Miss Vguyen-lee. That would be dead, too. You couldn't support a flea. Think about it."

"I will, Harry. I've got to. But I don't like it," answered Mallory. "You say you're really working on it?"

"I promise you."

"All right then, you win," said Mallory slowly, the sense of relief flooding over him again. "I'll go about my own business."

"I knew you'd be sensible." Gilroy laughed. "After all, it's in your own interests—and all of ours."

Mallory wondered why shame mingled with his relief and his dismay at the revelation of Humboldt's role.

20

The streets of Saigon flowered with color and movement, as the kaleidoscope whirled frantically again after the pause for the siesta. After another bottle of Dom Pérignon with Gilroy, Mallory returned to the typewriter and the telephone. On the quay the food peddlers had given way to sleek young men in sports shirts hawking jewelry, paintings, and smutty books. Among them, flaunting hips and bosoms filled out with sponge rubber, strolled the hectically-colored butter-flies of the evening. A sprinkling of Americans in cotton suntans was appraising the wares before making their se-lections.

On Rue Catinat the lights were flickering into life in curio shops, and the Beatles regurgitated "I Wanna Hold Your Hand" from a mirrored bar. Two diminutive policemen in white strolled slowly through the damp heat, husbanding their energy. Five American sailors rolled out of a bar, falling silent as they passed two Vietnamienne in white. They turned to watch the girls' slender backs recede, one big blond sailor holding his smaller darker companion by the collar. A heavily voluptuous woman in a crimson *ao-dai* spoke to them from a neighboring bar. Mallory could only imagine the conversation from his minute balcony, but he clearly heard the dark sailor's shrill wolf howl as the group charged into the bar.

A persistent throbbing intruded over the traffic's hum, the rough, surflike hammering Mallory had heard earlier in the day. The noise grew louder. Mallory thought he heard the word "tyranny" chanted over and over. As the chorus swelled, it became clear: TYRANNY . . . TYRANNY . . . TYRANNY!

The policemen scuttled into a curio shop, and in thirty seconds Rue Catinat was as bare of pedestrians as if swept by a broom. An Army jeep drew up on the quay and six police jeeps disgorged their white-clad cargo. Up Catinat, Mallory saw a fringe of students in white; the street was abruptly engorged with the demonstrators. The crowd was studded with placards reading: AMERICANS! DO NOT SUPPORT TYRANNY! DOWN WITH MILITARISM. The placards waved back and forth in time to the chant: TYRANNY . . . TYRANNY . . . TYRANNY. Those students who were unburdened shook their fists in the same rhythm. TYRANNY . . . TYRANNY . . . TYRANNY. The chant swelled to a falsetto and dropped to a bass, rising again to a shrill crescendo.

Checked by the cordon of police, the throng flowed into the hotel, disappearing from Mallory's field of vision. Policemen dived after them and, even from the fifth floor, Mallory heard the sound of breaking glass and splintering wood. From the balconies around him, American soldiers watched in silence. Finally, slowly and painfully, the crowd reversed itself, those in the street darting away to avoid being crushed by their retreating fellows. The chanting had stopped, and in the silence a stone tinkled through the hotel's window. It was followed by a volley of stones directed at the police. The edge of the crowd surged toward the police cordon, overwhelming it for an instant. A shot sounded, then three more. The crowd twisted and turned, seeking escape like an antelope in a net. Two minutes later it had dissolved. All the demonstrators had disappeared into side streets, except for six struggling in the grip of policemen. Abandoned placards littered the street.

An hour later, when Mallory passed through the lobby toward the taxi rank, waiters and bellboys were cleaning up the broken glass, the splintered wood, and the feathers spilled from ripped cushions. Their faces were, as always, closed. Since the taxis, like the American servicemen, appeared to have withdrawn to sanctuary, Mallory settled for a *pous-pous*. He made a noisy and solitary progress through the empty streets, watched only by squads of curious policemen.

The small door at 23 Rue Trongkyi opened to his first ring, and Tuyelle, in white, her hair hanging loose, gripped his shoulders. He was enveloped in a cloud of jasmine, forgetting the pain in his right arm.

"Gerry, Gerry," she said into his neck, her lips brushing his ear. "Gerry, I was so worried."

"Tuyelle," he said, holding her at arms length to see the green-flecked eyes and the tremulous lips. "It's good to be home."

"Welcome home, Gerry." She smiled. "Welcome home."

"I'm sorry I was late," he offered. "I ran into a demonstration."

"Yes, I know. But you are here now. Only that matters."

"Oh, Tuyelle, I missed you so."

"And I missed you—terribly."

"Maybe," he grinned, "we ought to get married soon. At least I'll always know you're waiting for me."

"I'll always be waiting for you anyway. Let's not talk about that now."

She came into his arms again, pressing herself urgently against him, her lips open against his. His hands strayed over her softness, pressing her closer. In the scented bedroom she slipped out of her clothing with rapid, flowing motions. Their coming together was even more urgent and more hectic than it had been the first time. Afterward, they lay depleted, her head pillowed on his left shoulder, her left leg thrown across his body.

She traced the purple-and-black bruise on his right shoulder, first with her fingertips and then with her lips. "My darling, it must have been terrible. Why did you stay so long?"

"It wasn't so bad for me. But for some others . . . I felt I had to stay, had to see it out. I'll tell you more later. What have you been doing?"

"The same as always." She shrugged. "Working a little—and worrying a great deal about you."

"Pretty soon," he said, "pretty soon, I'll be finished, and we can go away. Will you come with me, Tuyelle?"

"I'll come with you I think," she answered slowly. "But is this another proposal?"

"I suppose so," he said. "It certainly sounds like it."

"The answer is still I'll come with you, but I do not know about marriage yet."

"A girl who wants to live in peripatetic sin," cracked Mallory. "Every American boy's dream. You insult me. This is too serious for such a frivolous approach. I'll ask again—and again—and again."

"Do." She smiled.

He ran his hand slowly down her back, fingertips trailing over the smooth skin. But she pulled away.

"No, Gerry. I want first to hear what you have been doing. Have you found out any more about—about that business we talked of the other night?"

His face was briefly shadowed, but he smiled as he said, "Yes, it's all taken care of—all settled."

"Oh, I'm glad," she replied. "But how? Who was the man? What is being done?"

"Well," he answered slowly, "I don't know exactly who it is. But it's in good hands, and we can forget about it."

She sat up, pulling the sheet over her breasts and lifting his cigarettes from the table. She passed him a cigarette, and when her Camel was aglow, she asked again, "All settled, but you do not know who? Or what will be done? I do not understand."

211

"Look, darling, let's drop it. You don't want to hear the gory details."

"But yes, I do. You made me interested. Now I must hear all."

"I don't want to trouble you with this anymore. Let's talk about going away. How'd you like Paris this April, and New York in June? We can do it now."

She caught her breath. "I'd love it, Gerry—might even marry you if you insist. And we can stay at . . . But, Gerry, first you must tell me about this business with Johnny and the others."

"You won't like it," he warned, firmly turning aside a stab of suspicion. Why did she want to know so urgently? But, he answered himself, she was a woman after all and he *had* dragged her into the mess.

"Nonetheless. I am not a porcelain doll that must be kept in cotton wool."

"All right," he conceded, "I'll have to start at the beginning and tell you things I shouldn't, things that will make you think less of me."

"Not," she interrupted, "if you tell me truly. That, above all."

Sitting up painfully and slowly, addressing the tip of his own cigarette, he told her of his first conversation with Gilroy and their agreement.

"So that's how you knew of the spy," she said.

"Yes, because I was, in a way, one of them. But it's all over now."

"How over? You have still not told me."

"Tuyelle, you're not going to like this any more than the first part."

"Tell me," she insisted.

He told her as rapidly as he could, touching on Gilroy's suspicion of Thau but leaving Vao out for some reason, and then repeating Gilroy's description of Humboldt as an informer and an occasional homosexual. She listened quietly, her face unmoving behind her cigarette.

When he had finished, she crushed her cigarette out and turned to face him. Her eyes glinted green through the tears. "Gerry," she said deliberately, her voice rising as she continued, "you are right. I do not like it. And I shall tell you what I do not like. I do not like what you are doing. Everything you have done up to now I can understand. Even this spy business, I can understand, when a man is trapped. But to suddenly, now, just to say, 'It is over. It is not my responsibility.' That I do not like, because. . . ."

"But, darling," he interrupted. "It *is* over. There is nothing I can do. And Gilroy will handle it."

"Gerry," she resumed, unheeding, "you are more foolish even than Johnny was. He would never have believed such nonsense. You have come so far. You have seen so many die because of this man, and then you can say, 'It is over. I will forget.'?"

"But it *is* over," he objected.

"No, it is *not*," she replied. "It is just beginning. I thought you were a holy fool, like Johnny, but a man as well. Now, I think—I'm afraid—you are just a fool. But even if you are not a man, I still love you. I am the fool."

Mallory was silent, not trusting his tongue for fear it might destroy his hopes of life.

She resumed, her voice harsh. "One thing I can tell you. Johnny was no homosexual—concealed, part-time, or anything else. This I know. And if they lie about that to blacken his name, they will lie about everything else."

"Are you certain?" he asked. "Even Pierre said once. . . ."

"Oh, Pierre," she dismissed his doubt. "Pierre is a gossiping old lady. No, Johnny was not a homosexual. And why do they say Thau? Why do you Americans take the convenient way out? Always a Vietnamese who is the villain, never an American."

"But if he is, he is," Mallory insisted.

"It is not proved. You said so yourself. And if Johnny was the American—let us say he was indeed—Johnny giving this information and killing these men, then why does it continue now that he is gone?"

"I told you, Thau is now. . . ."

"I do not believe it. It is too convenient. First an American, then suddenly a Vietnamese. But there was, from what you say, never even a break in the business. Men died twenty-four hours after Johnny was killed. . . ."

"Somebody else taking over," he suggested.

"Without a break?" she countered. "And why, then, was Johnny shot? What was the purpose?"

"Gilroy says it was suicide, says there's no question."

"He would, wouldn't he? You are prepared to abandon the men yet unkilled, to forget this?"

"I'm afraid so," he answered.

"God help me," she said dispassionately. "I wish I had never met you. I wish I did not love you. Always compromises and pretending. Johnny—at least he—died for something. But you will live, and I want you to live and I love you."

She flung herself across the distance that separated them, muttering, "I will punish you."

Mallory felt her nails dig into his sides. Pain stabbed when her teeth nipped the skin of his right arm, below the bruise. He tried to calm her, stroking her back and touching her hair. But she was not to be soothed. She twisted around him, one moment alongside him, the next minute above, biting and scratching, her quick kisses like blows. Finally aroused and half angry through his sheepishness and his suspicion, Mallory responded, his hands hard on her body.

It was a rough, grinding coupling, Tuyelle astride him. But the moments of ecstasy were the most explosive they had ever known.

Afterward she was spent and demure. She lay, nuzzling

214

his neck and not speaking. Finally, he broke the silence.

"Tuyelle," he said tentatively, "if you want me to go. . . ."

She lit a cigarette, saying, "No, Gerry, don't go. I want you to be near me. And you may be right. Why should we destroy ourselves? It is hopeless after all."

"I'm glad," he began, "that you agree. I know it is not perfect, but. . . ."

"Gerry, I will marry you if you still want it when you have finished here."

21

The wave of exhaustion, long pent by emotion and desire, did not break over Mallory until the black door of 23 Rue Trongkyi had closed behind him. Tuyelle, her face bare of make-up and her moist body insecurely wrapped in a thin cream silk robe, had kissed him, first fiercely, then tenderly, murmuring, "I still think we are being cowardly, doing wrong. . . . But, Gerry, I do love you, I can't help it. And I'll do as you wish."

Alone in the humid night, except for the pariah dogs sleeping beside the garden walls, Mallory allowed his head to droop. Part of him rejoiced at Tuyelle's avowal and her promise. But the black clarity of night and exhaustion forced him to see the picture unadorned, like the hazily glowing image on a radar screen all the more exact because it was shorn of detail and nuance. Tuyelle and he would purchase their hope of happiness not only by Humboldt's uneasy sleep but also by the deaths still to come. Suddenly Gilroy's promises and rationalizations seemed as thin and specious to him as they had to Tuyelle. What hope of happiness, he wondered, could spring from such a beginning?

"Always compromises and pretending," she had said. "You are worse than Johnny was."

He forced the doubts from his mind, reminding himself that there was, quite realistically, nothing he could do. He could not fight Gilroy, even if the threat did not exist. All he could do was trust Gilroy and the CIA to find the informer in their own time.

He found a knot of *pous-pous* drawn together at the intersection under a dim yellow light, like Conestoga wagons camping on a hostile prairie. Their drivers, curled in sleep on the seats, were obviously not concerned about the Vietcong, though fear kept almost all citizens of Saigon behind bolted doors in the early hours of the morning. Mallory rapped on the side of the nearest vehicle, recalling that most *pous-pous* drivers were, if not agents, benevolently neutral on the side of the Communists. After haggling with the sleepy driver, he sank back gratefully onto the sweat-stained cushions, wondering if he were sitting on hand grenades.

Mallory closed his eyes, remembering by some quirk of the mind the wisecrack someone had made in Saigon years earlier: "You know what a glamorous foreign correspondent in Asia is? He's a general assignment reporter with dysentery." But it was not dysentery that troubled him; rather the intolerable aching and trembling of his arms, aggravated by the growing pain of the bruise. He hitched himself into a partially comfortable position and somehow fell into a doze.

He came to full wakefulness abruptly when the *pous-pous* began to jolt and sway. They had turned off the main road and were bumping down a back lane. All was darkness outside the weak yellow glow cast by the headlamps. He trusted in the driver's knowledge of Saigon until they turned into an alley so narrow that the sides of the cab brushed the houses on either side and the wheels slithered on the slime coating the broken cobblestones. He finally attracted the driver's attention by craning his body backward around the canopy. The Vietnamese, who had been so voluble a haggler five minutes ago, would only grin and say, "Majestic. Okay. Okay. *Vite.*"

Still expostulating, Mallory felt the *pous-pous* hit an obstacle and felt himself thrown clear of the stalled vehicle. Hands broke his backward fall and rough fabric was thrust over his head. Half-conscious, he was pushed into a car amid a flurry of whispered Vietnamese. When the car accelerated, pain stabbed from his right shoulder into his chest.

217

Frantic in the gray mist, his mind darted through mazes of fear. Was this death or merely abduction? And who held him? Was it Gilroy and the CIA underlining their threat, or had the bureaucratic machinery thrown a cog and ordered his death? Was it the Vietcong for some unfathomable reason? Or, perhaps, an unknown third group which had searched his room so clumsily? A trapped animal frozen by panic, he let go his hold on consciousness.

"Mr. Mallory, Mr. Mallory," the voice repeated, muffled and at a great distance. "Mr. Mallory, can you hear me?"

He started up to a clouded impression of three towering figures, but immediately sank back, closing his eyes against a stab of pain. His right side was rigid and unresponsive. Inching his left hand across his chest, he felt bands of broad adhesive tape binding his arm and shoulder.

"M. Mallory." A softer voice speaking the same muffled, distant French. "Please open your eyes, but lie still."

He slitted his eyes against the glare. The three figures danced in the haze of returning vision, one wearing a red bathrobe, the second in normal Western clothing, the third in Vietnamese coolie clothing. His eyes focused slowly on the three shining heads bent over him. They were identical —seamed yellow cheeks; long, drooping, black mustaches, and patent-leather hair—a triple incarnation of evil.

"It's all right, Mr. Mallory," said the first voice. "It's all right. I'm sorry. I didn't know of your injury."

"M. Mallory," the second voice took up, "I have taped your shoulder up. It appears to be only a dislocation which I have restored. But you'd better have it X-rayed tomorrow."

Two of the figures swam out of his vision. He heard a door slam as the man in coolie clothing spoke again. "I am sorry. But you'll understand we cannot repeat the same tactics twice. For your protection, too, not only our own."

The long, nicotine-stained fingers crept behind his head, cradling his left shoulder as he struggled upright. The smell of Chinese cooking and the clatter of mah-jong tiles would have told Mallory where he was if he had not seen the white-washed cluttered room and the Vietcong leader, whose strange humor had now led him to disguise himself in a Fu Manchu mask.

"Mr. Mallory," the Vietnamese continued, "my apologies again. I can only assure you that you have been seen by an excellent doctor. He has been taking care of my family and myself for years. . . ."

Determined to break the cozy, domestic tone the meeting had assumed, Mallory demanded truculently, "Well, you've got me here. Now what?"

"But you did say you wanted to talk again," the voice behind the mask said calmly. "And you will appreciate that we must use what methods we can. We are still not entirely free. I repeat my sorrow."

Feeling that he had been churlish, Mallory muttered an apology.

"Not at all, not at all. It is I who must repeat my apologies. Quite frankly, too, you'd be no use to us if you are so battered that you can't write."

Mallory leaned back drowsily against the cushions of the couch, feeling relaxed and sheltered. He surrendered himself to the sensation of security. The conviction and purpose that emanated from the wiry figure with the grotesque mask were overpowering, as was his certainty of ultimate victory.

He could understand Humboldt's defection. After so many men who did not know where they wished to go, much less how to arrive at their goal, this resolute figure was like a stern but kindly father. And his methods were, perhaps, no better but certainly no worse than Gilroy's machinations. Who was to say his cause was not just?

"Mr. Mallory," the voice was persistent, "try to pay attention to me. I had hoped for a talk, a good talk tonight. But the doctor had to give you sodium pentothal when he set your shoulder. I'll have to do the talking."

"Surely," murmured Mallory drowsily. "What did I. . . ."

"No," the booming voice was amused. "You didn't say anything about your personal life you'd regret. The doctor says only some react that way."

Mallory made an effort to rouse himself. But he could not cast off the blanket of comfort which dulled his senses.

"No," said the voice, "just listen to me. Don't try to talk. We have only a short time."

Laboriously, Mallory nodded his head.

"All right now. You still want to see us in the field?"

He nodded his head again.

"Fine. Tomorrow evening—you'll find the invitation in the morning mail—you are invited to a party at Mr. Hooghly's. You are to go and then you are to stay with Miss Vguyen-lee until midnight. Do you understand?"

"Go—Hooghly's party. Spend evening with Tuyelle till midnight. That right?"

"That's right, Mr. Mallory," answered the voice, warmly paternal. "But please do not forget to have your arm X-rayed. If you are incapacitated, do not go to Hooghly's. We will understand and try to make other arrangements."

"X-ray arm . . . If bad, don't go cocktail party."

"That's right," the voice was heartily approving, a patient teacher encouraging a backward pupil. "If you are all right, borrow M. Levoncier's car and take the Bien-hoa road, arriving at the sixteenth kilometer before Bien-hoa about four o'clock. Approach with your lights low, then turn off the lights and wait. Can you repeat that?"

"Levoncier's car—sixteenth kilometer before Bien-hoa about four. Lights low—turn off lights and wait."

"That's fine. And we will do the rest. You'd better tell Levoncier you're going to be away for a few days."

"Tell Levoncier going away," Mallory repeated. A thought was nagging at the back of his mind and, finally, with great effort he got it out. "Levoncier—he'll no believe. Want to know where. What say?"

"Appeal to his sense of intrigue," came the smooth answer.

"Hint you're going north on a counter-guerrilla mission so secret you can't tell even him. I'm sure he'll tell everyone else. That'll account for your absence. And tell him his car will be at the airport waiting for him."

"Car at airport okay," said Mallory. "All okay, very fine."

"And, Mr. Mallory, come alone. If there is anyone with you or any vehicle near you, my men will open fire. Do you understand?"

"Sure, understand fine. Levoncier—tell him going north, hint . . . And come alone, very important come alone."

"That's fine, Mr. Mallory. Just fine. You understand perfectly."

He reveled in the approval of the firm voice as he slipped comfortably off the hard edge of consciousness.

22

Mallory woke to a clouded memory of staggering through the lobby of the Majestic on the arm of the desk clerk and a pair of grinning bellboys. He was naked under the thin sheet, and the sour stench of yesterday's whiskey rose from the pile of crumpled clothing beside the bed.

"Oh, God, what happened last night?" he wondered.

His right arm was held immobile by broad bands of adhesive tape, and he remembered his talk with the Vietcong leader. Gradually the fragments assembled themselves from his unconscious. Tonight, he remembered, Hooghly's cocktail party, Tuyelle, then a rendezvous at four in the morning on the Bien-hoa road. Was there something else he had to do? Oh, yes, visit a doctor; that should have been obvious. And something else, something to do with Tuyelle? He felt a sense of diffused pleasure when he thought of her, but could trace it to no cause more specific than her mere existence.

When he finally stopped flogging his memory a bolt of joy illuminated the caverns of his mind. Tuyelle had promised to marry him, and that was cause for joy. But they had argued bitterly about his decision to abandon his search for the informer. Another "compromise"—that was the word she had used. He reassured himself, it was not fear, just realism that dictated the decision.

Sitting up gingerly, he reached for the telephone with his left hand, ordering breakfast and giving Tuyelle's number at the Ministry. During the fifteen-minute wait, he experimented with shaving himself left-handed, leaving streaks of blood on his brown cheeks.

"Allo." Her voice was tense.

"Hello, darling," he said softly. "Good morning. I love you."

"Oh, Gerry. You're all right?"

"Of course," he said, surprised. "Why not?"

"Well, darling," she answered crisply, "when a girl has just acquired a fiancé—even a provisional one—and she tries to call him to say good morning, it's a little disconcerting."

"What's disconcerting?"

"It's a little disconcerting to have the telephone operator advise—her voice dropped to a baritone—"M. Mallory, he got in very, very late last night. Perhaps you'd better not disturb him just now.'"

"Oh, that," he said lightly, glancing at his watch. The hands stood at 1:30.

"Yes, that. You didn't leave that late. What happened?"

"It's not what you're thinking."

"I am certainly not thinking what you think I'm thinking. My self-confidence is not that fragile. But what did happen? Were you celebrating—or what?"

"No, not exactly. I'll tell you later, but I dropped—was dropped—in on an old acquaintance. I'll tell you when I see you. I'm so happy, Tuyelle. I love you."

Her voice softened. "I love you too, Gerry. But you've got to take better care of yourself—not just for me, for yourself, too."

"Now," he said, "I know you're serious. You're ordering me around."

"Why not," she began indignantly, lamely finishing, "yes, I guess so."

"And why not?" he said.

The door opened after a light knock and a waiter entered behind a tray heaped with dishes, newspapers, and a pile

223

of letters. On top Mallory could see a heavy, square envelope, unstamped, addressed in the broad, black, backhand strokes embassy secretaries affect for social communications.

"Just a moment," he said, laying the telephone down.

"The Public Affairs Officer and Mrs. James Hooghly request the pleasure of the company of Mr. Gerald Mallory. . . ." Typed on a strip of onion-skin paper glued to the upper left-hand corner was the message: "To meet Senator Wilderman Sturtevant."

"Are you invited to the Hooghly's tonight?" he asked Tuyelle.

"Yes. Must we go?"

"I think I'd better. I want to check a few things. I'll pick you up at six-thirty."

"All right, Gerry," she assented. "If we must. Do you know something?"

"No, what?"

"I love you," she said. "Good-bye for now. Someone is coming."

Grinning with delight, Mallory washed his usual assortment of pills down with the glass of fresh orange juice that cost *Quest* $1.50. He leafed through the mail, finding two special delivery letters from the magazine stuffed with newspaper clippings on Vietnam. A long memo on attitudes in Washington and stamped "Confidential" he put aside to read later. There were a couple of bills forwarded from Hong Kong, and a letter from the Syndicate asking him to concentrate on certain subjects, "just as soon as you are free of your present assignment." They wanted another piece on opium and the Chinese Communists, he noted wryly, and another on tourism in Hong Kong. The covering letter didn't help much, though it apologized. "I am aware that these subjects have been done much, perhaps overdone. But I am sure that you can make them outstanding by applying your unique, detached, and well-informed approach." He'd keep the Syndicate connection, he mused, but he'd make it clear that they were going back to the original agreement—pieces on what he wanted, when he wanted to do them.

At the bottom of the pile was a large brown envelope, unstamped and addressed simply "G. Mallory, Room 536, Personal." He slit the flap with his butter knife and extracted a five by seven glossy photograph. Startled by the two naked figures about to embrace, he laughed. Who, he wondered, was favoring him with mildly dirty pictures? He glanced at the tableau again, his face dropping. He had, naturally, been looking at the girl, a thick-set, voluptuous figure with a broad Vietnamese face that lacked either distinction or expression. But the man was himself. The picture must have been taken, he realized, at Madame Jahn's on his first night in Saigon. Yes, he remembered the girl.

Mallory turned the photograph over in his fingers. On the back was a message typewritten in capitals. TEND TO YOUR OWN BUSINESS—NOT COUNTERESPIONAGE. OTHERWISE, YOU'D HATE TO SEE THIS PUBLISHED. THERE ARE MANY EAGER OUTLETS.

Mallory laughed aloud. The threat was as stupid as it was crude. They could send it to Tuyelle, of course, and there might be an unpleasant half-hour. But she was under no illusions as to his past behavior. And who would publish such a picture? Not even in Vietnam would the papers run a picture quite so explicit. Still laughing at the crudeness of the move, he tucked the photograph into his brief case and began to read the memo from Washington.

But his mind wandered halfway through the first paragraph. He could not, after all, dismiss the threat of the photograph quite so cavalierly. It was an eerie feeling to know that a third, unknown quantity—besides the Vietcong leader and the CIA—had definitely entered the delicate equation. He must have been closer than he had thought if the informer was willing to reveal his connection with Madame Jahn. And publication? There was one group which would delight in publishing a photograph of an American—a well-known correspondent—and a Vietnamese girl in a posture of obvious anticipation. What would serve the Vietcong's purposes better? And who could then prevent the South Vietnamese press from at least alluding to the handbills.

Rising to dress, he laughed at himself again. It seemed that Gilroy's security was somewhat motheaten. But he was, after all, dropping his extracurricular activities to concentrate on his story. The threat had turned into a laughable souvenir.

Nothing could spoil his good humor today, he reflected, not even being forced to dress left-handed. Not even, he concluded grimly an hour later, waiting in the embassy dispensary amid screaming children until the young doctor could finally see him.

Clucking gently, the doctor cut the adhesive tape to reveal the bruise. "A good job, beautiful taping." After a session with the fluoroscope, he advised, "A greenstick fracture, very fine, hairline, of the right clavicle, Mr. Mallory. We'll immobilize it again, and you'd better keep the arm in a sling for a couple of days. But nothing to worry about."

Strolling back to the Majestic in the heat, his arm dramatically tucked inside his shirt, Mallory's good humor even embraced the bulky figure of Gilroy, seated on the terrace before a bottle of Dom Pérignon.

"How are you, Harry?" he hailed. "Come to check up on me?"

"No, Gerry. I just want to say good-bye. I'm going back tonight and wondered if there were anything you wanted me to take back to Hong Kong. But what have you done to your arm?"

Mallory explained that he was now a wounded veteran of the Vietnam conflict, carefully omitting any reference to his rendezvous with the Vietcong. He debated, briefly, telling Gilroy about the photograph, but decided against it.

"Have you got any word for me, Harry?" he asked jovially. "How are the bloodhounds?"

"Nothing new, Gerry. I'm sorry. But we'll manage."

"Fine, Harry, just fine. I'll buy you a going-away bottle. Dom Pérignon?"

"Thanks," the heavy-set man said, studying Mallory intently. "Are you sure you didn't get hit on the head, too?"

"Of course. Why?"

"I haven't seen you so jovial in years. What's up?"

"I'll tell you when I see you next. Things are just going well."

"I'm glad." Gilroy paused before asking in a low tone, "Gerry, our understanding. It's still okay? You're not going to do anything foolish?"

"I've already told you," said Mallory, an edge of exasperation in his voice. "Why don't you leave it alone now? This wasn't entirely a social call, was it?"

"Well, not exactly," Gilroy conceded, blowing the bubbles off his mustache. "But I'm glad you're going to be a good boy."

"Goddamn it, Harry," snapped Mallory. "Lay off. I've already given in. . . ."

"Sure, Gerry, I just wanted to be sure you were being sensible."

"And if I'm not?" needled Mallory. There was no question in his mind, but he did resent Gilroy's patronizing paternalism.

"I've already told you. . . . But look, let's drop it. I'm satisfied."

"Well, I'm not," Mallory persisted, feeling his temper rising. "I want to know what you guys are doing about it. I didn't promise to sit by and let this slaughter go on indefinitely. There are a lot of things here I can't do anything about. But this I can. I can always write it—The Spy the CIA Can't Catch."

"Then we'll come down on you," reminded Gilroy.

"That would look pretty weak after the fact," Mallory sneered. "No, you've got to depend on my good faith. But

I'll give you a time limit, say, two weeks—then I write it."

"Don't threaten me, Gerry," Gilroy replied, setting his glass down heavily. He looked around the deserted terrace before resuming in a low voice. "Look, be reasonable. I promised you, and we will. But I can't go back and tell my people we're operating under an ultimatum from you."

"You should have thought of that before you got me involved."

"I didn't want to—I told them you wouldn't play the role. But they insisted," said Gilroy unhappily.

"What role?" Mallory jumped on the word. "What role was I supposed to play? Are you finally going to level with me?"

"For Chris' sake, Gerry," answered the big man, choosing his words with deliberation. "Look, this is personal. Between us two. I'll tell you why you've got to quit now. But, for Chris' sake, remember, this is personal."

"Okay, Harry. I'm waiting."

"Look, Gerry, one of the names on your list. . . . It's a prime contact of ours, an important agent. He works both ways."

"What do you mean, works both ways?" Mallory asked.

"Now don't push me too hard. But, roughly, the Vietcong think he's feeding them information. Occasionally he does give them something solid, but most of the stuff is sanitized first and it's harmless. For us, the contact with the VC and their thinking is invaluable. He really gets us solid stuff from them."

"Which one is he?"

"Gerry, you know I can't tell you that. But I can tell you that you were picked for this job for one reason."

"And that was?" asked Mallory.

"You were a diversion, a sprat to protect a whale. That's why we transferred that Sergeant you met at Thau's, to draw a little attention to you. That's why you're in danger, real danger, now. We—no, not we—*they* thought you'd thrash

228

around and make a lot of noise and distract attention. I was opposed to it."

"So what happens now?"

Gilroy smiled slowly. "You fooled them. You got too close to the bone. Now they want you out. And I advise the same. Get out of this."

"What about the spy? Are you really any closer?"

"Well, in a way, yes. We'll get him."

"Just in a way?" pressed Mallory.

"These things take time. But don't you worry about it. You've got to think of your own neck."

"So, I was the fall guy, was I?" asked Mallory, anger rising.

"You still *are* the fall guy, Gerry," Gilroy corrected. "If you don't leave things alone and get out fast as you can, I'd not bet much on your life. If the VC don't get at you, my people could."

"Your people? You?"

"Not me personally. But some of the boys are pretty rough. They knew Humboldt was marked, but they sacrificed him to protect their man. They'll sacrifice you, too. For Chris' sake, Gerry, I'm sorry. But this isn't a game any more. I'm powerless."

"Then, let me see if I understand," Mallory summed up, "I was the decoy, but I made the mistake of using my head a little. Now I've got to cut and run, leave you to handle the tip-off man—if you can find him. Is that right?"

"That's it, boy," Gilroy agreed unhappily. "But don't be so feisty. We'll get him, I promise. It's a matter of time till. . . ."

"Time—while men die and I run for cover," Mallory insisted.

"If you must put it that way."

"Look, Harry, thanks a lot," Mallory said rising. "I'll think about it. But the promise is cancelled. Will you sign my name to the check? I'll see you in Hong Kong."

"So long, Gerry," Gilroy said unhappily. "Don't forget what I've said. I *hope* I'll see you in a couple of weeks."

229

Mallory plodded up the narrow marble staircase, sick anger rising in his throat. "Compromise and pretending," Tuyelle had said. "You are worse than Johnny."

He had been carefully chosen as the whipping boy. It was not flattering, even if he had been somewhat more adroit than Gilroy's puppet-masters expected. Worse, there was no real prospect that the spy, whoever he was, would be neutralized. Men would die because Mallory wanted an easy, pleasant life—wanted his untroubled life so badly.

With self-loathing, he saw himself as Gilroy and his masters did: a broken-down alcoholic who could be depended upon to play the fool; a tool that was absolutely safe because, in whatever crisis, his cowardice would prevail.

The tracks were converging. The dilemma of the United States in Vietnam and his own dilemma were coming closer. His self-assigned task appeared hopeless. He could pull out, telling himself that he had done all he could in a fight that was not really his own. Gilroy and company, after all, were the professionals, and it was sheer presumption for him to doubt that they would find the traitor. He could write his story and his book, content that his responsibilities went no farther.

But, he asked himself, had he not come too far to turn back? Did direct responsibility flow from his deliberate involvement? What, exactly, did he owe to men like Harkness, to the bitter Vietnamese, and to the bewildered *montagnards*? For that matter, didn't he owe the United States more than a facile restatement of the perils and pitfalls of the war in Vietnam?

Sighing, Mallory put the questions aside. Perhaps Gilroy was right; probably he possessed neither the will nor the means to make a real contribution to the fight; probably it would be better for the United States, too, to withdraw with whatever honor it could still retain.

23

They mounted the stairs in regal procession between files
of Vietnamese guards augmented by a squad of American
MP's: Tuyelle's ruby bracelet and earrings set off her sinu-
ously flowing *ao-dai* of iridescent green, her blue-black hair
was drawn into an elaborately twisted knot, and her eye
shadow was a suggestion of emerald.

Mallory wore a dark tropical suit and a black sling. Levoncier was impressively bulky in starched cream linen and he
carried only his smallest camera as a concession to formality.

A queen, her consort, and a single equerry wearing the
badge of his office, Mallory thought, enjoying the glances
drawn by Tuyelle's perfection and his own badge of injury.
Deliberately he shook a cigarette out of a pack of Camels
with his left hand.

Martha Hooghly, blonde hair lacquered, full-bodied in a
strapless, ankle-length gown of scarlet, swept forward in a
cloud of Jolie Madame to greet them. Mallory marveled at
the artifice of the corsetière.

"My dears," Martha trilled, both hands extended, "I am
delighted that you could all three come. Now the party is
made."

She offered Tuyelle her cheek while her shrewd blue eyes
appraised the Vietnamienne's costume. "Tuyelle," she said,
"is always an ornament. But you are stunning tonight, my
dear."

"You look lovely, Martha," Tuyelle murmured. The conventional female response was overwhelmed by the mo-

231

mentum of their hostess' enthusiasm as she turned to Mallory. "And Gerry. You always bring a note of intellectual distinction. But what have you done to your arm?"

He explained briefly, barely finishing before Martha bestowed her accolade on Levoncier. "And Pierre, that exciting French rakishness, spine-tingling as always."

"Extras courtesy of the Vietnamese and American governments," Jim Hooghly observed dryly. He had come up behind them while his wife was rhapsodizing. "I feel like a five-star general with that turnout."

"Evening, Jim, what's the occasion for the troops?" asked Mallory.

"You won't believe it, Gerry. But we had a four-hour debate today at the embassy. Should we hold this cocktail party or cancel it in deference to the inflamed sensibilities of the local students? Decision, signed and sealed, was to go ahead—stiff upper lip, show the flag. But we've got to make sure the Senator isn't disturbed. Therefore the troops."

"Who exactly is this bird, Jim?" Mallory asked. "I'm out of touch with the Washington pecking order."

"Senator Wilderman Sturtevant," the Public Affairs Officer answered, "is deputy chairman of the Foreign Affairs Committee. Expert on Asia because he comes from the West Coast and was in the Solomons during the big war. A fighting liberal, says his campaign literature. A pain in the ass, say I. He's so Goddamned liberal he's convinced everything the United States does is wrong. It's been a rough couple of days. Almost wish I'd been with you guys up on the Plateau."

"You would have been very welcome, Jim," Levoncier interjected. "A nice change for you from desks and offices and Senators."

"You can say that again, Pierre." Hooghly laughed. "I'm smart like you. I wouldn't forget to duck."

He gulped from his tall glass, his eyes, as ever slightly bloodshot, glowing.

"But let me get you drinks," he said, signaling a waiter.

232

The throaty belching of motorcycles and the low, petulant whine of a siren cut across the tinkling of glasses.

"That must be Sturtevant now," Hooghly said. "Excuse me."

The Senator, dark, compact, and stockily powerful in a rumpled gray suit, bounded into the dimly lit room trailing his entourage like a cloak. His brown eyes roamed restlessly in his fleshy, athlete's face.

"Good evening, Mr. Hooghly, good evening," he declaimed in a full bass voice. "Lots of interesting people to talk to, I hope. You have got lots of Vietnamese, haven't you? I'm tired of talking to Americans and cabinet ministers. Want to know what the people are saying."

"Yes, sir," Hooghly answered, subdued. "They'll be along in a little while. In the meantime I'd like you to meet Gerald Mallory."

"Good evening, Mallory. Know your stuff, like it—usually," Sturtevant barked. "What do we do about this mess here? Pull out and let them come to some kind of terms, north and south? Then keep the peace stable with our Navy and Air Force?"

"I'm afraid it's not that simple, Senator," Mallory said. "Sure it's a mess. But we can't keep the peace after we've pulled out. The Communists will take the south for sure, and then. . . ."

"Interesting, Mallory, interesting," Sturtevant interrupted, a note of irritation marring the melodious voice. "Of course, it's not that simple. But we've got to make a decision, can't be bogged down. If these people can't—won't—work for themselves, what can we do?"

"There's not much hope the way we're going," began Mallory, "but still. . . ."

"Look, Mallory," the Senator interrupted, "I want to hear everything you've got to say. Why don't you speak to George here—George da Costa, Gerald Mallory—George is my administrative right-hand. We're leaving tomorrow evening, but how about the morning? George?"

"Could you meet the Senator at the Ambassador's residence at ten tomorrow morning, Mr. Mallory?" asked the tall, thin aide, his down-turned lips barely moving in his long, lugubrious face.

"That'll be all right then," said Sturtevant. "Let's go meet some others."

He squeezed Mallory's biceps, drawing him toward the center of the room. Mallory, for the moment inextricably part of the Senator's entourage, grinned at Tuyelle. She smiled back. The Senator had not spared her a glance.

The room was beginning to fill up, fans battling the rising smoke, and white-clad waiters moving at a brisk pace. A martini was pushed into Mallory's hand, and the Senator took a light scotch and water. Glancing around the room, Mallory saw Colonel McGuffey in dress whites making for the bar and Vao glowering at Tuyelle from a corner.

The hectic atmosphere was so familiar, so commonplace that Mallory could feel the tension leaving his neck and shoulders. The lamps threw soothing rays of light across the smoke, picking out American and Vietnamese faces in polite conversation. Behind him a woman laughed shrilly and a glass splintered. Uniforms constantly moved among the bright dresses in the intricate revolutions of a modern operetta.

Mallory reflected that this was, after all, reality. Vietnam was a hard, nasty fight, enlivened by moments of grace like the present one. After a brace of martinis, his elaborate suspicions seemed pure fantasy. Undoubtedly not one but dozens of informers of varying effectiveness served the Vietcong in Saigon. Yet they were certainly not to be found among the men his own excessive ingenuity had discovered in Humboldt's rubric.

With a start of pleasure, he saw that he could tell Tuyelle they were not only free of Gilroy but free of the burden he had contrived for his own conscience.

The pressure of the Senator's hand on his arm increased.

"Isn't that Dr. Thau?" demanded Sturtevant. "Over there? Let's go talk to him."

They cut through the throng, towing a wake of hangers-on. Sturtevant began the conversation abruptly, ignoring the circle of onlookers that formed around himself and the white-haired Vietnamese, who was dressed for the party in a straw-colored tropical suit, the shoulders tight and the skirts of the jacket skimpy in the French fashion.

"Dr. Thau," said the Senator, "Mallory and I have been having a good talk. We're pretty much in agreement that we can't accomplish anything here—we Americans—unless you people can do more. What can you do?"

"Very little, I'm afraid, without your assistance, Senator," replied Thau, his broad, seamed face turned inquiringly toward Mallory.

"I've thought about what you were saying, Dr. Thau," Mallory said, "and I'm sure you're right about the Chinese. The Senator and I are not quite in full agreement. But I'd second his question."

He turned to Sturtevant, explaining, "Dr. Thau argues that Chinese ambition to conquer the underdeveloped world is so strong and Chinese strategy so dangerous that a victory in Vietnam could double our troubles throughout Afro-Asia— and even in Latin America."

"Come now, Mallory," the Senator snapped, "surely you don't believe that? The problem is hunger and degradation, not a fancied threat from a bunch of wild-eyed opportunists in Peking who don't know anything about the world."

"If you'll forgive me, Senator," Thau wheezed, "the problem is hunger and degradation, of course—but just part of the problem. Let's go back to Vietnam. Hunger and degradation are, by the way, not really so bad, but what can one do about them as long as all effective authority is destroyed by the Vietcong? The first problems are exerting control and creating military authority. Only when there is effective authority can men and governments attack the problems of hunger and degradation. But, at this moment, here we see. . . ."

Sturtevant, straining at the conversational leash, interrupted. "Look, Dr. Thau, we know that revolt springs up in the soil of discontent. End the discontent and the revolt ends. Naturally it takes time and effort to put down the revolt, but it begins withering when the taproot is cut. And that taproot is discontent."

"Perhaps, if the revolt is spontaneous—and relies mainly upon its own resources. Unfortunately, revolts rarely do. There is almost always someone—the Chinese in this case and in many other cases—who ignites and fans revolt. You must cut *that* taproot. Of course, I agree that the ultimate solution is social and economic."

Mallory, debating with himself the advisability of accepting another martini, and finally yielding, was startled to hear the Senator laugh. "Well, sir, I'm glad we're in agreement. Fundamentally it comes down to the same thing. Cut the taproot of misery and the rest will follow."

Dr. Thau, amazement widening his eyes, began, "But, Senator Sturtevant, I can't. . . ."

The Senator cut him off. "Very good to have spoken with you, sir. And you may be sure I'll take heed of your feelings, report them where they'll do the most good. You're right, of course. The only real and effective solution is economic and social. But you mustn't expect Washington to do everything. We have our own problems . . . can't carry the world."

Mallory smiled his apologies at the Vietnamese, murmuring, "I'll see you later, Dr. Thau."

Why, he wondered, did the bad ones make the junkets, while the good ones stayed in Washington, making laws? Sturtevant wheeled about in quest of more information, his grasp still propelling the correspondent.

McGuffey, decorations shining over his white pocket, was bearing down on them, a lean cruiser cutting through the wash of the party. From the other side George Dietrich was

236

approaching at a slower pace, a ponderous battleship thrusting the other guests aside by sheer weight. The Senator was well cut out, but McGuffey got there first.

"Good evening, Senator," he said, the small face beneath the domed forehead obsequiously attentive, a Leprechaun bent on deception. "The General wondered if there were anything more we could do. Do you have everything you need, sir?"

"Hello, Colonel," answered Sturtevant. "Everything's fine as can be expected. Except I'd still like to know what you do with all the men you've got here. Damned lot of men, damned few results."

"Well, sir," answered McGuffey, "I hoped the table of organization I sent you this morning would answer some of your questions. Did you see it?"

"George?" said Sturtevant to his sallow, lugubrious assistant, without taking his eyes off McGuffey. "Did we get it?"

"Yes, sir," murmured the administrative assistant deferentially. "It came with that batch of papers this morning."

"Fine, Colonel, I'll take a look at it. But, I warn you, it'd better be good. Awful lot of men, awful poor results. Is there anything else?"

"No, sir. Except the General hoped he'd see you before you left."

"You have a tentative date for 3:30, if the Foreign Minister doesn't," da Costa began.

"Fine, Colonel, tell the General I'll try to see him. Good-bye, Colonel. Thanks for your help. Good-bye."

Dismissed, McGuffey said, "Good-bye, Senator. See you, Gerry." He drifted into the crowd, pausing on the way to relieve a waiter of a tall glass. Mallory watched him go, wondering again at the labyrinth of suspicion he had erected.

Thau, first? No Vietcong agent would speak as he had. Obviously it would have been worth the slight risk of breaking cover to bolster an influential Senator in his half-formed belief that the United States should pull out of Vietnam. If

237

Sturtevant's view prevailed, the Vietcong would have won. No, Thau just couldn't be working for the Vietcong.

As for McGuff? Over the crowd Mallory saw the bald head tilted back in the attitude of a man relieving a well-earned thirst. McGuffey, newcomer to Vietnam, would barely have time to make any clandestine connections. The lean Colonel was interested in doing the best job he could for his country, getting his stars, and protecting his boss—in that order. Mallory had known McGuff too long not to know the PIO's motivations almost as well as his own.

He rejected the vagrant thought. It was not the glow of the martinis which was smoothing out his problems but a belated access of clarity. He laughed at his own dismay of that afternoon. Why should he care that the CIA thought him such a weak vessel? His job was not skulking in corners scavenging dropped bits of information. His job was reporting, and he was damned good at it.

George Dietrich was towering over the Senator. He had suspected Dietrich as well. The publisher was speaking, his rolling periods apparently having silenced the Senator's barking for the moment. ". . .therefore, we must exert our full efforts. Anything less would be a betrayal of all we have stood for in Asia for a century. Freedom and free enterprise can only grow under an umbrella of American protection. But that is what we want, is it not, sir?"

Sturtevant looked puzzled as the ponderous publisher extracted a starched handkerchief from the breast pocket of his sharkskin jacket and wiped the drops from his glowing brow.

"Free enterprise?" Sturtevant finally snapped. "Yes, of course, though we can't expect exactly the same institutions to flourish here as flourish at home. Must adapt to local conditions. But it's gone too far here. Take our stand down the line, right?"

The question was obviously rhetorical, characteristic of

238

Sturtevant's highly personal style of discourse. But Dietrich took it up, replying, "No, I do not think so. We must take up the challenge right here or else we shall find ourselves discredited. Of course, it will take an immense effort. But our great country should exult in that effort. Too long have we allowed others to dictate the course of events, though we possessed the ultimate power. The effort will, however, as you say, sir, be immense."

"That's right," said Sturtevant, "the effort would be immense. Even our resources are not inexhaustible. You're absolutely right. We can't go on taking losses forever in a hopeless cause. Thank you, sir, I shall consider what you say most earnestly, be assured. Good-bye, sir."

The man held on like an absent-minded bulldog, Mallory reflected, feeling himself wheeled around again. In the midst of saying, "Ah, good evening, Mr. Mallory, I am glad. . . ." Dietrich abruptly shut his mouth and watched the Senator recede. But Mallory crossed another name off his list. Advocating massive American intervention was just what the Vietcong wanted least. Dietrich, too, was in the clear.

There was still Hooghly, though. Hooghly, as Dietrich had stressed, had been a prime mover in the decision to let the discontented and ambitious generals overthrow President Ngo-dinh Diem, and Diem's passing had unquestionably given the Vietcong great opportunities. Cynical after long government service, he might have turned his coat in despair of success and greed for gold. There was certainly no specific evidence to rule Hooghly out. But it was, of course, impossible to prove a negative, and the only indication that Hooghly, who certainly had access to all information, might be the traitor was the tenuous possibility of identification in Humboldt's rubric. Verdict not proven, Mallory decided, and that had to mean "not guilty" for lack of further evidence.

Gratefully reaching for another martini, Mallory turned away. He completed the gesture automatically, though the room was suddenly black behind the lowered jalousies. A woman screamed, another giggled, and a man swore fluently amid a torrent of breaking glass.

"Nothing to worry about, folks." Hooghly's voice cut the swelling noise. "Just a failure of the lights. The guards are having a little trouble, but it'll be all right in a minute."

Mallory pushed toward the door faintly outlined by the moonlight. He ignored squeals and curses as he trod on toes and knocked a glass out of someone's hand. Despite the glow cast on the porch by the moon and a distant streetlight, he stumbled into a small, dark figure.

"Take it easy, buddy," the man snapped. "Oh it's you, Gerry. Still working press, I see."

"Hello, Sid," Mallory answered, glad to see the dapper, hard-headed *Times* man. "What's up?"

"Look for yourself," Rosen answered, leading him around the corner which obscured their view of the street.

Sitting silent in the roadway were several hundred schoolgirls in white *ao-dais*. Guessing in the dim light, Mallory thought they ranged in age from twelve to eighteen. They carried placards reading: STOP KILLING VIETNAMESE! AMERICANS, LEAVE US ALONE! On the edge of darkness he had the impression of an equal number of male students. A loudspeaker clanged in sing-song English: "All we ask is you leave Vietnamese work out Vietnamese problems. Senator Sturtevant, do you hearing us? All we ask is working our own problems. This is Vietnam's problem, not America's problem."

A whistle blew and several hundred schoolgirls began weeping bitterly. Some sat motionless, tears dripping down their childish faces; others writhed in the dust, sobs choking out of their throats. As the loudspeaker began its litany again, a big black car fluttering an American flag inched its way through the crowd. A girl screamed and the male students, as if released by the signal, pushed their way through the seated girls toward the guards, who had been watching mesmerized.

An American MP Sergeant stepped forward and crumpled. A shower of rocks followed the first missile, and the guards huddled together for an instant, hands over their faces for protection. In the background the loudspeaker continued monotonously: "Not your problem, Americans. Our problem, not yours. Stop killing Vietnamese. Go home, Americans, go home."

An American voice screamed, "Who ordered that car? Go back, go back, you fool."

The car reversed, and another girl screamed in pain.

"Just hold it! Stay there, you fool!" shouted the American voice again.

But the car continued backing, accelerating to shake off the students clinging to the sides and tearing at the doors. Abruptly, the limousine halted, and an elderly Vietnamese in a light-gray chauffeur's uniform was jerked through the window by clutching hands. The driver disappeared in a writhing tangle of dark heads and white-clad bodies.

Mallory heard the order just before the execution. "Fire" —and a volley rang skyward from the MPs' pistols. The Vietnamese soldiers did not raise their rifles, but they joined the Americans charging into the crowd. After the briefest scuffle, the street was clear except for the chauffeur, his gray uniform stained and his head bent at an impossibly sharp angle. In the limousine's headlights Mallory saw two schoolgirls, one clutching her leg and screaming, the other bent forward from the waist, head between her legs like a rag doll.

"Another job for the meat wagon," said Rosen tensely. "I'm getting tired of this, Gerry. My nerves are going."

"Sid," answered Mallory, turning away, "don't grieve too much. The people who staged this show are happy to throw away a few schoolkids for the headlines. Practically every correspondent in town was here to see the Senator besieged."

"Yeah, Gerry," Rosen agreed. "Let's go see how the great man took it."

Mallory laid his arm over the smaller man's shoulders as they pushed through the screen door into a room alight once more. Men and women were chattering and waiters were sweeping up broken glass. A small group boiled around the Senator, but Mallory spared his affronted dignity barely a glance. Against the far wall Tuyelle stood close to Vao. Her face was turned up, and his arm clasped her waist protectively.

24

Mallory furiously pushed his way through the throng, thrusting a startled Vietnamese general out of his way. His vision, narrowed by rage, saw only the complacent pair across the room. But they were spotlighted against the light green wall in their graceful attitude, half-conspiratorial and half-affectionate.

The revelation was as painful as the jagged explosion of a migraine, but Mallory knew that he was, at last, seeing clearly through the haze that had shrouded his mind. Vao and Tuyelle, always Vao and Tuyelle, laughing at him and distracting him from his purpose. Vao, always around the corner, always appearing in the least likely places, and always shadowy. And Tuyelle herself, first reluctant, trying to put him off the search, then urging him on toward false quarry. Who else could have corrupted Johnny Humboldt but Tuyelle? Who else but Vao, masquerading as a newspaperman, could have been everywhere, putting together a jigsaw puzzle of bits and pieces of information which finally resolved into a picture of death?

The war might be hopeless. But he could destroy this pair of conspirators.

Had she believed she could corrupt him too? Or was she seeking only to distract him from her own role in Humboldt's death? How he had been besotted by her kisses and her body. How he had been deceived by the meaningless scribble of Humboldt's she had passed off as the key to the puzzle.

Almost upon the pair, his lips shaping a scathing denunci-
ation, he paused. The cautious thought came immediately after the incandescent revelation. Far better to move slowly,
watching with his new awareness until he had the corrobora-
tion he would need. Did the Vietnamese, he wondered, hang
spies or shoot them?

A hand was tugging at his good arm, had been tugging
for some seconds, he realized. Levoncier's voice intruded upon
his rage. "Gerry, Gerry, *mon cher*. It was not that bad, this
little riot. Come back to us."

"Yes, Pierre," he said slowly. "What is it?"

"Ah, that is better, *mon cher*. Look, I think I have some
good pictures. McAllen will love the oh so murky tones and
the agony in bad light. But I must ship them now. Air France
leaves in an hour. Do you still want the car?"

"The car? Oh, the car. Maybe I could use it later."

"Good. I shall leave it at the Majestic then. And Gerry, if
I do not see you for a few days, if you do go on this expedition,
au revoir—and good luck!"

"*Au revoir*, Pierre," he said automatically.

Tuyelle was smiling at him across the few feet that still
separated them. It was an effort to smile back. When he
came close, Vao put out his hand, murmuring, "*Au revoir*,
Mr. Mallory, good luck."

Suppressing his rage, Mallory answered, "*Au revoir*." But
a thrill of confirmation tingled along his spine. Vao must
know of his rendezvous. Why else wish him luck? Was he so
contemptuous that he was dropping his guard? Mallory
watched Vao's thin back disappear through the door before
turning to Tuyelle with his forced smile.

"Another drink or shall we go?" he asked.

"Let's go now, Gerry. I saw that through the jalousies—and
I would like to go."

Mallory was silent in the taxi, occasionally glancing under
lowered lids at the model of perfection beside him, groomed
for the role to the tiny hairs of her moth-wing eyebrows.

He would, he reflected bitterly, rather be sharing a car with a tigress. It was less dangerous. Tuyelle seemed content with silence, though she puffed nervously at her cigarette. She spoke only once, asking, "You do not wish to go out for dinner?"

He shook his head, grunting, "No."

In her living room, the seamed faces of Pierre's portraits looking down with all the pain and laughter of Vietnam in their eyes, he poured two large scotches. She accepted hers with low thanks and let the cigarette smoke trickle luxuriously through her lips before asking softly, "Gerry, you must have been wondering why I was so quiet."

He had not. Her silences, her moods no longer concerned him. But he asked, "Yes?"

"Gerry," she rushed on, "I am so happy, I was just thinking about it. Everything is clear and beautiful—and our life, it will be good."

Disgust rose in his throat, but he managed to ask, "Why, Tuyelle?"

"It is strange." She laughed. "But it is because Vao is going away. I never cared for him as you thought, but he was so much a part of the old life that. . . ."

"Vao, going away? Where?" Mallory interrupted.

"Gerry," she chided, laughing, "you should be listening to me and my rhapsodies, not worrying about Vao. But he is going to India to be press attaché in our legation there. He says, bad as this government is, one has, after all, no choice. Better to perish with it, than to serve the. . . ."

The elaborate structure of Mallory's suspicion tumbled. He could almost feel the physical impact. If Vao were leaving Vietnam, he could hardly be the informer. No apparatus would wantonly destroy a brilliantly successful combination.

He discarded the theory with a perverse pang of deprivation. This, too, a fantasy? But, then there was no longer any reason for suspicion of Tuyelle. He turned to her, taking her hands in his own and urging, "Yes, go on. Tell me.

Why has Vao's departure made you so happy? That's a strange parting from an old friend, not to mention an old lover."

"Not an old lover, Gerry." She smiled. "You have less reason to be jealous of Vao's memory than of Johnny's—and no real reason to be jealous of Johnny. Why so happy? Because I saw the whole thing clearly for once. The entire old life passing and letting me go free of the past into the new life. Oh, Gerry, I know we'll be happy."

Her mood was beginning to kindle a response, but he could not refrain from asking, "And Vietnam? Are you giving up, then?"

"No," she answered seriously, "I cannot give up Vietnam. Even if there is little hope, I shall do what I can. And you will do for me what you can. I shall serve—my task is you."

"Then we give up the search for the informer, write the story—and get out? Is that what you want?"

"Yes, Gerry, yes. We can do so little. But we shall, of course, return."

"That's wonderful, Tuyelle, wonderful. But it will have to be a delayed honeymoon. First the book, then Europe and New York this summer. And, Tuyelle, I have a wedding present for you."

"What's that?" she asked. "Wouldn't you rather wait and surprise me?"

"No, this one you must take now. Tuyelle, I'm all through with my fantasies. I know that someone's tipping off the Vietcong, but it's not anyone we know. There is no debt to Humboldt any longer. We're free."

For fifteen minutes he explained the process by which he had discarded the suspects they had conjured up from Humboldt's scribbling. "And I'd even eliminated Vao," he concluded, laughing.

To his surprise, her face was grave. She started to speak, hesitated, and stopped. Finally she spoke slowly. "Gerry, are you so sure? Quite so sure? Johnny was no fool you know."

"Of course I'm sure. Despite what Gilroy said, Humboldt was probably no more involved than you or I. Let's forget it," he said conclusively, raising his glass. "To you, and me, and the future."

She was still pensive as she put her glass down. "Gerry," she said again, "it's one thing to recognize defeat, another to deceive oneself. I, too, have been brooding and—but first let me ask you: Why did your friend Gilroy make so much of Johnny if he were not involved? Why was he rushed away? Why was he killed? Or why did he suicide?"

"I guess we'll never know, Tuyelle. For my purposes, for my story, it's good enough that he did commit suicide in disgust. I'm not tilting at windmills any more."

"Sometimes," she spoke in a voice so low he had to lean closer to hear, "sometimes it is necessary to tilt at windmills— I have been thinking—and I do not know, but let *me* ask some questions this time."

"Sure, go ahead." He smiled. Her persistence actually reassured him that all his fantasies had been just fantasies. Hadn't he been convinced, only half an hour earlier, that she was the root of the evil?

She continued. "You may think me mad, but I have been thinking hard. Tell me, was George Dietrich's luncheon for you a success?"

"Why, no," he replied, puzzled. "I've already told you. Those types he produced were so horrible it was embarrassing. Enough to make you despair."

"Suppose it weren't you, then what?"

"What do you mean?"

"I'm not sure. But I wonder, if some other correspondent had been at that lunch, someone who knew very little about Vietnam—what would he have felt?"

"Hell," he laughed, "that's easy. I almost felt it myself. Any country represented, truly represented, by a crook, a playboy, and a senile old man—why there'd be no hope."

247

"Maybe that's the conclusion Dietrich wanted you to reach," she suggested.

He rejected the tenuous theory impatiently. "Look Tuyelle, I've just been through a week of fantasy, real deep-dish Oriental fantasy. I don't want to plunge back into. . . ."

"But," she insisted, "do you think Dietrich is a fool?"

"No," he conceded, "he just had bad luck."

"Bad luck with men he's known for years? That's not likely, Gerry."

"No, I suppose not," he mused. "But it was just a fluke."

"Are you sure?" she insisted.

"Of course. Why his line is hard as Gibraltar. Plunge in and save Vietnam at any cost. Why, only tonight, talking to Sturtevant—my God!" His voice trailed off.

"Yes, Gerry?" she probed.

"No, it's too fantastic, but still. Look, tonight Dietrich knew Sturtevant's reputation, knew his position. But he kept stressing that we had to involve ourselves here regardless of the cost. He kept stressing that the cost would be astronomical, but, of course, we could pay it. And Sturtevant, not surprisingly, went away even more convinced that the only thing to do is to get out. But it was just a miscalculation on Dietrich's part, I'm sure."

"He miscalculates often, doesn't he?" Tuyelle asked.

"Don't we all, Tuyelle?" Mallory smiled. "Look, this guy is no Einstein—not even Aaron Burr. He's just a fat, high-living, pretentious slob who wants as much money as he can get—and covers his greed with a flow of cant about free enterprise. Pierre says he was mixed up with Raul Salan and the opium trade in the old days. If that's not high-class, wholly unprincipled greed. . . Dietrich just wants to keep the United States here so he can keep raking in the shekels."

"Opium," said Tuyelle, "that speaks much more than simple greed. You have seen heroin addicts, Gerry, ruthlessness

248

even sadism, not just greed. Gerry, do something for me while I get more ice. Think about George Dietrich as I have."

Wrestling with the "quick-opening" aluminum cap of the bottle, Mallory conceded, "I'll go along with you this far. Dietrich could be the man Humboldt meant, the double-agent Gilroy wants to protect. That figures. Dietrich fits Humboldt's rubric perfectly. It has to be a fat man. That first reversal, you remember. Taut, meaning fat. And it has to be a man with a ruddy complexion. Emeralcund for rubicund. So Humboldt thought he had something. But all he had was a double-agent, working for us."

"But Johnny was shot," she reminded him.

"Yeah, that was a bit rough. Why not just get him out of the place? Unless the others, the VC, wanted to protect their man Dietrich, and if they did, then they must have known of his double role."

He took a deep draught of his scotch and ice. Rubbing his palm over his hair in perplexity, he said, "But Tuyelle, we're just going round in circles. Did they know that the others knew that they knew that the others knew? And so on, ad nauseam."

"Go on, anyway, Gerry," she suggested.

"All right. Humboldt was convinced Dietrich was the man —probably that he was supposed to be our double-agent, but was really working for the Communists. Therefore, Humboldt's anguish about making the revelation. Point one for your side. Point two, Dietrich was a rabid anti-colonialist when he got here, then did a quick switch. Pierre thinks it was just dough that made the difference. Still I'll give you the point."

"Where are we proceeding?" she prodded.

"I supposed," he answered slowly, "to the conclusion that Humboldt felt certain Dietrich was the man responsible for giving the Vietcong foreknowledge of our plans."

"Point three, Gerry?" she insisted.

249

Mallory grinned sheepishly. "Look, Tuyelle, I told you that somebody was trying to frighten me off this, somebody who didn't fit into the pattern—neither CIA nor Vietcong. Well, that outfit finally came down to blackmail. I'll tell you the details later, but it had to be somebody who was mixed up with the opium business. And that we know Dietrich was— and maybe still is. But an American agent would still want to protect himself."

"What else do we know?"

"Well," he continued, "the ink box at my friend's, the Vietcong leader's—that's pretty damning if it was the same one. But a double-agent would have to be in touch, wouldn't he?"

"So, everything we know could point two ways, could it?"

"That's about it, Tuyelle. We're no wiser."

"But I must always ask again—why was Johnny shot? That was too much, if Dietrich was only a double-agent and not really working for the Vietcong. You did not know Tham," she concluded somewhat irrelevantly.

"We can go around on that bit forever," Mallory answered patiently. "Did X know that Y knew that X knew. . . . Can I stop now?"

"Surely." She laughed. "But look, Gerry, Johnny was no fool. He knew something that told him Dietrich was more than a double-agent for the Americans, that his loyalty was given to the Communists. And so Johnny was shot."

"I'll accept your judgment—on the basis of your shrewd appraisal of Humboldt's character. And if you ever analyze me as shrewdly, I can't hold out much hope for this impending marriage. But, Tuyelle, I'm no fool either. And that means I'm smart enough to know when we're licked. You've got me half-convinced Dietrich is a bad boy, a really nasty specimen. But what can I do? I can't convince anyone else with the evidence we've got, can I?"

"I suppose not, Gerry," she conceded.

"Then let's have another drink and a sandwich and I'll go quietly home."

"We'll have the drink and the sandwiches, Gerry. But I don't want you to go home," she answered.

"So much the better." He grinned. "I didn't want to outstay my welcome."

"Oh, Gerry," she said, exasperated.

But she could not leave the matter alone. Over brandy and coffee she returned to the attack.

"Then, Gerry, we've decided Dietrich is a killer; he killed Johnny—or had him killed. He's killed dozens of others, maybe hundreds or thousands. He's one with the people who sacrifice schoolgirls no older than my little sister. And we leave him alone. He survives untouched, a traitor, a murderer, a profiteer, and a man who twists others' souls with drugs. He is to survive."

"I'm afraid so, darling," Mallory answered deliberately. "I know it's terrible. But there is nothing I can do, short of shooting him myself."

"Talk to your friends," she urged. "Tell them, expose him."

"I've already tried. But I can't convince even Gilroy with our present evidence, much less anyone else. No, I'm getting off this trolley car. I'm going back to being a reporter. I've got a big story and that story is important to our future. No more fiddling around. There are things a man can do, and things no one can do. That's realism. I'm reconciled. I'm not a superman."

"No, that's clear," she snapped. Then, instantly contrite, she added, "I'm sorry, Gerry, I suppose that's the beginning of maturity, knowing what you can't do."

"Or of decay," he muttered. "But I'm reconciled to my limitations. I don't even feel bad about this."

"Then why are you drinking so much?"

"Habit, I suppose." He shrugged. "Tuyelle, maybe I'd better go home after all."

"No," she urged. "Don't go, Gerry. Don't leave me to-night. I have the feeling everything will be all right if only you stay. But if you go, something will be terribly wrong for-ever."

"I want to stay," he said. "But let's talk about the future, not the dead past."

"Yes, Gerry," she answered meekly. "And, I think you're right. Better to be alive and loving, better to survive for another battle than to destroy oneself in vain. But just one more question?"

"All right." He grinned. "I should have known better. Okay, go ahead. We'll close the subject when you're ready, not I."

"It's not *that* subject. Just this: What about Vietnam?"

"That's a nice topic for a little bedtime story, isn't it? But I did say all right. Skipping all the verbiage and the back-ground, leaving out the sound, color, feel, and smell stuff, this is about it. . . ."

"What's going to happen?" As he talked, his ideas became definite for the first time. "Sturtevant, the Sturtevants and the Dietrichs and all the little men will have their way. We'll pull out because we can't see how important it is that we stay. And that will be that. The Vietcong will have won their victory through psychological warfare directed at us, not at the Vietnamese people at this stage. Finished."

"And what could you do, what should we all do?" she per-sisted as he emptied his glass.

"That's simple, simple and nasty. We must stay and fight it out, knowing we can't gain any decisive victory. But too much is at stake, too many men and women we can't abandon, not to speak of our own honor. We must stay and fight, how-ever hopeless it appears, and hope we can hold on until the other side begins to change because it realizes that *it* can't win. Hopeless causes are not attractive, but sometimes they're the only causes worth fighting for."

252

"Thanks, Gerry," she breathed. "Well said, eloquent and honorable. I do love you."

"Thanks, darling," he smiled. "Now let's go to bed with one last drink. I'm tired."

"Tired?" she mocked. "Tired? Is that the only reason you want to go to bed?"

"Well, not that tired," he answered.

He lay under a thin sheet listening to the thunder and the rain outside while waiting for her to reappear. The temperature had dropped, but it was still hot and sticky. Brandy, he reminded himself sipping slowly, was fine for Paris, but it was hell in Saigon.

The door opened and Tuyelle was silhouetted against the light. Her thin nightdress, a gesture rather than a garment, fell in two broad folds from her breasts, and her hips swayed under the transparent fabric as she came to the bed.

He grasped her eagerly, straining to fit himself to every curve and hollow of her body. She responded with a gasp, and they caressed each other, slowly and langorously, excitement mounting. He slipped the nightdress over her head and ran his fingers down her spine. She turned back to him, her mouth hot and demanding.

"Now," she breathed huskily.

But Mallory could not. "It must be the whisky or something," he muttered shamfacedly. "I'm sorry, darling."

"Never mind, sweetheart, never mind," she soothed him. "Of course it's the liquor—and we're both tired. Just lie back."

She caressed him expertly, surprising him with her dexterity and her ingenuity. But after ten minutes he shook her off.

"It's no use, Tuyelle," he said harshly. "It's no use. I'm no good tonight. I'm going."

He began flinging his clothes on, stopping only to pour and gulp down another glass of brandy. He ignored her pleas.

"Gerry, stay with me tonight. This doesn't matter. It doesn't matter that much. Stay with me, please."

Fully dressed, he mustered a lopsided grin and said, "Look, Tuyelle, let me go. Maybe it doesn't matter—or you have to say so. But it's not right. I'm no good to anyone tonight." He bent over and kissed her, barely brushing her lips.

Opening the black door, he was assailed by a tide of rain. But he turned up his coat collar and began walking toward the nearest intersection. Before he had gone a half-block, he could feel the water rolling down from his drenched clothing to squelch into his shoes. But he did not care.

25

The rain leached much of the alcohol out of Mallory before he found a *pous-pous*. He was cold, shivering, and half-sober when he slumped onto the stained cushions, gratefully allowing the driver to enclose him behind the filthy canvas weather sheet. This night he could ride a *pous-pous* unafraid, shielded by his appointed rendezvous with the Vietcong.

His bitterness mounted as the alcoholic glow dissipated. Struggling to light a damp cigarette, he saw that he had been on an emotional roller coaster all that day and the three days preceding. From the moment he landed on the High Plateau, time had become an endless, empty corridor wholly lacking the customary divisions of sleep and night that impose order and continuity on our lives. His memory fragmented by brief intervals of rest at odd hours, he could barely remember that first day of the ambush on the Plateau. Hardly ninety-six hours past, it might have occurred weeks earlier.

The slaughter on the Plateau and the riots in Saigon had wrung his emotions without threatening his own identity. But the sour talk with Gilroy had shredded the husk of his self-esteem. He had, though briefly, become the bumbling derelict Gilroy saw, the irrational drifter who had made the horrifying discovery of Tuyelle's treachery. That grotesque fantasy had scarred him, despite his later joyous release from suspicion.

Was he becoming a manic-depressive? The violent gyrations from elation to despair he had always known had become so intense and so telescoped in time that he feared he might truly be losing his grip on reality; the dangers of Vietnam were not all physical.

He was half-convinced that Dietrich was the informer. But was he sure? Could he find enough certainty to convince even himself?

Tuyelle, he knew, could only feel contempt for him; not only for his physical failure, though it must lie heavily in the balance. But how else could she feel when she contemplated his cowardice? He had said he would do nothing about Dietrich because it was hopeless—and dangerous. But he had declaimed that Vietnamese and Americans must continue to fight even though the cause appeared hopeless, presumably with Gerald Mallory comfortably ensconced in Hong Kong gracefully accepting praise for his brilliant analyses. He simply did not know whether he could ever go back to Tuyelle again.

"Hopeless, hopeless, hopeless," he said aloud, paying off the driver and adding a tip three times the exorbitant fare. It was a meaningless gesture, since he felt no particular good will toward the man. But it would have been nice to see that dark face smile sullenly, or even look surprised. It did neither. The Americans had been in Saigon too long.

"Hopeless," he repeated to himself as he climbed the stairs. "Hopeless, hopeless, hopeless," he chanted aloud, tilting the brandy bottle over an empty tumbler in his room. The words ran together, syllables linking into new forms and deteriorating into meaninglessness. "Lesshope, lesshope, lesshopeless, hope. . . ."

He shuddered as the brandy burned along his esophagus and flamed in his stomach. But the shock broke his maudlin litany. He tossed down the rest of the brandy and stripped off his wet clothing. He could just manage, though he had only an arm-and-a-half to work with. His jungle gear lay in the corner, musette bag still packed and boots stuffed with thick socks. Automatically, he began dressing again. He would keep his rendezvous despite the pain in his arm. He would go and see the other side for himself. He was still a working reporter, and that much he could do. Let Tuyelle worry; let them all worry. He could still do his job.

Pulling his stained bush jacket on, he felt a weight in the side pocket. Levoncier's little revolver slipped into his hand, and, for a moment, he toyed with the weapon, raising it halfway to his head. Laying it down gingerly, he poured another brandy. The parallel was too close. Gerald Mallory would not go out with a pistol bullet in his head as John Humboldt had.

He sipped the brandy cautiously and stared hard at the little weapon. The screws and hatchings on the plump hand grip began to form a pattern. He stared longer and Dietrich's face smiled unctuously from the polished metal. "Murderer, traitor," Tuyelle had called him. But he would survive and prosper while other men died to make him secure. To denounce Dietrich would be pointless, since no one would believe him. He shuddered, remembering Humboldt's death.

"Unless I shoot him myself," he had told Tuyelle to demonstrate how ridiculous, how hopeless—that word again—it was to think of their destroying Dietrich when they had no real evidence against him. But why not? Here was the evil he knew. Here was the deed he, and no one else, could do. Perhaps he owed a life to Tuyelle and Harkness, to Vietnam and America.

It might be Dietrich's; it might be his own. If he could slip away unseen, would Gilroy blame the Vietcong and bury the matter? If he were caught, might they still not prefer silence?

With a start, he read his own resolution and pushed the speculation aside contemptuously. This time he would act without examining the consequences. Here was the courage Tuyelle and Gilroy both assumed he lacked. After all the cowardice and all the pretense, he would confront the evil directly, without thought of consequences.

257

Fondling the butt of the revolver in his pocket, he strode through the lobby.

"Mr. Mallory," the desk clerk called, "Mr. Levoncier left an envelope for you."

Mallory took the envelope, feeling the weight of metal. Outside in the night the battered Citroën waited, rain flowing down its ungainly flanks. He could just manipulate the gear-shift lever that protruded from the dashboard. When he found the switch, the headlights cast a weak yellow glow, but the windshield wiper dashed aside the sheets of rain with fine abandon. Driving slowly, he found the square dominated by the apartment house which was crowned by Dietrich's penthouse.

The car had taken all his attention, but as he rode in the automatic elevator he began to wonder what he was doing. He did not, after all, *know* that Dietrich was the traitor; he only *felt* it in his nerve ends. Contemplating the actual deed, he feared he could not pull the trigger unless he were certain that he was executing the right man. But he crushed the doubts into the corner of his mind. He had come too far to turn back.

Mallory pressed the discreet white-plastic bell in the polished teak frame and was rewarded with a peal of chimes. He rang three times before the door swung open.

Dietrich's bulk was swathed in a fawn-colored dressing gown of pongee, and he wore pajamas of a finer silk in the same shade. His graying hair clung closely to the round contours of his massive head, except for one vagrant forelock. Although the broad, florid cheeks were pillow-seamed, the small blue eyes were alert. His face was as smooth as if he had just shaved.

The publisher appeared unperturbed by the apparition he saw before him. Mallory's dark, cropped hair, still wet, was a palisade of irregular spikes. His wide gray eyes were bloodshot, and his drawn cheeks were speckled with the cuts he had inflicted while shaving that afternoon. He was suddenly

258

conscious of his filthy, torn, jungle green jacket and trousers, which exhaled a musty odor of sweat mingled with brandy fumes.

Dietrich stepped aside with a bland smile of welcome. He waved Mallory into the air-conditioned living room, which still smelled faintly of sandalwood.

"Come in, Mr. Mallory, come in," he said. "I will not go so far as to say I was expecting you. But I am glad that you have decided to take advantage of my standing invitation. A drink, perhaps?"

"Brandy, if you have it," said Mallory, lowering himself into the depths of a green leather chair. Their pinpoint lights transformed the aquariums into a single broad band of murky iridescence that threw shifting shadows across the room.

Dietrich returned with a bottle of *marc de Champagne* and two brandy snifters. He placed them on the broad teak coffee table.

"I seem to remember that you like *marc*, Mr. Mallory."

"Thanks," responded the correspondent briefly.

"What can I do for you, my dear fellow?" Dietrich inquired. "Surely you have not come to discuss the progress of the war at this time of the evening—and in that garb."

Mallory set his glass down on the table beside the statuette of Kwan Yin. "Mr. Dietrich," he said abruptly, "we seem to have a mutual friend named Gilroy, Harrison Gilroy."

"Oh, is that so?" asked Dietrich noncommittally.

"You do know Gilroy, don't you, Mr. Dietrich?" Mallory persisted.

"I have had some business dealings with him," the publisher admitted.

"Then there was the matter of young John Humboldt."

"Tragic case. Tragic young man," said Dietrich. "I knew him casually."

"I think you knew him well," Mallory said. "Just as you did Pham-quot Tham, who shot him."

259

"I'm afraid, sir, I don't quite follow you. I understood that Humboldt had shot himself."

"You will, my friend, you will follow—if you don't already," Mallory said, thrusting at the curtain of blandness. "Then there was the massacre at Hieptre and the slaughter on the High Plateau only yesterday. Have you heard of those?"

"Naturally, I follow the news. I have read about the catastrophe on the High Plateau. But I'm afraid the name Hieptre means nothing to me."

"So much information passes through your hands that you can't remember each case?" jabbed Mallory.

"My dear fellow, I have no special reason to recall each battle in this ceaseless struggle," Dietrich said placatingly.

For a sickening moment Mallory was half-convinced by the fat man's deprecating air. He had a quick vision of himself—filthy, half-soaked, and exuding brandy fumes—an obvious madman seated in that overelaborate, overcivilized room. But it was easier to go on than to turn back.

"Mr. Dietrich, I have evidence—testimony and documents —that prove you've been feeding information to the Vietcong. You don't deserve it, but I've come to warn you— that information will appear in *Quest* magazine next week."

The fat man's hands curled in his lap and he flushed angrily, but he replied with a half-smile. "I'd be sorry for *you*, very sorry. Bankruptcy through a libel suit would be the least of your worries. You'd probably end up in an insane asylum." Dietrich deliberately raised his snifter to his lips, sipping delicately as the flush faded from his cheeks. He added. "And the way you look—and act—right now, it's obvious that's where you belong."

"Nonetheless, I intend to go ahead. I know you're the man who. . . ."

"What tommyrot," Dietrich exploded.

". . . has been killing hundreds of Vietnamese and Americans for your own profit—a dirty, money-grubbing monster."

260

Dietrich's fleshy forehead creased, forcing the heavy gray eyebrows down over the small, blue eyes. "Go ahead, Mr. Mallory," he said in a low voice. "Dig your own grave. Isn't alcohol fast enough for you? Must you destroy yourself with your own fantasies?"

"I have the evidence, and I will go ahead," Mallory goaded. "I'll draw a picture to horrify the world—obese, pretentious, sanctimonious, drenched in blood and drugs, a traitor to his country and to humanity."

Dietrich's aplomb was forced, and he gulped the remnants of his *marc* before pouring another heavy dollop in his glass. But his voice remained low. "Go ahead then, Mr. Mallory, go ahead. Coming from a gin-soaked, womanizing correspondent who couples with attendants in opium divans—who will believe it?"

"Everyone," said Mallory triumphantly, "everyone who'll wonder how you know about my personal habits. I can prove your connection with Madame Jahn's, and you've just driven the last possible doubt from my own mind."

"Nonsense! Everyone knows your habits. It's common gossip."

"Nonsense to you, Dietrich. I've been to Madame Jahn's only once this trip. Yet you know about it. I'm sure you even had me photographed. A *voyeur* too. That will be the final condemnation for the moralistic American public."

"And would you like to see such a picture published?" asked Dietrich, his eyes almost hooded by the heavy eyebrows and the pockets of fat under them.

"Go ahead. It won't hurt me one-tenth as much as what I'm going to do to you. Ruin, disgrace—I wonder who'll shoot you, the Vietnamese or the Americans."

"Mallory," said Dietrich, rising, "you almost force me to a decision."

Mallory fumbled the revolver out of his pocket. "Sit still, Dietrich," he said. "Sit still. Let's not have any more melodrama than we must. I warn you truly, I'd rather shoot you now than later. Stand up slowly and keep your hands on your head."

Grimacing with distaste and pain, Mallory pushed his right hand into the pocket of Dietrich's dressing gown. It was empty, but the second pocket yielded a small revolver.

"Sit down again, Dietrich," he commanded. "And, remember, I'm a bit distraught, high-strung at the best of times. And this is not one of my best."

The fat man settled himself comfortably, crossing his legs and leaning back in his chair. He sipped his *marc* delicately. "Mr. Mallory," he said jovially, "we seem to have reached an impasse. If you do write these lies about me, you'll find yourself in such trouble that you'll never get out of it. That money in the Bank of China simply can't be explained away. If you shoot me, on the other hand, it would undoubtedly inconvenience me considerably. There will also be this large body of mine to dispose of—most unpleasant for you. This is not the Vietnamese countryside where one body more or less, even one as large as mine, causes little comment." He looked down complacently at his bulk.

"What do you suggest?" Mallory prodded.

"Why don't we strike a bargain, Mr. Mallory? One that would be of mutual benefit. In order to avoid inconvenience I am prepared to pay two hundred thousand dollars. I'm sure Miss Tuyelle—who, by the way, has expensive tastes, as I know—I'm sure Tuyelle would prefer an affluent correspondent to a broken man."

"Point, game, set, match," said Mallory, speaking low. "No false charge is worth quite so much to cover up. I'll think about it, Dietrich. Since you're so sure of your analysis of my character—and Tuyelle's."

"My dear fellow," said the publisher with a placating sweep of his heavy hands, "no judgment on your character was implied. It just seemed a sensible solution."

"I'll think about it on one condition," Mallory repeated.

"And what is that?"

262

"That you tell me why you're doing this."

"You want me to add fuel to your fantasies, do you?"

"Look, Dietrich, I told you, I know. But I want to know why. It's worth the gamble to you, isn't it?"

"Mr. Mallory," the big man smiled warmly after a moment, "you have given me the opportunity I have long wished for— to explain my rationale to a man who is obviously much less unintelligent than I had thought. You were not convinced by my lunchtime charade, I take it?"

"No," said Mallory shortly, "I wasn't. Now start talking. I'll think about your offer as you talk."

"Mr. Mallory, assuming your suspicions to be true, what would motivate a man like me to do the things you ascribe to me? If you were a little more sophisticated of course, I wouldn't have to explain."

"Just go ahead, Dietrich. I'll try to follow."

"You must forgive me, my dear fellow." The publisher laughed. "I meant no disrespect to your intellect. I've already told you what a pleasure it will be to explain to you, to be able to drop my sometimes fatuous mask for a while. I merely meant that you would understand if your mind were free, as mine is."

"Free?" Mallory's voice cracked with disbelief.

"Yes, Mr. Mallory, free. You act as you do because of where you were born. Your loyalties were chosen for you by your parents; I chose my own. If you had been a Russian, you would be defending Holy Mother Kremlin with the same fervor and the same epithets. A Chinese, and your dedication would verge on mania. But I have risen above circumstances, above the accident of my birth. I have made a decision freely. I am a free man with a free mind, one of very few alive today."

"And that decision?" prodded Mallory.

"That decision—the theoretical decision—is that there is no possibility of anything but a victory for the Communists in Asia. It would, incidentally, be best for the United States

263

to get out, rather than waste its substance. But that is not my immediate concern. Having made my judgment, I have protected my own interests."

Mallory's mind clanged shut like a bank vault. He had been turning over Dietrich's offer, wondering what devices the publisher would suggest to keep the transaction secure, wondering if he might raise the offer another hundred thousand. But the phrase "protected my own interests" shut off the speculation. He was, after all, not sitting with a murderer at two in the morning to protect *his* own interests; there had been too much of that in his life. Dietrich would never know how close he had come. Mallory hoped the decision did not show on his face.

But the publisher was continuing undeterred. "Mr. Mallory, I shall not pretend that my decision was wholly unemotional. Do you understand the attraction of power to the unhampered mind? I myself work with the National Liberation Front in good part because it holds the power. The doctrine of inevitability is the strongest weapon we have, irresistible because it is true. No man will fight the inevitable unless he is mad, and most men in Asia today can see that our triumph is inevitable."

"Then you're a believer?" Mallory interjected. "That makes it a little more palatable."

"Anxious as I am for your good opinion—both in the abstract and, tonight, as a means of extricating myself, extricating both of us from this predicament— I shall not lie to you. No, I am not a believer in historical determinism, dialectical materialism, or even the benefits of communism for the rabble. I am merely realistic enough to recognize the inevitable, spiritual enough to be drawn to power, and crass enough to benefit from my realistic conclusions."

"And what about the dead, the men you've killed? How do they fit into your bookkeeping?"

"Mr. Mallory, you are, obviously, at liberty to believe that I am toadying to your good opinion in my reply. But

264

I tell you, quite honestly—the time for pretense has passed—what you should see clearly for yourself. If I have precipitated the deaths of a few men, I am saving the lives of many more by moving this stupid conflict toward a speedy conclusion. The sooner it ends, the fewer men will die. Guerrillas can be opposed successfully, but only by men as besotted and as insensitive as they themselves are. Neither the men in Saigon nor the men in Washington are equipped to fight these guerrillas. They are too frivolous. It's a blessing to end this war rapidly."

"What about Humboldt? How did his death serve humanity?" Mallory asked.

Dietrich ignored the sarcasm. "He got in my way, in our way. First he was providing me with information. Does that shock you, Mr. Mallory?"

"Not as much as it should," Mallory conceded.

"Then he turned on me. I had let down my guard with him, as I am afraid I am with you. He threatened to expose me, as you are threatening. My defenses are strong, but they are not perfect. What else could I do?"

"From your point of view, nothing," said Mallory. "Just as you would eliminate me—will eliminate me—as soon as you can."

"Mr. Mallory," the fat man beamed, "it is a delight to talk with an intelligent man. We must discuss safeguards for you as soon as I've finished answering your questions. The matter is at the moment just as vital for me as it is for you. Humboldt never held a gun on me. I know I must prove that you will live to enjoy your money. Can we move on? Are you through with this line of questioning?"

"Not quite," Mallory said, admiring the publisher's composure in spite of his disgust at the man. "How did you keep your information so fresh after Humboldt's death? You'd lost your source, hadn't you?"

"I had expected more of you than that. Of course, I hadn't lost my source, just *a* source. Mr. Mallory, have you ever heard of corruption, Oriental corruption? Of course you have. There is Occidental corruption, too, and no man is immune. There were—there are—American officers assigned by the CIA to give me certain information to bolster the role I play. They even receive payment to give the transaction versimilitude. A few payments made much too high in error, a few thousand dollars here and there. The excess not reported. It tempts the greedy man; you see, don't you?

"Then the information, too, increases in quality. Often it is not even necessary to say a word. These transactions have a way of working out without words, without explicit agreement. In a corrupt war it is impossible to fight without corruption. Since corruption cannot be controlled, it is impossible to secure all possible sources of information."

"And the relay?" Mallory asked, curiosity overcoming repugnance.

"I thought your evidence was complete," Dietrich sneered. "I understand the Liberation Front possesses a most efficient radio network. In Saigon, with the assistance of the CIA, passing information is about as difficult as ordering a bottle of wine."

"I see," Mallory said shortly. Caution still asserted itself against the fat man's braggadocio, he noted with perverse amusement, to keep specifics and details secret.

"Can we discuss the matters vital to both of us?" Dietrich pressed him.

"No, not here," Mallory answered abruptly. "Get dressed Dietrich. We're going for a ride in the Vietnamese countryside, where the bodies are as common as rice paddies."

Dietrich flinched, and Mallory added, "No, I haven't made up my mind yet. You can relax for a while. But I've got to convince you I'm in earnest, too. Let's go for a ride and talk about our mutual problems."

"But it's comfortable right here," the fat man expostulated.

"Move, Dietrich. I'm not fooling with you. Move. Get your clothes on," Mallory said, gesturing with the revolver.

266

Fascinated and revolted by the mounds of pendulous flesh, he watched the publisher dress. First silk underwear, embroidered with the ornate initials GH in red, then a silk shirt, and finally the inevitable sharkskin suit. As they walked toward the door, Mallory warily behind, the publisher carefully drew on a light, transparent nylon raincoat.

"Shall we go?" He twinkled at Mallory. "I need hardly add that I am yours to command."

26

Dietrich grunted as he forced his bulk behind the wheel of the Citroën. He tucked his raincoat around his white suit with a series of flicks so precise they lent his elephantine figure an ephemeral grace. His air was less that of a man facing death than that of a businessman anxious to finish an unpleasant transaction and get back to his desk. Was Dietrich, Mallory wondered, so certain that he would compromise?

Twice the fat man tried to start the aged engine, and twice it sputtered asthmatically into extinction. Exasperated, Mallory leaned over to check the gauges. The gas tank was three-quarters full.

He dug the muzzle of the revolver into the publisher's ribs, daunted by a fleeting sense of unreality. But his harsh words carried conviction even to himself. "All right, Dietrich. If you don't want to take a ride in the country, we won't. I'll just pull the trigger and dump you out. Nobody would connect me with a corpse found on the street, even one as large as yours."

The engine caught on the next try, chattering in its accustomed demented rhythm. After further fumbling, the publisher managed to get the headlights glowing.

"The Bien-hoa road, and keep the speed between seventy-five and eighty kilometers," Mallory ordered as the battered Citroën drew away from the curb, tires casting up freshets of white water in the rays of a solitary streetlight.

The corners of Dietrich's mouth drew down and his broad

268

face seemed to shrink under the speckled shadows of the rain-drops on the windshield. "Bien-hoa, Mr. Mallory?" he asked. "You know that the road is somewhat dangerous?"

"What better place to be alone, Dietrich?" Mallory replied. "What better place to think about a couple of hundred thousand dollars—or maybe three hundred thousand?"

Dietrich's tongue darted nervously between his pale lips, and he countered, "That's a bit high, but I might be able to. . . ."

"We'll see, Dietrich, we'll see," Mallory interrupted "I haven't said *yes* yet."

The black car settled to its pace, wide-set tires gripping the wet road. They crossed the bridge and turned right for Bien-hoa without seeing another car. Under the glow of the last streetlamp, Mallory's eye was caught by a slip of red paper protruding from the glove compartment. Working the catch open, he found that the paper was tied to the neck of Levoncier's silver brandy flask. Scrawled across it were the words: "Bon voyage, Gerry." He took a long gulp, his eyes fixed on Dietrich over the flask.

The trees, white-washed for visibility, flickered by in an endless procession of earthbound wraiths. Mallory settled himself as comfortably as he could, his back against the door, and tried to envision his next move. He could just see the car stopped and Dietrich standing before him in the rain. His finger tightened sympathetically on the trigger, but he could not complete the mental picture: the flat explosion and the heavy body falling into the mud. Judge he might be, but executioner he apparently was not.

Could he write the story as he had originally threatened, he wondered. But that road was blocked. He could not expect authority to deal with Dietrich on the evidence of a guarded confession which only one person had heard. No more could he expect any editor to print that farrago of charges without overwhelming evidence. He knew, as Deitrich did not, that few editors would take such a chance even with full documentation. McAllen of *Quest* was not one of those few.

Mallory shivered, remembering Humboldt's blood puddling in the pink dust before the candy-striped sentry box. Even the counsel of cowardice was vain. Mallory could not hope to flee; he would never leave Saigon alive. He was, quite simply and quite inextricably, committed. He must destroy Dietrich or Dietrich would destroy him. Once more he considered accepting the bribe. Were private vengeance and the moral debts he owed worth almost a quarter of a million dollars?

He shook off the fantasy. The compromise might mean safety for Dietrich, but for himself—if he lived—it would mean years spent wrestling with the memory of this night in a succession of bars. They might be the world's plushest bars, but there was little joy in the prospect. Apparently he could not commit the final betrayal. His was the dilemma of an eighteenth-century bankrupt who could only redeem his honor by suicide. If the deed were done, honor would be satisfied, but he could not preserve life and honor both.

He reluctantly formulated the decision which had been poised in the back of his mind: let Dietrich's allies do the job for him. The Vietcong leader had said, "Come alone to the 16th kilometer stone—or my men will fire." A spurt of hope told him there was a slender chance that he might survive. They would probably fire first at the man in the driver's seat.

He accepted his decision with uneasy fatalism. If he survived, it might mean redemption. If he did not, justice would have been executed on himself as well as on Dietrich. It did not occur to him that Dietrich might survive while he perished.

Nylon crackled a sharp complaint as the fat man shifted his weight behind the wheel. Mallory shook off his revery and raised the revolver.

"Mr. Mallory," Dietrich's voice piped high and thin above

270

the drumming of the tires and the rain, "had I realized that *Quest's* resources ran to no more than this automobile, I should have been more insistent that we continue our talk in the comfort of my apartment."

"Talking is the condemned man's privilege," said Mallory, "but I'm doing the insisting tonight."

"I should like to discuss realities," the fat man persisted. "The opportunity to talk without restraint is quite compelling. And I am sure I can show you that there is only one practical solution to our encounter."

"Go ahead," Mallory answered. "You fascinate me."

"I put it to you, Mr. Mallory, that historians will rock with incredulous laughter at the response of the mighty United States to the deadly pinpricks of the Vietcong." The words were well-reasoned, almost glib, as if he had rehearsed them innumerable times in his mind, but Dietrich's normally bland tenor was jerky and harsh. Mallory realized that he was listening to a man pleading for his life. "The world's most powerful nation frustrated by a few tens of thousands of half-educated guerrillas scampering through the jungle."

"You have a point," Mallory conceded. "It's insane that these people are beating the hell out of us."

"I have thought much about the dilemma." Dietrich's voice was settling down, though the grating edge of anxiety remained. The compulsive flow continued, squeezed out of him by fear and vanity. "Basically, I believe, it is simple. The Vietcong possesses both a specific desire and the will to pursue it. The United States possesses neither."

"What exactly do you mean?" Mallory deliberately encouraged the fat man's monologue. The reactions instilled over twenty years were operating, and he was still the reporter, ever curious. Light on his own perplexities might come from even this unlikely source, but the monologue also served to keep him from thinking of his own fears.

"My principals, I'm sure," said the fat man, shifting in the driver's seat and dashing globules of sweat from his fleshy

271

forehead with the back of his hand, "must roar with laughter when they watch Americans debating the Vietnam issue. *Is our position moral? Can we properly impose our will on the Vietnamese? What do the Vietnamese people want? Can our forces be effective?* Really, it's so ludicrous it's delightful."

"I'm glad you find it amusing," Mallory said bitterly.

"My dear chap, even you must admit it *is* amusing. The Chinese have said time and again that they will destroy you. They have even given you a blueprint of their strategy. But your politicians talk as if Vietnam were a minor skirmish and not the opening battle of a war to the death."

"I don't see how all this justifies your actions, or how it makes the sheer dazzle of three hundred thousand dollars even more attractive."

"Two hundred thousand," parried Dietrich automatically, "though as I said, I might go a little higher."

"I'm still confused by your reasoning."

"Mr. Mallory, a passport is just a sheaf of paper."

Mallory heard the quickening tension. The publisher was coming to the heart of his argument, unable to conceive in his absolute arrogance that he might be unable to convince.

"When another passport becomes more convenient, I shall change. As I told you, I have risen above the accident of birth."

"And that justifies treachery?" Mallory persisted.

"A nation forfeits allegiance when it can no longer defend its vital interests," the high voice said tensely. "The Vietnamese peasant changes sides when the government cannot protect him. I am doing no more. The so-called Western democracies are failing to protect their citizens' vital interests —and the citizen is no longer bound."

"Isn't your judgment a little premature?"

"No, Mr. Mallory, not premature, just prescient."

"So you take the cash and let the partiotism go?"

"If you wish, though I wouldn't put it that baldly." The fat man forced a chuckle. "More important, however, I move

272

with the movement of the world, rather than perishing like the dinosaur, defending the sacred principle that all animals must be at least thirty feet long."

Mallory was desperately sorry he had allowed the discussion to begin. Brandy, exhaustion, and the throbbing of his shoulder provided no proper foundation for theoretical disputation within a world of morality wrenched askew. Dietrich's facts were, by and large, beyond dispute, though his conclusions were odious. Why, then, was it so difficult to refute them?

Feeling the hard edge of his resolution begin to crumble, Mallory demanded truculently, "What makes you so sure we're acting like dinosaurs?"

"Your inexplicable refusal to assert control or to use your true power." Dietrich's voice was a high, hypnotic purr. "And your exceeding ineptitude on the ground. Ngo-dinh Diem, horrible little man, at least held things together. You permitted his destruction—after alienating him by the alternating obsequiousness and bluster of your so-called ambassadors. And today. . . ."

The fat man wrenched the wheel over hard, skidding around a log that reared suddenly through the slashing rain on the slick, black roadway.

"And today," Mallory prompted.

"Yes, today, look at the farce, the parody of Machiavellianism perpetrated by the CIA and your other cloak-and-dagger Boy Scouts." The fat man was enjoying his own eloquence, his vanity apparently telling him that Mallory was already half-convinced. "They gave me license for my activities; they almost pushed me into them. Americans do not play the game well. They should not be allowed to play. But, you know, even my own activities are helpful, yet not essential."

"How so?" Mallory prodded, monosyllabic in his physical and psychological pain.

"These charades of students and Buddhists that echo so

273

much louder in Washington than in Saigon," Dietrich said, his self-assured tone more fitting for the lecturer addressing attentive students than a prisoner pleading with his captor. "—of course we encourage them. But there is no real need to. Your obsession with representative government provokes demonstrations and you take them seriously. With or without me, the end is inevitable."

Mallory was silent, fighting both his inclination to agree and the tide of physical exhaustion that was creeping over his senses.

The high silken voice spoke out of the darkness. "You are silent, Mr. Mallory. Thinking about my points?"

Mallory did not answer. He saw again the tangle of men and oxen and carts harried to desperation and mangled death on the matted trail through the jungle of the High Plateau. And he heard the dry tones of a half-forgotten teacher of logic repeat: "No man can predict the future with accuracy. Therefore no man can justify his actions by citing their harmony with the shape of the future. Nor can he argue that he merely assists the inevitable in coming to birth."

"Mr. Mallory?" Dietrich's voice cracked with anxiety. "Mr. Mallory, are you reconsidering my offer? At least three airliners will leave Saigon by ten this morning. Once you're out of the country you are beyond my power. But you'll still hold the evidence you claim, and you'll still be able to publish if I don't pay—shall we say a round quarter of a million dollars. How does that appeal?"

"I'm still thinking," said Mallory, abruptly realizing that he was dealing with the madness of complete self-belief and utter self-assurance. "Meanwhile, slow down."

As the Citroën's pace slackened, he craned his neck to see the edge of the road. With half an eye on Dietrich and the revolver, he waited till a squat, gray milestone crept up beside him. BIEN-HOA 18 KM.

"A little faster," Mallory snapped.

The car pounded through the wet night, isolated in the

274

yellow tunnel of its own headlights with only occasional flashes of lightning throwing the checkerboard paddy fields on either side into sharp relief to show that the world still existed. Mallory's cramped left arm began to jiggle involuntarily, and he propped his wrist on his knee. His throat closed and he bit down a surge of bile. The taste of copper pennies mixed with brandy fumes and stale ashes in his mouth. He washed them away with another draught of brandy. Screwing the top of the flask down carefully, he let it drop to the floorboards.

The next milestone read: BIEN-HOA 17 KM.

"I want you to stop exactly at the next milestone," Mallory directed. "Stop and kill the engine."

"But my dear fellow," Dietrich protested, "in the middle of nowhere? What about my offer?"

"Do as you're told, Dietrich," said Mallory, "or the gun may go off before we can discuss your offer again. Anyway, I can talk better if we're not moving."

He saw the milestone fifty yards away and directed, "All right, there it is. Put your brakes on. And dip your lights."

The Citroën obediently began to lose speed. Sour bile almost choked Mallory, and he dug the butt of the revolver into his thigh to keep it steady. He wished fervently that he were anywhere else. He fought down the desperate impulse to fling himself out of the car. It was too late, much too late.

The Citroën stopped precisely beside the milestone, and Mallory flicked on the overhead light. He let it burn for ten seconds, his body tensed, before ordering, "Kill the lights."

Dietrich fumbled in the darkness, complaining, "I can't find the switch."

Finally, Mallory heard the click. Instead of darkness, high beams drenched the empty road with yellow light.

"Sorry," said Dietrich, "wrong way." The switch clicked again and the light died.

Muscles involuntarily drawn taut against the bullets' impact, Mallory hardly heard the muttered apology. Ten seconds passed, twenty seconds, thirty, and the night remained quiet except for the monotonous lashing of the rain. He craned his neck out the open window.

A heavy hand closed over his own. He slammed his fist down on Dietrich's wrist and, for an instant, the grip loosened. He inched his arm back, clinging desperately to the revolver. His finger was still on the trigger, but the muzzle pointed down at his own thigh. He felt the savage fingers slip a millimeter and he struggled harder. But a second massive palm thrust itself under his chin, fingers groping for his eyes. Pain shrieked from his shoulder and he was hurled back into the corner, his hand empty.

"I am sorry, Mr. Mallory." The unctuous tones pierced the darkness. "But you really left me little choice. I prefer to save the money."

Mallory, huddled in the darkness, did not hear the words. The shrill voice was merely a distant dirge for his failure. But he became aware when Dietrich prodded him with the revolver.

"Now we'll change places, Mr. Mallory," said Dietrich evenly. "I hardly think I'll need this toy of yours, considering your state, but still. . . ."

The car lurched forward with Mallory driving. Dietrich was talking again, and Mallory wished only that he would be quiet, that he would leave him alone with his bitter thoughts. He could not even commit suicide effectively. His fleeting vision of himself as an instrument of justice dissipated, and he resolved that in the future, if there were a future, he would stick to reporting. But the necessity for decision would probably be spared him.

". . . hard to believe you were unaware," Dietrich was saying, "that I knew of your arrangements with my friends, or that we would have our own signals. Why do you think I suggested a drive in the country? It's all very convenient, thanks to you. We'll not need that fool Gilroy's assistance now. We'll arrange our own accident."

Mechanically Mallory concentrated on keeping the Citroën on the road. The heavy front-wheel steering forced him to use his bad arm, despite the constant pain. The high voice droned on, assaulting the perimeter of his self-absorption.

". . .because we are strong and you are weak. We will win. You had wit enough to see that you could never convince your bemused countrymen of the truth of my role. You even had courage enough to face me yourself. But you were venal enough to snap at the lure of a bribe. And you were too weak to shoot me yourself—if that is what you really intended. . . ."

"Dietrich," Mallory interrupted, his voice low, "no man can see the shape of the future clear, neither you in your megalomania nor I in my towering professional pride. We are all creeping in the dark toward a fate we cannot know."

"And what does this metaphysical diversion mean?"

"Just that you are convinced that I will be dead within the hour. And I see no reason to disagree. But anything could change it. A rut in the road, a bad skid. . . ." He moved the wheel suggestively, and felt the revolver's muzzle in his ribs.

"Don't try it, Mr. Mallory," the publisher warned. "Savor the minutes remaining to you."

"Anything could intervene," Mallory resumed, speaking with the calm of a man who has accepted the inevitable. "But you have the effrontery to forecast the culmination of events five years, ten, perhaps even a generation hence. I could respect you if you believed—or even if you had acted intelligently so as to avoid becoming a pariah in the only world you know. But your greed and your arrogance have undone you. Not conscience, but the world you are creating will destroy you."

"Mr. Mallory." The publisher's self-satisfaction seemed in-

277

finite. "To set your mind at rest, I can tell you that I have made my arrangements. My Chinese friends can find useful employment for me in a host of places. Or, if I choose, I can simply disappear and enjoy the considerable fortune that has accumulated through my efforts."

"*If* the Chinese would let you disappear, you fool," Mallory goaded, "and that they never will. You're trapped. Besides, you're now committed to arranging an entire series of accidents. Do you really think even Gilroy will be stupid enough not to connect my accident with you?" Mallory himself wonder about this, but his threats seemed to be unsettling the publisher.

"Mr. Mallory," Dietrich blustered, "you are not unintelligent. You managed to pierce my—ah—cover. But the others, no."

"You have already destroyed yourself, regardless of what I do," Mallory persisted. "I am as great a menace to you dead as alive."

"You won't experience the discomfort of discovering how wrong you are," bleated the publisher.

"But I recommend one thought to you," Mallory went on. "There are degrees of evil, just as there are degrees of stupidity. You are deep in both. We Americans bumble. We even do injustice in the name of justice. But our ends, insofar as we can see them, are good, just as your employers' may be—though not your own. We are saved by one thing. We have no sweeping, all-comprehensive plans. We do not become the slaves of our own visions as do your friends."

"This is all very interesting, Mr. Mallory, but hardly pertinent."

Mallory knew quite suddenly that he desperately wanted to live. He wanted Tuyelle. He wanted responsibility. He even wanted the pain of the perpetual indecision which is the fate of men who are not fanatics, that perpetual indecision through which they must always choose not the single, correct path but only the path which seems best at the moment.

278

And the choice must be made again and again, as long as the spirit survives.

Yet all he could do was harass the obese megalomaniac beside him. Still a chance remained, and he went on. "Enormity carries its own defeat. The more violent a revolution, the greater the strength of the counterrevolution. Not even your Chinese masters are immune. They are creating their own nemesis. They will kill and murder and sow terror like a plague across the land. They will offer to stop in the name of humanity—if we grant them all their desires. Then, of course, the real terror begins, the days and nights of fear, the destruction of human beings, as they have destroyed you. Dietrich, the grotesque, warped monster you have become will destroy itself."

"Very biblical, Mr. Mallory, very biblical indeed," sneered the fat man, his voice shrill with anger. "In the meantime, do as I tell you. You'll see a lane in a moment. Turn and drive slowly till I tell you to stop. Dip your headlights."

Mallory made the turn, fighting the wheel, which bucked and turned in his hands as the car's wheels slithered and skidded in the rutted mud. His exhaustion crowded out all sensation except the fact of the steering wheel slipping in his hands and the hungry mud boiling in the pale yellow light. They entered a clump of trees, and Dietrich ordered, "Stop the car and flash your lights on high once."

Painfully, Mallory found the key. The engine spluttered for thirty seconds, then died, sighing in finality. He fingered the knurled switch, flicking the lights up to disclose a group of figures moving toward the car. Their sleek black raincapes were pushed into sharp peaks by the muzzles of submachine guns. He moved his hand again and the night was black around them.

"You see, we do have our alternative arrangements." Dietrich's voice was smug again. "My men were, naturally, waiting elsewhere, leaving only a courier. Did you really imagine that...."

The darkness was total, but a precise equation glowed in Mallory's mind. The chance was one in a thousand that he could overpower Dietrich and turn the car to escape before those dripping black figures came too close. But he could certainly close with the shaken publisher and fire the revolver once or twice, grasping one kind of success on the verge of the grave.

Bracing his feet on the hump of the transmission between the seats, he hurled himself, shoulder first, into the fat man's solar plexus. He heard the outrush of air in the dark at the instant before two hands came down, groping for his throat. Disdaining to defend himself, Mallory grasped the revolver with both hands, wrenching a clammy finger back till it cracked. The fat man screamed shrilly. Mallory forced the revolver around, ignoring the single hand that clutched at his windpipe as he ignored the bones grating in his shoulder. He forced the muzzle into the soft yielding flesh of the fat man's stomach and fired three times.

The shots spawned an everlasting echo. Outside his enclosed black world, reverberating with shock waves and stifling with cordite fumes, Mallory heard a string of shots. A blow to his shoulder touched off a Roman candle of pain that consumed him.

He awoke to the feeling of water on his face. He was propped against a tree with a raincape beneath him. Rough hands were tearing at his shoulder, and he almost fainted with the pain. Down the road the Citroën was burning. He knew a moment of regret. What would Pierre say?

His eyes focused on a tableau across the road. Five black-caped men were standing around the mountainous figure that sprawled in the mud. As he watched, one put his hand on the shoulder of another. The second stepped forward, submachine gun muzzle pointed down, and fired a quick burst. Dietrich's legs drew up convulsively. His knees jutted stiff in the firelight for an instant before they relaxed and his feet fell to lie, splayed and motionless, in the mud.

The first figure detached itself from the group. Although Mallory could not see the face in the darkness above him, he recognized the long, nicotine-stained fingers in the light of the burning car. They placed a burlap-covered canteen beside him.

"Mr. Mallory," said a voice surprisingly melodious without the covering mask, "I'm sorry that our expedition will have to be postponed. But you will live to write of our inevitable triumph."

The Vietcong leader turned and strode down the road. He stopped briefly and Mallory just heard the soft voice speaking across the distance. "Mr. Mallory, we do not have accidents. He had served his purpose. We have known for a time that he was about to betray us."

27

Sundered boughs lay thick on Magazine Gap Road, the approach to the once gilded eminence called The Peak, where hundreds of Britons, Americans, and Europeans still led lives of uncrowded comfort. In Wanchai, the fevered strip along the shore, where the Chinese lived in a perpetual turmoil of light, noise, and rubbing propinquity, emergency squads were hacking at the debris of two tenements that had collapsed under the hammering rains and 150-mile-an-hour gusts of Typhoon Matilda.

Matilda had already swept on to confound the precise planners of the People's Republic of China by washing away earthen dams and flailing the young crops of Kwangtung Province, before disappearing into Kwangsi and Szechwan Provinces. In their capitals of Kweichou and Chungking, trembling provincial officials were already pondering the manner in which they would falsify their reports in the vain hope of avoiding condemnation for failing to prepare for the catastrophe.

But in Hong Kong the storm had passed, leaving the June morning scrubbed fresh by its violence. Crossing the harbor on the green-and-white ferry that imperiously ignored sampans and lighters bobbing on the white-flecked green waves, Gerald Mallory reflected with an awareness which, for a moment, rode over his elation that things might have worked out much worse.

The worm that seemed to hide in every shining apple had revealed itself. *Quest* had tired of waiting during the three weeks he had spent recovering from his wounds. True, they had run his story and they had paid him in full without complaining. None of his conclusions had been altered, but they had given him no more than fifteen hundred words which, somehow, was not the same as the twenty thousand originally planned. McAllen, full of sincere concern, had explained in a hideously expensive telegram that the pages in the allotted issue had been filled with stand-by stories. "EDITORS FEEL," he had added, "IT WOULD BE ANTICLIMACTIC TO ATTEMPT REVIVE FULL-DRESS TAKEOUT AFTER BEING FORCED RENEGE ON MAJOR PROMOTION EFFORT."

Mallory couldn't help feeling that McAllen's attitude wasn't quite logical, considering the publicity the magazine had gained through him. But he knew better than to expect consistency from either politicans or editors. Besides, his relations with *Quest* were excellent, perhaps because McAllen felt guilty at dropping the takeout after making such a play of Mallory's injuries on *Quest's* behalf. They were already discussing a major piece on Indonesia.

The manuscript of his book, *Vietnam—Two Minutes to Midnight*, had been completed only a week earlier, and his publishers were planning rush publication to take advantage of the glamor invested in him by his brush with the Vietcong. He did not know whether his anguished candor would keep the book off the best-seller list, but a respectable sale seemed assured. He might not be standing on the pinnacle, but he had come a long way back up the slopes—under his own power.

Jostled by dark-haired clerks in neat, white shirts and their sisters in tightly-cut silk sheaths, he hurried down the long gray corridor of the Kowloon pier. He ignored the gaudy advertisements, which sought to compel the flow of tourists' dollars, and cut through a queue of red busses to the taxi rank. In the green Hillman Minx, which circled through the textile factories to the airport, Mallory turned his thoughts from the sometimes sordid, sometimes heroic, but always complex processes by which events are processed for public consumption.

Tuyelle was on the Air France Boeing 707 which was at that moment making its final approach over the scattered southern islets of the Crown Colony. It had taken almost five months for her to obtain permission to leave Saigon for six weeks—five months of letters and static-distorted telephone calls. But, finally, the future was coming to him to grasp as he could.

As he dodged through the arrival hall, side-stepping tourists boasting of their purchases in Tokyo, a film of concern slid over the surface of his elation. Tuyelle had insisted that they make no definite plans, but simply spend a month together before even thinking of the future. Nonetheless, he could not help wondering, half in hope and half in fear.

His shoulder sent a peremptory twinge to his brain, reporting contact with the arm of an immensely fat Chinese in a summer long-gown of blue silk.

"Every time it hurts," Tuyelle had admonished him on the phone, "remember your own words. No one can predict the future. Let us not try to direct it exactly."

The open bus was rolling away from the Boeing across the heat-slick tarmac. Mallory saw a splash of yellow silk below the sheen of black hair. In that instant the future seemed wholly clear to him.

ABOUT THE AUTHOR

Robert S. Elegant graduated from the University of Pennsylvania before he entered Yale's Institute for Far Eastern Languages. He holds two Master's Degrees from Columbia— one in journalism, the other in Chinese and Japanese studies. From 1951 to 1953, he was a war correspondent in Korea and then spent the two following years in Southeast Asia studying guerrilla conflicts in Malaya, Indonesia, and other areas as a Ford Foundation Fellow. From 1956 to 1962, he was in India and Hong Kong for *Newsweek*, which then sent him to Bonn until 1965. In this same period he was the winner of the Overseas Press Club Citation for Best Magazine Reporting from Abroad. He now heads the news bureau of the Los Angeles *Times* in Hong Kong.

Mr. Elegant is the author of a number of nonfiction books on Asia, including *China's Red Masters, The Dragon's Seed,* and *The Center of the World,* and he has written for such magazines as *The Reporter, Business Week, Look, The New Leader,* and *Reader's Digest.* The authentic background for A KIND OF TREASON is the result of more than a decade of experience as, to quote William J. Lederer in *A Nation of Sheep,* "one of the six best American foreign correspondents . . ."